PRAISE FOR RICHARD ANDREOLI

"From the first page, Richard Andreoli catapults you down the rabbit hole and immerses you in the crazy world of comic conventions. But this isn't simply a sardonic examination of fans; it's a love letter to heroism and the people who believe in it most."

—C.J. ABEDI, BEST-SELLING YA FANTASY
AUTHOR OF THE FAE TRILOGY

"*Battle at The Comic Expo* is, firstly, just one of those ingenious ideas. So obvious. So on point. So intrinsically funny. But the execution of this novel lives up to its premise -- written by an insider, someone who knows what goes on in those cavernous convention halls filled with the stale sweat of nerds in stormtrooper outfits. Andreoli captures the absurdity and the beauty within this tribe of lost souls, and along the way manages to tell a compelling yarn. But the real pleasure of this novel is in its authenticity of place and character."

—MICHAEL RYMER, DIRECTOR AND PRODUCER,
BATTLESTAR GALACTICA, HANNIBAL, PICNIC AT
HANGING ROCK

"Replete with tension, action, and anxiety, *Battle at the Comic Expo's* injection of dark humor permeates a gripping story that excels in the unexpected while remaining firmly based in comic culture. Readers will relish its ability to teleport at warp speed between various genres while retaining a sense of originality and drama that makes the story vivid, unpredictable, and nearly impossible to put down."

—DIANE DONOVAN, CALIFORNIA BOOKWATCH

By
Richard Andreoli

For more information,
visit **www.battleatthecomicexpo.com**

First Edition: May 2018
ISBN: 978-1-7322724-1-5
Library of Congress Control Number: 2018905393

Edited by Alissa McGowan of Red Pen for Rent
Book design by James Harless
Cover illustration and logo designs by Michele Svengsouk
Interior illustrations by Frank Svengsouk

For Steve. My hero.

ISSUE #1

"HEROES"

Summer's here, and it's time for America's Finest Comic Book Expo! Join the largest gathering of comic book, TV, and film fans from around the world for special movie screenings, Japanese animation, a masquerade competition, and seminars on everything from breaking into the comic book industry to independent filmmaking. There will also be a host of special guests, including Enduring creator Ron Lionel. So join us July 20–23 at the San Diego Convention Center in beautiful San Diego, California!

**—Commercial for America's Finest
Comic Book Expo**

Joe Cotter was having a craptastic morning, which wasn't a good sign considering that the Expo hadn't even opened to the public yet.

It wasn't that anything had gone wrong and required him to step in as head of security—yet. He just knew something was off; he could feel it. He was tired, but not exhausted in the physical sense. Yes, he'd awoken at 4 a.m. to begin the day's preparations, but he'd gone to sleep at eight the night before, like he'd done every year for a decade. He'd slept soundly in the posh hotel room the CBE provided its senior staff, awoken without any jarring surprises, and even had time to eat something and drink a large coffee. There had been no last-minute problems with exhibitors, no fights in the attendee line that snaked around the convention center, and no one yelling at him to fix the unfixable for some unruly movie studio executive. (Yet. That would undoubtedly come.)

Everything about the morning was perfect on paper.

But not in reality. Joe couldn't put his finger on what was wrong; he just knew he didn't feel right. As he stood alone in the skybox overlooking the Exhibit Hall, he picked at the feeling, as though it were a scab he'd discovered on his body but didn't remember earning. He knew he was ... not tired, now that he thought about it, but almost bored —like back in school when he'd been forced to attend a prerequisite class to graduate. What was his problem?

A trickle of sweat dripped down between his shoulder blades, and he shifted uncomfortably in his dark blue polo shirt. The skybox seemed hot, even though he could feel the air conditioning blasting in preparation for the myriad of volunteers who would be streaming in and out of the room. The scent of sticky, sweet donuts on plastic silver platters mixed with that of rich, burning coffee in large metal carafes— treats for the morning crew. It was all suddenly overwhelming, like the fumes were being pumped in to suffocate him. Joe looked down at his palms and saw that they were sweaty, too.

"Stupid..." he muttered, picking up a napkin from the nearby pastry table and using it to wipe his hands clean.

"Joe, we need you up front," came a woman's voice over his walkie-talkie earpiece. Amy Fogderude, one of his team from Superior Staffers —the company Comic Book Expo hired for jobs that regular (and non-vetted) volunteers couldn't necessarily handle, such as crowd control, escorting celebrities throughout the event, or handling money in the registration halls. It was also where Joe worked as the vice president of operations when he wasn't volunteering for America's Finest. "It's Klingons," she said gravely. "Outside the Hall A lobby."

"Roger that," Joe replied into the microphone clipped to his shirt collar. He smiled slightly as a bolt of energy shot through him; this anxious excitement was what he normally felt before opening—and it was good. He picked up the stationary PA mic in front of the skybox window and looked out over the hall below him. To his left were aisles of mom-and-pop businesses selling everything from comics, books, toys, and games, to costumes, vintage collectibles, TV series, and movies. In the center section were the major exhibitors, with their multi-level, ornate, interactive displays where fans could learn everything about their favorite projects. From comic book companies and Hollywood studios to toy manufacturers and everything in between, these were the booths most attendees rushed to see when the doors opened. And to the right sat Artists' Alley, the sci-fi and fantasy illustrators section, the Small Press area, and finally the fan art show. Everything appeared to be where it belonged, despite Joe's tingling spider sense.

He pushed through the strange sensation, clicked on the microphone, and announced, "Attention, please. The Exhibit Hall will open in thirty minutes. Please clean up the area around your booth as soon as possible. Comic Book Expo staff will be inspecting the aisles shortly."

Clicking off the PA, Joe turned from the window and raised his elbows to the sides so the blasting air could dry his now-wet armpits. He held them like this as he passed the couches and chairs that would eventually be filled with exhausted volunteers, raised them higher so he could maintain his balance while hurrying down the metal steps from the skybox, and only lowered them once he opened the heavy grey doors that led out onto the Expo floor.

This year, the Exhibit Hall was approximately 610 steps, or slightly more than a quarter of a mile, from the edge of Hall A through H. Joe's best friend Robert, CBE president and one of the biggest nerds who ever lived, had worn a pedometer and walked the entire floor just to be sure. *"This measurement did not include the distance from the lobby doors to the back loading dock,"* Robert had recounted to Joe and the other department heads at their pre-show meeting the night before. *"Nor did it take into account weaving around all the exhibitors, but it's pretty dang accurate if you ask me."*

In short, the Exhibit Hall was huge. But this was Joe's 25th Expo, so he knew how to easily cruise the room when it was loaded with fans, much less during the set-up period. There were the occasional carts delivering supplies or equipment, janitorial staff vacuuming the blue carpets that matched the event logo (and Joe's senior staff shirt), and a few random people wandering about, but otherwise the room was relatively empty. So even though the skybox was in Hall E, and Joe had a pretty good walk ahead of him, he could probably make it to the Hall A lobby in three minutes, barring any interruptions.

Unfortunately, there were always interruptions.

Through the Dark Horse Comics booth, Joe saw a short weeble of a man precariously standing on two stacked chairs as he tried to hoist up a well-worn sign that read "Ragnarök Comics." Joe rolled his eyes at the name, sucking in a breath at all the things that were wrong with this scene. He quickly made a detour.

"Hi, excuse me," Joe said, trying to sound as polite as possible. "Yeah, you can't do that."

The Weeble huffed and hopped/fell off the chair but maintained his balance and gave Joe a crazed, caffeine-fueled look.

"Ron Lionel is signing here," he snapped, large sweat beads shining on his balding head like clear Chinese checker balls sitting in their holes.

The sign flapped loose and fell to the ground. The two men stared at the crinkling paper for a moment, then Joe turned back to the Weeble, unfazed.

"Yeah, well, that's cool," Joe said, wondering who Ron Lionel was, "but here's the situation. You can't stand on a chair to hang signage because it's an insurance hazard. If you need help, you have to call Exhibition Services to do it for you." The Weeble started to speak, but Joe talked over him, which he thought was much nicer than just telling him to shut up. "Second, you were trying to hook your sign onto the back wall of the booth behind you, and it was coming dangerously close to piercing their merchandise. I don't think they'd appreciate that."

"It costs money every time you call Exhibition Services," the Weeble returned, as though the union fees had been established to penalize him personally. "And, well, I'm sorry about their booth. I didn't damage anything, did I?" He started to look, but Joe shook his head. The Weeble turned back. "Anyway, as I mentioned, Ron Lionel is signing here, and he's an invited guest of the Expo, so I have to get that sign as high as possible."

Joe blinked, remembering that he had heard the name tossed around at some of the pre-event meetings, but since he didn't really read comics anymore and didn't know any of the current celebrity creators, it hadn't stuck with him.

Rather than admit that, he said, "And do you think Ron Lionel would appreciate a tired old sign being strung up like you're at some school dance? Come on, man, you know him better than that..." The words hung there, like a razor-edged pendulum that could swing down and slice your head off at any second. And though Joe didn't know this Ron Lionel guy, he could tell from the Weeble's expression that he'd struck a chord. "Printing and shipping services are in the back, and they can make you a nice new banner within the hour. It will be worth it." The Weeble nodded, looking defeated, and Joe understood that this had less to do with CBE rules and more to do with the guest this guy was hosting. Now he felt bad. "I'll send one of the exhibitor liaisons over to help you out. It'll be fine."

The Weeble nodded his thanks as Joe turned, continuing toward the lobby doors and his original mission. But just then, a soft, subtle scent hit his nose: the dry, dusty, aged smell of old comics, magazines, and paperback books.

A chill ran up Joe's arms to his shoulders, neck, head, and then down his back. When people talk about the smells of a convention like America's Finest Comic Book Expo, they often joke about fanboys with an inability to practice proper hygiene. Joe knew those tales were true. He'd been caught downwind of soiled clothes on a sweat-soaked person (gender didn't really apply to these stories). But for Joe, the real scent of a comic book convention, and this one in particular, was this—the smell that had invaded his soul when he was 15 and attending for the first time. Back then, the scent had heralded all the adventures waiting to be discovered in those aging pages. A few years later it became the scent of possibility. That, too, was a simpler time, when Joe still lived at home and didn't have to worry about rent or a car payment or utility bills. A time when he could spend hours drinking coffee and writing—story ideas, character studies, and possible scenes—in the leather-bound journal his high school English teacher had given him as a graduation gift to encourage him to continue following his passion. It was this sense-memory from a time when he knew—*knew*—that his would be like all those other writers' words: printed on paper, sealed in plastic protective bags, just waiting to be devoured by some eager fan.

Joe felt safe. Warm. Out of his funk. He smiled ... until he spotted someone who shouldn't have been in the Exhibit Hall before opening. Anger scratched the inside of his skull.

"You!" he shouted at the young man, who was in full Renaissance Faire garb. "Out! Now!"

Xander Thompson was resplendent in his grey breeches, white pirate blouse, grey cotton cloak with magenta silk lining, and wide-brimmed magenta silk hat accented by obnoxiously long peacock feathers that threatened to tickle the face of anyone standing too close. Though Joe (and anyone else with a half-passing knowledge of history) recognized that the outfit wasn't period accurate, he also knew that Xander's flair and personality would keep any costume police off his back. The young man's mysterious power to charm most men and women he met really pissed Joe off.

Xander tried to cover his look of disappointment by removing his hat, swooping it down in front of his chest so that the feathers fluttered past his face, and bowing. "Milord Cotter," he said with the full flourish he always used when wearing his Faire costume. "'Tis a most glorious morning now that I have seen thee."

"Yeah, well, 'thee' says you need to leave." Joe took Xander's arm— firmly, but not past the edge of threatening—and began escorting him toward the large grey metal doors that led to the convention center lobby. "You know you're not supposed to be in here before show opening. It's an insurance thing."

"Is it?" Xander asked in feigned confusion.

Honestly, Joe wasn't sure; he'd made up that excuse five years ago when Xander first started sneaking into the Exhibit Hall early. At the time, Xander had sworn he didn't understand that the rules applied to him—having just been elected "Fan of the Year" for the first time—so Joe made up the insurance excuse and thought the situation resolved. Now he understood that the temptation to see the Exhibit Hall early and report on all the surprises inside was too great for Xander to resist; each year he somehow found a way to slip in. Normally this kind of behavior would be grounds to revoke Xander's membership and kick him out—it just wasn't safe, having attendees roaming the aisles with delivery equipment and shipping materials all over the floor, not to mention the risk that something could be stolen from an unmanned booth—but Robert had shut down that idea. Xander was hugely popular among everyone from cosplayers to comics' fans to *Rocky Horror* devotees. His antics were mostly harmless, and no one ever suspected him of being a thief, so rather than piss off someone who could start a social media smear campaign against the Expo, they just played the "What Can Xander Get Away With?" game every year. Joe suspected the real reason was that Robert liked the kid. He had no idea why.

"Alright, let me go!" Xander said, dropping the Ren Faire accent and yanking his arm away from Joe's hand as he continued walking toward the exit doors, returning the magenta silk hat to his head.

Joe stayed on his heels, and for a moment he felt victorious. He didn't like it when people felt entitled to something—like their birthright or bank account or job or popularity meant that they should be treated better than anyone else. Getting the chance to knock Xander down a notch made Joe happy.

But then, Xander hit the horizontal release bars on the hall's metal doors. They opened, revealing a sun-drenched entrance on the other side. Xander exited into the lobby in a flourish of fabric and light that seemed to ignite the entire city block. Fans turned, some cheered, and Xander beamed. His world was perfect once again. Joe's annoyance returned.

"Xander!" shouted Robert, and the young man removed his hat, bowing once more.

"Well good morn', Milord Robert!" Xander beamed, seemingly unfazed by the encounter with Joe. "How doth the president of America's Finest Comic Book Expo fare on this fine summer day?"

"You're not supposed to be in there!" Robert said, but he didn't shuffle uncomfortably in his suit coat or offer the nervous laugh he'd squeak out during a real confrontation, so Joe knew his friend wasn't really upset. Xander must have known as well, because he continued speaking as though Robert hadn't mentioned his trespass.

"And where is thy beautiful wife, the Lady Louise?"

"Working," Robert said with pride. This, too, bothered Joe. He'd known Robert longer than anyone, and the truth was that Robert wished Louise loved CBE as much as he did. But she didn't. And, as he always did, Robert just smiled and made an excuse for her absence, which invariably involved her job as a pediatrician. "Babies continue being born, whether or not it's Expo weekend..."

"Robert," Joe interrupted. "Klingons are storming the front entrance." He hooked his hand on Xander's bicep and dragged him along. Robert stepped in line next to them.

"Milord Cotter, I must object to this barbaric behavior!" Xander protested as he put the hat back on. The peacock feathers brushed Joe's face; he was sure the kid did it on purpose. "I need to be at the Expo opening ceremony. Ron Lionel's going to be there!"

"Why do you get to go?" Joe asked.

"Milord Cotter!" Xander said, indignant, as he gestured toward himself with his free hand. "Fan of the Year. Again."

"Yeah, well, I'm not a fan. And I'm not done with you yet, either," Joe said. While he wasn't a violent person and had only used force a couple of times when working events (and never CBE), Joe was trained in both boxing and aikido, so he knew how to be physically persuasive when necessary.

"Joe! Robert!" shouted a woman. Joe paused despite himself. He didn't have the willpower to see Pam right now.

"Can't talk." Joe started walking again. "Klingons."

"Oh, I love the *Star Trek* fans," she said, joining their mission. "They're so passionate!" Unlike the other full-time staffers in their color-coded polo shirts, Pam wore normal street clothes. (As the CBE treasurer, it wasn't a good idea to have her stand out in the crowd.) Though, to be fair, Pam's idea of "normal" was office attire, making her look like a company executive compared to the T-shirt and shorts most Expo attendees wore. Joe took in the fitted blouse that showed off her cleavage and scooped in at the waist, the slacks that cupped her ass. She may not have looked like the bikini-clad models in the Exhibit Hall who were hired to hand out promotional cards for the latest movie, but that was fine by Joe. They were hot, but Pam Dailey was sexy.

"Hi, Xander!" she said, leaning forward to look him in the eye. "You in the masquerade this year?"

"I wouldn't dare miss it, Milady!" Then, with a scowl at Joe, he snapped, "You're wrinkling the blouse!"

Joe glanced at Pam. She smiled at him with an "I know what you're doing right now" look. So it was obvious to her (and probably Robert) that he was avoiding her, but at least her expression was playful, not angry. That was one of the things that had drawn Joe to Pam. She wasn't one for needless drama. She could see through the games he'd sometimes play and force him to face his own behavior. It was one of the first qualities he'd fallen in love with.

Now, three months after they'd broken up, that look wasn't comforting. It was uncomfortable.

"How are things on the romance front, Milady Pam?" Xander asked.

"Seriously?" Joe said, tightening his grip on Xander's arm and walking faster.

Robert, who with his pudgy frame and heavy suit had been huffing to keep up, suddenly ignited a burst of speed and put his hand on Joe's arm, halting the group.

"Okay, that's enough," he wheezed, and Joe let go. "Xander, stop going where you know you shouldn't be. Okay?"

Xander nodded.

"Stop sneaking into the hall early!" Joe interjected, causing all three to do a double take. "It's not fair! Everyone else has to play by the rules. You're no more special than any other person paying good money to get in here. It's just..." Joe trailed off as he saw the concerned looks on Pam and Robert's faces and knew he was sounding really emotional for such a trivial matter. "It's just not fair," he said, bringing the volume down.

Robert looked at Joe for a beat, then turned back to Xander with a firm stare, like a patient uncle who was running out of patience. It was the type of quiet authority Joe had never seen in Robert when they were younger.

"Of course," Xander said to Robert and Pam. "My true apologies." He nodded solemnly, then gave Joe what could only be described as "shade" before walking toward the escalators that led to the third-floor lobby.

Seemingly satisfied, Robert returned his attention to Joe. "Now, where are we headed?"

"Hall A," Joe said through clenched teeth, frustrated with Robert for stepping in like that. But if he was honest, he wasn't annoyed with his friend but with his own behavior. And the fact that they'd already made it to Hall A, but he hadn't noticed.

Joe turned to the glass doors leading to the street and saw them: a band of Klingons bearing down on Amy. She wore a yellow Superior Staffers polo shirt, which indicated that she'd been hired to help the Expo but wasn't an actual volunteer for the event. However, most beings—including Klingons—wouldn't recognize that; they just noticed the blond bombshell with big hair and even bigger boobs. She often got mistaken for a cocktail waitress or undercover stripper when Superior Staffers was hired to help run events. That didn't bother Amy. In fact, she used it to get people to do what was needed, either by joking or flirting, or playing the unexpected hard ass if necessary.

Joe respected Amy's ability to not take other people's reactions personally, and to use her assets to her own advantage. As a result, he'd quickly moved her up in the ranks. Her skills also made her the perfect choice to manage crowd control. While 99 percent of fans attending CBE were good, normal people, right before opening they were always really anxious and excited. This was especially true when dealing with fans who had arrived at 10 p.m. the night before so they could be first inside the next morning. Having a firm hand attached to a hot body with a great personality was helpful when keeping people in line.

But Amy had never faced a Klingon ground troupe before.

"What's going on, guys?" Joe asked as he stepped out of the air-conditioned lobby and into the already warm July morning with Robert and Pam right behind.

"'Iv chaH DaHar'a' puny Humanpu?" the Klingon Commander asked the others in his group as he slowly turned, glaring down at Joe. This loosely translated to, "Who do these puny humans think they are?" Then to Amy he spat out some more unintelligible words that loosely meant, "Go back to your knitting, she-flesh, before we have to teach you the ways of Klingon passion."

He took a step toward Amy, but she didn't budge, instead pressing her chest out like a drunk dude about to get into a bar fight—which was impressive given the size of her breasts.

"Fuck you. You're not Klingons," she snapped, clearly having come to the end of her patience. Seeing as it wasn't even 9 a.m. yet, Joe knew that was a bad sign.

A second Klingon laughed, deep and dirty. He looked at Amy and said to his commander in the alien tongue, *"She is a sturdy one. She might even make a fine morsel for a human!"*

The six Klingons laughed sinisterly.

"Speak English, or I swear to God I'll have you hauled away by the SDPD," Amy shouted back.

Even though Joe himself had been in a foul and somewhat irrational mood moments before, nothing can restore clarity in a person faster than seeing a friend or coworker he truly likes stepping to the edge of getting themselves into a whole heap of trouble.

"Okay, that's enough," he said, sliding his body between Amy and the Klingons. Out of the corner of his eye, he saw Robert, and realized his friend had used a similar technique on him minutes before. "Seriously, guys, your costumes are awesome and the fact that you know Klingonese is crazy amazing. But you can't get into the show early, or without a badge. So explain to us what's up, in English, and hopefully we can help you."

The Klingons looked at one another. Joe could see that they were at the end of their patience, too, but he suspected it was because they were burning up under all that makeup and costuming.

The commander sighed. "We're doing the Age of Ascension ceremony during the masquerade intermission on Saturday. We need our professional badges into the show, but she won't let us inside." There was a slight nasal tinge to his voice.

"Then perhaps speaking the native language would help, wouldn't it?" Joe asked, showing Amy he had her back. However, he didn't wait for their response. He pointed behind them. "Industry Registration is in the Hall C lobby. This is Hall A. You want to turn around and follow the signs. We have to keep this area clear because of fire department regulations; otherwise we would have let you in here. Sorry." The commander nodded. "And make sure you wear those badges at all times or my security won't let you inside. I know it sucks for the costume, but you can take the badges off during the masquerade."

Satisfied, the Klingons all turned and walked to the correct entrance. Yes, it's true that the Klingon Empire posed quite a problem for Starfleet, but the United Federation of Planets never had Joe Cotter as their security chief.

Joe turned back to Amy. "Sorry about them."

He noticed Pam smiling at him. She looked proud, and Joe's heart dropped just a millimeter. Pam must have seen the look on his face because her smile dipped slightly—an acknowledgment of the sweet-sad confusion they now shared.

Robert's phone alarm sounded. He shut it off and looked at his watch. "Oh, God, we have ten minutes until Ron Lionel does the opening call."

He turned and rushed inside the lobby toward the giant escalators Xander had ascended moments before. Joe nodded to Amy, who stayed in her position as he took off after his friend with Pam by his side.

Joe turned to Pam and whispered, "Who the hell is Ron Lionel?"

ISSUE #2

"STEPPING TO THE LEFT OF NORMAL"

This is the tale of Dexter Trent, whose loving parents were accidentally electrocuted after he spilled water on a faulty string of Christmas lights. Orphaned, the 15-year-old is condemned to a Dickens-style foster care facility. But, one night, as Dexter mops the hallway floors—having disobeyed the sour headmistress yet again—he sees a darkly beautiful world reflected in the dirty water. This is the land of the Enduring, which is being attacked by an all-powerful, unseen creature. Hearing a cry for help from people inside this place, Dexter inadvertently takes a step "to the left of normal" and falls in. Now, without any special powers, Dexter goes on a journey to stop the dark overlord and save the people of the Enduring.

**—Original pitch for *The Enduring*
comic book series**

"Well, look who cleans up very nicely," Sarah Cisneros said to Ron

Lionel as he stepped into the air-conditioned limo the studio had provided. He took the seat facing her as she handed him a large, black drip coffee. She sniffed the air. "Freshly showered. I'm impressed. The fans won't even recognize you."

"The fans don't know me."

"They know what you've led them to believe," Sarah said with a knowing look, then gave his outfit an approving glance. "Thank you for listening to me. You keep this up, I won't know what to do with myself."

Ron slid off his gold aviator sunglasses and looked down at his black button-down shirt, black jeans, and boots. All designer names, incredibly comfortable, and a perfect fit for his frame. It was an outfit that gave confidence, and Ron liked that. Seven years ago, when he'd sold *The Enduring*, his dress code had involved torn blue jeans, a retro T-shirt for a cigarette company or band, and an old suit coat if he was trying to look fancy. He said he didn't care about appearances and even went to extremes to keep his ratty look going once the comic took off, but when Sarah started repping him, she called him out. She knew he was full of shit. The truth was that Ron didn't know the first thing about how to dress or look cool, and he felt stupid about that. While his bravado had made it work among comic book fans, now that he was moving in Hollywood circles, he needed to dress up his game.

"You don't have to know everything," Sarah had told him during their first meeting over a mediocre steak dinner at a swank Hollywood hot spot that had since gone out of business. "In fact, you'd be an insufferable asshole if you did. What you have to do is know what you don't know, and surround yourself with people who, collectively, do know their shit. It's like when you were a kid and too scared to dive into the swimming pool because it looked too cold. Once you held onto your balls and jumped in, you found out it wasn't so bad after all. And, actually there were a bunch of others in that pool willing to help you swim. That's what me and my team are here for."

Ron now looked over at Sarah's perfectly tailored blue suit, high heels, and expertly coiffed pixie haircut as she scrolled through her phone for any emails or messages she needed to answer right away. She was 50-something but looked 40, like so many women he'd met on his visits from Vegas to LA. But unlike the beanpole agents and studio execs who worked with her, Sarah was a tank of woman—not fat, but broad and short—the kind of person who doesn't walk into a room, or traipse or float or glide. Sarah's movements were a cross between storming and bustling, like a person who's always on a mission. In the years that she'd been his agent, Ron noticed that wherever they went, people wanted to meet Sarah because she looked, moved, and sounded important. He envied that about her.

"I should make you a character in one of my stories," he said.

"Bite your tongue," she replied without missing a beat, still looking at her phone. Then she glanced up. "But if you put my Stan in the book, you don't need to get me a present this Christmas."

"I didn't get you a gift last Christmas."

"And I haven't forgiven you for it, either," she said, clearly enjoying their banter. She put her phone down and looked at Ron with a smile. "How did last night feel?" His eyes widened in horror. Recognition crossed Sarah's face, and she scowled. "Not her! I meant how did it feel to be recognized by fans!"

Ron sat back in the black leather seat and laughed, trying to play off his embarrassment. He sipped his coffee and looked out the window, vaguely realizing they'd only progressed one car length since they'd turned onto Front Street.

"What? There's nothing wrong with it," Sarah said as she met Ron's eye and he felt his cheeks flushing red. "You've worked hard to get here. You need to recognize that and be thankful for those moments." Ron averted his gaze but could still feel Sarah staring at him. "You hear me?" Ron smiled and nodded, but he couldn't look at her for some reason. "Good. A lot of people don't have this gift that you've got. Or they have it and never make the right connection to the right people at the right time. I know. I've met plenty of them. Hell, I've repped plenty of them. And every day I thank God for my boys and girls like you because you *did* do it. You did."

Silence. Then Ron looked up, changing the subject. "I can't believe you carded her."

"She was a *girl!*" Sarah said, louder than necessary (but that was her nature). "I wasn't about to let you go home with a minor."

"I have my ways of finding out their age," Ron replied and looked out the window again. Only three car-lengths closer to the convention center; too many cars and fans swarming the streets.

"Sweetie, having hair down there doesn't make you of age," Sarah replied, acting as though she was going to throw her phone at him. "If that was the case, I'd be twelve."

"Ohh?" Ron perked up as if interested. Sarah nudged him in the shin with her red-bottomed heels. "Seriously, if you were only twenty years younger ... and single ... and without a kid ... I would so ask you out."

"You see absolutely nothing insulting with what you just said to me, do you?" Ron laughed, but Sarah pressed on. "I'm not joking now, okay?" she said. "I am not gonna let you screw up your entire career by getting your rocks off with some cute little girl who may or may not be eighteen and an ethics major at San Diego State University. Period."

Ron hopped over to the seat next to Sarah and leaned into her. "Well, thanks to you, we know she was of age." Sarah clicked her tongue dismissively. "And she was pretty good, too."

"You're disgusting." She pushed Ron away. "Please tell me you didn't leave her in your hotel room."

"I'm not bringing some fangirl there so she can snap a selfie of us in bed together after I've dozed off. I don't need that getting posted all over the Interweb." Ron leaned back into Sarah. "You've taught me well." Sarah nodded. "We went to her dorm room..." Sarah's hand came up to his face and halted the conversation. Ron laughed, watching the throngs of people walking past their limo, many trying to look through the tinted windows to see who was inside. "Should we just get out and walk? How far is it from here?"

"Five blocks. And no, I'm not walking down the streets of San Diego in Louboutins. From car to carpet, thankyouverymuch." She looked at her phone. "You've a little time until the opening ceremony, and they can wait a minute if we're running a little late, I'm sure." She started flicking through her contacts. "I can call that Robert guy and let him know we're caught in traffic."

"Want me to call him for you?" Ron asked with a slight laugh.

"We don't need a 'Ron Lionel meltdown™' before the Expo even starts," Sarah replied, still focused on her phone. "I'm still a little nervous about you hosting this masquerade thingy."

"I don't have meltdowns!" Ron snapped, sounding more annoyed than he'd intended, which annoyed him even more. "The fans just take everything I do and blow it up like a fucking nuclear bomb."

"And you've had no part in any of it..." she said, still scrolling.

"Don't!" Ron commanded, an edge to his voice.

"Don't you 'Don't' me," she returned sternly, looking up from her phone. "You've got to see it from their perspective." He did. He'd tried to be the J. D. Salinger of comics, not letting his publisher give out any personal information about who he was in hopes of creating an air of mystery. "For God's sake, you pretended to be British!"

It was true. But it wasn't as deliberate as Sarah made it sound.

When it was published, *The Enduring* #1 sold out right away, due in large part to his publisher, the Weeble, not having the investment money to print enough copies, nor enough technical experience or fore-thought to publish online. That low print run and perceived snub toward the digital comics industry made it a must-read. And, to be fair, the book was very good, so word got around. Profits from that first issue paid for second and third printings, and when issue #2 hit the stands (but not the web), it was considered better than the first. The comics were unlike anything the industry was currently printing. Where main-stream books often featured big images and sparse words to show epic battle scenes, *The Enduring* was crammed with incredibly detailed drawings and dense copy, with words sometimes making up the images in order to convey the surreal and unsettling world Dexter had fallen into. And then, just as the reader was on the verge of feeling overwhelmed, a turn of the page would reveal a beautiful painting with no words at all but a rich tapestry of emotions—a breath of fresh air amid the chaos. These juxtaposing styles allowed Ron to play with concepts like space and pacing, deliver richer details, and make the reader feel as though they were on the journey with Dexter.

Fans had quickly begun discussing *The Enduring*, wondering about the author's origins. Was he an established writer using a pen name, or a real unknown as the publisher claimed? They'd debated all the plot points, teases, and allusions laid out in those pages. They'd called it the new *Harry Potter* or *Hunger Games*, with touches of *Promethea* and *Saga* mixed in, but unique and fresh unto itself. Articles about the series had appeared in mainstream publications like *Entertainment Weekly* and *Rolling Stone*. Some even wondered if the lack of a digital version was actually a larger statement about the impermanence of art in the modern age. And since all of that was fueling sales, Ron had made the Weeble keep quiet.

Then, as *The Enduring* reached its first anniversary and a highly anticipated Christmas issue was about to hit stands, Ron had decided to celebrate—at a small, local convention in Las Vegas where fans were hosting an *Enduring* panel. Since Ron wasn't talking—or attending conventions of any kind—readers had taken it upon themselves to discuss and debate the books. Why did Dexter's parents really die? Was it the evil Faerie Queen testing her power to see if she could reach into our world? Or was it really the US government who had uncovered this mythical land and needed to send someone in to find out how dangerous things really were? Or perhaps the plot was even more nefarious? Did Dexter's new friends Falstaff, Ariel, and Puck orchestrate the accident so that he would "step to the left" and save their land?

Ron had wanted to experience one of these panels firsthand. However, as he'd stood in the back of a meeting room packed with nearly 1,000 fans and risking closure from the fire marshal, he'd started to lose patience. The assemblage of "experts" were tossing out theories left and right, speaking as if they knew Ron personally, had seen his notes and discussed the book with him for hours over wine and cheese. They pulled out their fancy literature degrees from such-and-such college, their art history experience from a 10-day guided tour of Europe, and they dropped names like Joseph Campbell, Ayn Rand, Max Ernst, and Neil Gaiman. And although some on the panel proposed theories that Ron decided to use in future issues, what really got under his skin was that they spoke with such authority about his creation. His creation! Not theirs!

"You blithering idiots!" Ron had screamed from the back wall, his small, round sunglasses almost falling off his chiseled face in the process. He wore ripped black jeans and an old black and red Marlboro T-shirt. "How can you think that Falstaff is the Faerie Lord when he doesn't even have wings? Don't you even look at the bleedin' pictures? That's why they're there, for Christ's sake!"

"Sir, there is no need for that kind of rudeness," said the moderator, a plain-looking woman with glasses and frizzy grey hair.

"The hell there isn't, Fat Fanny!" he snapped, and everyone in the room sat up at attention. In a flash, Ron understood the dangerous situation he'd just created—like a hunter suddenly surrounded by his angry prey: When you're at a convention populated by fans who have spent their lives being mocked for their appearance, you don't call someone out about their weight. You may think someone is stupid, and you may hate them until hell freezes over, but *that* was just not done. Still, he was too pissed off to let that stop him, so he followed his father's philosophy on life: Go big or go home. "You all are crucifyin' the story with your daft theories. Has it ever occurred to even one of you acne-ridden gits that part of the joy is the mystery? Is the curiosity of seeing what's to come?"

Ron could tell from the looks on their faces that they were intrigued, wondering who he was. He saw women holding their breath and men eyeing him warily as he slowly strode to the front. He suddenly felt sexy—dangerously sexy. He twisted the thick black leather band circling his wrist and continued forward.

"This isn't some pissy little superhero book," he schooled them, finally realizing that he'd adopted a British accent but not caring. "You have to pay attention to every word, read the books two or three times—maybe more than that, by the looks of some of you—because it's the only way to really grasp the nuances. The details. You need to examine every line that's been scribbled out for your personal pleasure because I lay it all out in such detail, and triple check my work every issue so that I know it's all there. You have to pay attention!"

"You..." said Fat Fanny, clearly surprised. "You're Ron Lionel?"

"Better believe it, Fanny," he said as he reached the front table where the panelists sat and flicked a piece of her wild hair.

"How do we know?" yelled one brave soul in the back. "Ron Lionel's never been seen before."

"True enough," he said as he pulled out his wallet. "But now you can beat off to your heart's content because here I am."

He showed his ID to Fat Fanny. She looked at it, then at him, and said, "He lives in Las Vegas!" And then she shouted, "And he's British!"

Ron was not British. As far as he knew, there was no English blood in his family. He did, however, deliver a spot-on accent that came about from watching lots of British TV shows as a child and practicing while playing alone with his toys. There was even a period in kindergarten when he'd tried to tell his classmates mid school year that he was now English and going to use the accent the rest of his life. The combined teasing of those same classmates and his parents' stern reaction put an end to that phase, but Ron continued to assimilate the tone and syntax of people he met—particularly ESL speakers. Whether it was at a party or a fast-food drive through, Latino father or Filipino mother, he would pepper in slight hints of broken

English. He wasn't trying to be mean or funny; it was just something he did.

In truth, Ron had no idea why he'd started speaking like that at the convention, but he considered it a blessing. After that weekend, reprints of the first eleven issues spiked, and while there was no evidence to back up his theory, Ron believed the accent was to blame; comics' fans seem to have a thing for British writers and artists.

It was only a matter of time before the truth came out. Ron had known that; though, to be fair, he wasn't expecting it to happen only four months after his "coming out." Still, he had prepared himself, so when an angry fan interrupted his first official *Enduring* panel at Project A-Kon in Dallas, Ron was ready.

"I have proof you're not British!" Angry Fan screamed, shaking papers in his hand as if he intended to pass them out to everyone in the 3,000-seat room. "It says here…"

"You're right, I'm not British," Ron said, bored. "Now shut the fuck up and sit down." The fan—and everyone else in the room—was stunned by the nonplussed admission. Angry Fan slowly sat down. "I never said I was British. You all did. And I let you. You want to know why? Two reasons: sales and art.

"This book was doing okay. It was getting attention. But the second people thought I was British, sales skyrocketed. People who don't read comics even picked it up because they'd heard about this transgressive British author who was turning the American comics industry upside down. Bullshit! All bullshit. Every article after that Vegas convention—every single one—made a point of mentioning that I was British—from a long line of respected British authors, even. Not that I was a flaming asshole, which is completely true, but that I was British.

"And why? Because you idiot fuckers think everything artistic or literary that comes from outside of the US is genius and brilliant, and everything here is reductive. Well it's not. There are thousands of struggling artists who are producing provocative, thrilling, challenging, inspiring work that gives my brain a boner like you wouldn't believe.

And those poor sons-of-bitches can't get the fucking time of day because no one in the industry, and none of you fanboys, will give it to them. And it's a loss. A terrible, terrible loss." Ron paused, calmed himself a little too quickly to be genuine, and looked out into the audience. In a softer voice, he said, "To all of you in this room who are artists trying to make your mark, and who can't because for whatever reason people don't think you're 'enough,' keep fighting. You will make your mark one day ... even if you have to let people believe you're a Brit to do it."

And with that, Ron owned his fans once more. He shook his head to clear the memories and turned to Sarah. "The British thing paid off."

"You're lucky it did. It could have bit you in the ass."

"But it didn't..."

"You're not hearing me," she said. "Being you, the you that I know, works. The real Ron Lionel can be as successful and respected and wealthy as this a-hole you've created." He started to speak but she took his hands and squeezed them. "You want to be right about things, and I get that, but there's going to come a time when you can't fight your way out of a situation. When you're going to have to listen to what's being said, take it in, and realize it's to help you, not attack you."

Ron heard the stress in Sarah's voice. He stared at her for a moment, saw her expression crack ever-so-slightly, then return to normal. In that instant, he knew what had happened.

"The studio didn't like my draft," he said, the fear he'd been suppressing for a month vomiting through his soul. Sarah squeezed his hands. Her palms were sweaty. He pulled away and looked out the window as his eyes started stinging. "When did you find out?"

"Last night."

"Why'd you wait to tell me?"

"They wanted me to wait until after the Expo." He felt her sit up. "And the fans last night. When I saw how they reacted to you at the restaurant, I wanted you to enjoy that moment."

"Studio didn't want me to talk shit about them this weekend," he said.

"Will you?" she asked.

"If I do, it won't magically produce a good script."

"Your script wasn't bad..."

"Clearly it wasn't any good, either!" Ron snapped, glaring at her. He tried to discreetly wipe the corners of his eyes before putting his aviators back on.

"I'll back you up either way," Sarah said calmly, "but know that it almost bit Anne Rice in the ass when she talked bad about the vampire movies."

The car stopped, and Ron opened the door. As he stepped out and onto the sidewalk, Sarah leaned over.

"Where are you going?"

"To walk."

"What about the opening ceremony?"

Ron shut the door and started down the street toward the convention center. He moved at a quick pace, like a New Yorker on his way to work. He wove in between fans in street wear, spandex superhero costumes, and Japanese cosplay outfits—all of them so excited about the approaching event that they didn't notice the star in their midst. But that didn't register with Ron anyway. The heat from the morning sun immediately latched onto his fitted black shirt, and he felt sweat beading up between his pecs and shoulder blades.

You can't fuck this up, he warned himself. *This is your money. This is how you live.* Silence, and then: *This might be it...*

Ron shoved the invading thought out of his mind and instinctively reached into his pocket. He felt the vial, and a smooth excitement rushed through his veins. He didn't know what was going to happen this weekend, but whatever it was, he was going to do it big.

ISSUE #3

"NON-FICTION"

Mirror-Mirror Universes: The Birth and Rebirth of Fan Fiction

Saturday, 11:30–12:30, Meeting Room 2Z, Basement

From Star Trek, Star Wars, *and* Robotech *to* Riverdale, Blake's 7, *and* X-Files, *fan fiction is almost as popular as the TV and movie series that spawned it. Join popular fan-fic authors for a discussion on why this genre continues to grow—even for shows and films that ended decades ago. Plus, can fan fiction writers actually transition into mainstream work?*

Panelists: Alec Orrock, Mike Morimoto, Joe Cotter, and Diana Jess

—Text from the America's Finest Comic Book Expo events guide

"Look at them all..." Pam whispered as she stared at the crowds below the giant three-story windows. It was mostly to herself, but Joe heard and watched as she walked over to the stainless-steel railing for a better view. He stepped away from Robert and Xander—both busily texting on their phones—and a couple hundred attendees standing by the stage that had been assembled on the third floor above the convention center lobby. They were all eagerly waiting for Ron Lionel to show up and lead the opening ceremony, but Joe was more interested in Pam. He joined her at the rail and followed her gaze outside.

Long lines of fans wove in both directions down the front of the building on Harbor Boulevard and around the corner to the back. The throngs of button-wearing boys, girls, men, women, and possibly animal-human hybrids in T-shirts, jeans, skirts, spandex, and costumes braided around one another like long, colorful ribbons on a Maypole. Joe recognized many of the references quite clearly: a family of Sand People with Jawa children stood next to the Sandman and Death; a Deadly Gladiator's Desecration orc admired a clan of hobbits; and three Harley Quinns from various eras posed for photos with two naughty Squirrel Girls and one Silver Age–accurate Thing. From Joe's perspective, they seemed to be entwining the convention center's cement columns to strangle it, but he understood why an outsider and relative newcomer like Pam would still feel awed by the sight.

"There's so many..." she whispered, as though they were observing an undiscovered island and didn't want to attract the natives' attention. "They look so ... happy. Excited.... Excitedly happy." She turned and Joe saw the light in her eyes, like a little girl on her first trip to Disneyland.

In a manner of speaking, that was the case. Although it wasn't Pam's first Comic Book Expo, it was still new enough for her that she would invariably get swept up in the energy—unlike Joe or Robert who had spent decades watching it grow. He loved her obvious joy while watching fans wander the halls. Pam had been hired three years ago, when the Expo's board of directors thought it might be wiser to bring in an outsider to handle the finances. They hadn't expected Joe and Pam to start dating, or to break up three months before this year's show. Fortunately, Pam took her job very seriously, and regardless of her past with Joe, the CBE's needs came first. And because Joe loved America's Finest Comic Book Expo more than almost anything in his life, he truly appreciated that quality in her.

Joe found himself smiling. Without thinking, he reached out and hugged her to his side. Pam leaned in, placing her head on his shoulder. Joe heard her sigh, felt her smile, and both bodies relaxed. For an instant, their problems vanished.

"Joe! Pam!" Zack McCullock, the head of Industry Registration, was sliding through the crowd toward them. Zack was always easy to spot (even among the costumers), with his long blond mullet, black leather trench coat, black denim jeans, and red T-shirt. He was often mistaken for a character from *Blade* or some post-apocalyptic video game or sci-fi epic, but Zack had developed his look long before the term cosplay was invented. "Hello my brother and sister!"

Joe and Pam separated, and Joe felt a dull, annoying ache creep into his sternum once more.

"I just met some folks at DC and Marvel, and they invited me to their company parties tonight," Zack said, causing a few fans' heads to turn. He pulled a pack of cigarettes from the inside pocket of his coat and looked up at the duo through sunken eyes. "Really cool, guys, I gotta say." He tossed his head to the side so his thinning, wispy locks whipped out of his face. Then, with a quick brush of his hand over his overgrown brownish-blond beard, he placed the unlit cigarette on his bottom lip, where Joe knew it would dangle for the rest of the day. "You guys want to come?" he asked. "They said I could bring anyone."

The silence lasted a beat too long before Joe said, "Maybe. I need to see how the day works out."

Pam nodded in agreement.

"Cool," Zack nodded back, either ignoring or oblivious to the pause. "Oh, Pam, I need change for the cash registers."

"Already?" she asked with a laugh. Joe could tell she was trying to cover for the awkward silence. "They're not killing you guys already, are they?"

Zack shrugged. "If I could handle fighting off the Bloods while living on the streets of LA, I can handle professionals charging Industry Registration and demanding badges."

Neither Joe nor Pam responded. They didn't question his statement or even make a funny face. They simply smiled politely. That was the agreement the entire senior staff at CBE had made years ago when Zack first joined their ranks. It had been in effect before Joe or Robert became volunteers, and Pam became a part of that pact after she'd proven herself at her first event. Because, among the many colorful characters who populated the America's Finest Comic Book Expo staff —like Destino! who ran the masquerade and supposedly had the exclamation point legally added to his name, or Lady Margaret (no one knew her mundane name), who rode a motorized scooter and ran Deaf and Disabled Services claiming to be handicapped, though in truth she was just overweight—Zack was possibly the most unique. He was a compulsive liar.

Zack's lies never involved anything major. They were usually fairly outlandish, like claiming he'd served in Special Forces, or that he'd lived on the mean streets of Los Angeles even though all the older volunteers had known him during that same time period and confirmed that he had never been homeless. But then, sometimes the stories would end up being true—like actually getting invited to an A-list Hollywood party because he'd helped some professional during the Expo. His tales always held plenty of well-researched details, which made fact-checking somewhat difficult. They also contained just enough realism that no one could tell truth from fiction. And, since Zack was a nice guy who made Industry Registration run smoother than it ever had in the CBE's 42-year history, no one questioned him.

"You think they can hold out for another half hour?" Pam asked, already walking away. "I need to check with Robert about the opening."

Joe tried to catch her eye, hoping she'd help him escape the way she had when they were dating. But, like a waiter who knows she has five tables needing ketchup, extra napkins, and iced tea refills, Pam smoothly glanced everywhere but where she was needed. Joe supposed he deserved it. He had broken up with her, so he was on his own now. Hug or no hug.

"Sure thing," Zack nodded, taking the cigarette from his mouth with his index and middle fingers, and raising it to his head in quasi-salute. He then turned to Joe. "Excited about Saturday?"

"I haven't gone to the masquerade in years," Joe responded, because other than the panels in Hall H, that was definitely the biggest event on Saturday.

"I meant your panel," Zack said. Joe hadn't forgotten, but unlike past years, it just wasn't on the top of his mind. Zack offered him a curious glance. "I'm looking forward to it. You know I love your writing."

"I know..." Joe replied, embarrassed.

"I was at that first panel when you'd written that 'lost' *Robotech* story." Zack paused for only a second, then his eyes lit up. "About how Roy Fokker became the leader of Skull Squadron before the Zentradi attacked Earth!" Joe nodded but stared down at his feet. "You were, what? Fifteen?" Zack beamed.

"Seventeen."

"And how's your dad doing?" Zack pressed on. "Is he coming again?"

It was a question longtime attendees always asked, after that first year, when he'd been introduced as the youngest writer to ever appear on a Comic Book Expo stage. That year marked the first time Joe had ever shown his writing to people outside of an English class, so to have people enjoy his work so much that they would invite him to speak on a panel with other fan writers had been mind-blowing. His ecstatic parents, Maria and Joseph, had also attended the event. Leading up to the panel, this had caused Joe unending embarrassment, and he would walk five paces ahead of them so none of his Expo friends would see them together. However, at the actual program Joe had been forced to introduce them to the panel moderator, who'd then introduced them to the room. The couple received a standing ovation from the attendees, most of whose parents thought comic books and science fiction were a waste of brain cells. For years after, Maria and Joseph continued attending America's Finest Comic Book Expo, just because they thought the "kids" at the Expo were "a hoot." Times had changed.

"The show's too big now," Joe said. "Too many people. It's too hard getting around."

"Lady Margaret in Disabled Services could get him a scooter or wheelchair," Zack offered. "We could get a volunteer to help..."

"Yeah, I don't know," Joe said. "Things change."

Zack took this in, sticking the cigarette behind his ear. Joe could see he was still interested, which made him even more uneasy.

"What new stuff are you writing?"

"Nothing much," Joe said. "Been busy. The job and promotion to VP and everything. We get so many contracts now." Zack's smile fell, ever so slightly, and Joe felt like he'd disappointed him in some way. "Been getting to travel a lot, though, which has been great. Pam and I went to New York this past spring and... Well, you know."

He and Pam had broken up on that trip, and everyone in the main Expo departments knew it.

Joe saw Zack studying him, and felt sweat beading up in the center of his back once more. He started to laugh, to find a way to make a joke, but Zack propped one of his booted feet up on the railing and leaned in like a swashbuckling pirate. He withdrew the cigarette from behind his ear and flipped it between his fingers.

"She still likes you, my friend. Every time I see her looking at you, it's with pride." Zack paused, watching the cigarette move between his fingers. Joe saw his eyes travel a million miles away. With dread, he sensed where this was going. "You know, I loved a woman once," Zack said with a small, sad sigh. "But I was too caught up in my ego. My pride. I never said what needed saying, and by the time I'd gotten the nerve..." He stopped, shaking his head. Whatever happened to this "love," it obviously wasn't good.

"I know what Pam's problem with me is," Joe said, annoyed with Zack's melodramatics. "Wrong place, wrong time. She wants one thing right now; I want something else."

"Maybe it's time to change the time table. Make yours match hers," Zack said with a nod. "You can't live with regret, my friend. Trust me." He sighed deeply, then pointed the cigarette at Joe. "I know."

Joe shoved Zack's foot off the rail, taking the older man by surprise. "The convention center will charge us if you scratch that," he said, then marched over to Pam, who was now chatting with Xander. Robert stood behind them, still hurriedly texting. Joe knew something must be wrong, but asking Robert in mid-crisis was never a good idea. He'd wait.

"So this will be your last masquerade?" Pam was asking Xander.

"Verily so," he replied as he finished posting a photo of the waiting crowd to his followers.

"Can you just speak regular English?" Joe asked.

"Ignore him," Pam said. "I want to hear about you going to LA!"

"The move is two months nigh, but before that happens, I'm planning a performance most extravagant for the America's Finest Comic Book Expo masquerade," Xander explained to Pam and anyone else within earshot, which at this point amounted to Expo volunteers, industry professionals headed to their panel rooms and signings, and the occasional Superior Staffers employee. It also included the 300 attendees who had paid extra to be a part of the opening ceremony—which was starting in five minutes but didn't seem to have its host. Joe suddenly understood why Robert was glued to his phone. "I have always been an actor, milady. For me, to act is to live! And none of this reality show nonsense. I mean *acting!* 'Tis past time that I journey to where my heart beckons."

"So one last show for the fans, is that it?" she asked.

"Indeed!" Xander beamed. "The masquerade has always been a joy, but it's really a fancy costume contest for the groundlings, and not a grand ball as the name implies. But if this is the year when I leave behind my 'fan' status..." he used air quotes to accentuate the word "... and become a professional, then I must leave this place in a way that 'twill be spoken of for years to come. After all, who knows where I may wind up next summer? Working on a mini-series? A feature film? Gearing up for the new pilot season? Being a guest on one of the panels for next year's Comic Book Expo? The opportunities are endless!"

"Your parents must be so excited," Pam said.

"They'll be there." Xander smiled. "Mother is working on the costumes, and Father has developed some secret surprises that you'll just have to wait and see on Saturday night."

Xander's parents had been America's Finest attendees for years; he was named after their favorite character in *Buffy*. (They'd once told Robert, who'd later told Joe, that technically their favorite male character was Angel, but being Wiccan, they didn't feel comfortable giving their son that name.) Xander's mother had been a convention costumer for years and worked for the Old Globe Theatre in San Diego, while his father created high-tech gadgets for cars, such as flaming tailpipes and hydraulic jumpers. Joe knew that whatever was planned, it would be big. For some reason, the thought made the muscles on the back of his neck tense up.

"This isn't about winning, you understand," Xander said, with what Joe considered a little too much sincerity. "For me, this is all about the performance." Dramatic pause. "And my farewell."

"How did your audition for UCLA go?" Joe asked, the words flying out as though he'd been possessed. Pam looked over, surprised, and even Robert put down his phone. Xander raised his chin.

"It went well. I got very good feedback," Xander replied, his defiant optimism pissing Joe off even more.

"Oh, good," Joe said, just as positively. "What did the professors say?"

Xander paused, shooting a quick glance at Pam and then back to Joe, as though he were about to break the connection with a scene partner but knew better. Joe's head swelled. He could feel a victory coming.

"They said my audition pieces were very bold choices," Xander said carefully.

"What did you choose?" Joe pressed with false interest.

"Why do you suddenly care?" Xander shot back, and Joe's sense of superiority deflated. He felt his own smile slowly sink as Xander quickly covered his frustration. The young man raised his head once more. "They said I needed to do some more work. Take some classes, and then I could audition again." He smiled meekly at Pam and Robert. "To be asked back..."

"Is huge," Pam interrupted. "Most people don't even try."

"Xander," Robert stepped in. "Sorry, but I could use some help. Have any of your followers mentioned seeing Ron Lionel? He's late, and I'm worried."

"I'll check!" Xander said, stepping to the side with a dramatic unfurling of his cape. As he began clicking through his phone, Joe noticed Xander's hands shaking slightly. He felt like an asshole.

"That went too far, and you know it," Robert said, and Joe did. But what was worse was watching Pam walk away toward the water fountain and knowing he'd disappointed her.

"Robert Griffis?" A smartly dressed woman in a blue business suit and heels approached. She was slightly out of breath from hustling up the escalator and fighting her way through the crowd, but not as much as the Weeble, who trailed behind her. He had changed clothes and was now wearing a blue dress shirt and tie, neither of which seemed to fit very well with his pleated tan slacks. "Sarah Cisneros from Creative Artists. Have you seen him?"

Robert stared at Sarah for a moment.

"Oh my God, you're Heidi!" he shouted, but before she could respond, a tall, handsome man appeared from the side, put his arms around Sarah and Joe's shoulders, and pulled them into a brief hug.

"You're mixed up, man. Her name's not Heidi," he said loudly, then reached out to Robert and shook his hand. "Ron Lionel."

"Yes, I recognized you," Robert said with obvious relief.

Just as Joe started to move away, Ron pulled him and Sarah back into a hug. "This lady and this dude are my dream team!"

Annoyed, Joe worked himself out of Ron's grip and turned to look him in the face. The bright-eyed man blinked twice, saw the Weeble standing on the other side of Sarah, then scowled at Joe. "Well, okay, I don't know who the fuck you are." He turned to Sarah. "But this lady! She's the one who's always got my back." He moved over to the Weeble and shoved both hands onto the man's shoulders; the Weeble leaned his head back slightly, as though worried he might get strangled in the process. "And this guy! I made him a fortune!" Ron laughed, a little too loudly for Joe's comfort.

Finally, he shoved the Weeble aside and wrapped his arm around Robert's shoulders. "You must be Robert. Let's get this shit show started."

ISSUE #4

"EARTH-R"

DEXTER STEPS INTO THE ROOM.

This is it—the moment when Dexter finds out who murdered his parents and brought him into the land of the Enduring. But as he steps into the dark, cavernous room, he steps on something — making a noise.

The figure turns.

FOUR PANELS IN SUCCESSIVE ORDER REVEAL:

The Faerie Queen transforms into Myranda, then into the evil head-mistress from the Peekskill Orphanage.

Finally, she changes into woman we don't recognize.

On Dexter, his eyes growing wide. Then, in shock...

DEXTER
Mom?

—Last script page for *The Enduring* #84

Fingertip against the left nostril, snap-inhale with the right, and Ron Lionel felt the sharp sting of the cocaine. He released both nostrils so the overly air-freshened scent of the convention center bathroom could enter his nose, sniffed deeply, and enjoyed the tingling in his head. It rapidly warmed the back of his skull, running down to his spine and over his shoulders until it melted into his fingers.

Ron looked down at the inch-long glass vial with its bullet-shaped plastic blue head, held tightly above the piss-splattered toilet in the stall. He turned it upside down, twisted the small arrow crank so the tip pointed up toward the vial, and felt it slip slightly in his sweaty palm.

In sudden panic, Ron clamped his left hand down over the bullet. He exhaled and let out a small giggle of relief. While it was the start of the Expo weekend, and the restrooms were still relatively clean, had the vial fallen into the bowl or ricocheted off the edge and onto the wet tile floor—and miraculously not broken—there would be no going back. He wasn't that desperate.

Crisis over as quickly as it had nearly begun, Ron turned the vial upside down once more and rapidly flicked it three times with his right fingernail, then held it up as he twisted the entire vial back around. Looking into the bullet's tip, he could see a small sample of the white powder sitting in its nest, waiting.

Placing his index finger over the small, almost invisible hole on the opposite side of the crank, Ron put the vial up to his left nostril and did another snap-inhale. The powder flew into his nose, but this time the sting was smaller, and a tiny sour drip ran down the back of his throat.

Ron felt good again. And guilty. But mostly good. What Sarah had told him wasn't the end of the world. It wasn't great. It wasn't what he wanted to hear. But it wasn't the end of his career.

That was what Sarah had been trying to tell him in the car. You may fall down—you *will* from time to time—but there's always the big picture to look at. He was still Ron-fucking-Lionel, a shit-ton of people came to see him this weekend, and he still owned *The Enduring*. Not the studio. Him. And maybe his script wasn't the best, but...

No. Fuck that. Fuck all that.

Ron was self-taught, and he'd succeeded. Big time. So what if he hadn't gone to film school and been in the Hollywood Boys' Club his whole life? Tough shit. A lot of groundbreaking work came from outsiders like him. He would learn their game, then make it work for him—same as he'd done in the God-forsaken comic book industry.

Ron looked down and rolled the vial in his hand, watching the coke form walls, mountains, and craters against the glass edge, then collapse down into different patterns with each spin. For a short second he felt sad. Defeated. Disappointed. Not just because the studio didn't like his script and probably wanted to bring in an experienced writer (he knew this was the last draft he was allotted under their contract), but because he'd taken a bump ... and it wasn't even 10 a.m.

The smell of pee and shit and indigestion was already invading the bathroom and would only get worse once the Expo weekend started.

The Expo. This fucking convention. How would he get through four days of it? Hosting the masquerade would be easy, even though he only partially understood what he was doing, and that he would be doing it in front of thousands of people who may or may not like his work. That was fine. He knew how to work a crowd. And even four days of questions about Dexter and his family and friends would be easy. He'd left the readers with a massive cliffhanger about Dexter's mom, so he could tease them with hints and clues that he may or may not actually follow through on in the next year.

But the fans only "kind of" cared about that. It was the studio deal they'd ask about. The movie was supposed to start shooting in the fall.

The fans would want to know about the script, his meetings with the director, preliminary casting, the design and wardrobe teams... They'd want to know everything, and he didn't know anything other than the fact that the studio hated his script and he was exhausted from the whole God damn process.

"Bullshit..." Ron muttered, angrily wiping the sides of his eyes with the heel of his palm. It was all bullshit. He could spot it, and his fans would spot it too, and when they did, it could all be over.

Suddenly, Ron felt a swelling in his chest. Excitement. He looked up at the white tile wall above the toilet and squeezed the vial tight.

His fans. They could spot bullshit a mile away, especially if he told them it was bullshit. And the studio knew that. The director-fuck knew that. So the execs might not like what he'd done so far—and maybe it did need some work—but they *had* to work with him. They had to. Because Ron Lionel was *The Enduring*.

That was what Sarah had been telling him when she'd talked about his team. It wasn't just her or the agency, the lawyers or the publicists. It was the fans. And as much as he was *The Enduring*, the fans were the biggest and best assets on his team.

A wave of warmth rushed through him. He swallowed the bitter drip in his throat and thought about Sarah. She really did care for him. More than the Weeble, more than his parents, more than any chick he'd met and fucked at any of these conventions. Yes, she got paid from his work, but that was fair; she protected him. She navigated him through a world he didn't understand. And whenever the shit hit the fan, she was there for him. He couldn't fuck that up now. Ron shoved the bullet in his pocket, turned, snapped open the stall lock ... and stopped. He locked the stall door again, pulled out the bullet, and loaded it once more. He held it up, looked at how much was left. Sadness started to creep in, and not just because of the finite amount.

No...

Later...

Maybe later.

Ron turned the crank back, the powder fell back into the vial, and he slid the device back into his pocket. At the sink, he lifted wet fingers to his nostrils and sniffed some water in to clean any residue. Ron looked up, tilted his head back to make sure nothing was showing around the edges, and then walked out to the third-floor lobby where he was supposed to host the Expo opening.

To the right, Ron saw them all—the guys, girls, and gays who'd paid extra to see him perform this silly ceremony. They were so eagerly watching for him to come up the escalator that no one noticed him standing behind them. He smiled ruefully. How stupidly single-minded they all were. He had wanted commission from the ticket sales —demanded it, initially—and he would have raised holy hell had Sarah not intervened. Turned out, the Expo donated the profits from this opening event to a literacy program in San Diego.

Literacy? It's all about the fucking pictures with these people.

Sarah pointed out that it was for a good cause, and said he'd look bad if he caused a problem, but he still felt like he was being taken advantage of. Maybe he could write the time off for his taxes or something since it was his name that got this group of oddballs up here in the first place. He'd have his accountant look into it.

Suddenly, something seemed wrong. Different. Odd. Ron had felt this feeling before. Like an oddly cool, windy Las Vegas day when he could sense that a storm was coming, but a twisting in his gut told him there was something bigger happening in the world. It was the kind of feeling that old people get "in the bones"; Dick Van Dyke looking into the sky before Mary Poppins arrived. As a child, the feeling had inspired adventures in the backyard or at the nearby playground. As an adult, he'd always brushed it off because it never really amounted to anything.

This day felt different. Ron looked down at his arm and saw goose bumps appear and disappear with his breath. His breath. He could hear his breath, even with the crowd.

That was it: the room seemed very quiet, even though things were happening nearby. And it was cool. Outside, the rising sun reflected off the many-windowed condominiums of downtown San Diego, flooding the glassed-in lobby with brilliant, ethereal light. Yet there wasn't any warmth.

A chill shot up Ron's spine and he spun around, realizing there was a person directly behind him: a short woman with two square suitcases in hand.

"Ja'harrah!" she yelled, clearly as startled to run into him as he was to find her there. She raised her right hand in a claw shape, with the middle and ring fingers slightly bent inward, then made an infinity gesture in the air.

She was dressed in an orange skirt and sweater, with black patent leather shoes like you'd see on kindergarten girls. Her dull brown hair was the oiliest Ron had ever seen, and it was roughly chopped in a bowl shape at her cheek. Thick glasses with large black frames rounded out the look.

On almost any other girl, it would have been retro-hip, but that wasn't the case here. Ron stared at her, wondering if she was one of those annoying comicaze players—or whatever the fuck they called themselves—but realized there wasn't enough thought in the outfit for it to be a costume.

"Ja'harrah," she repeated, keeping her voice low. Then, looking up and making hopeful eye contact, she added, "Lord Lionel."

"Lord Lionel" was a name the haters had given him after that first convention as a kind of "fuck you" to his attitude. Ron actually respected the ballsy person who came up with it. But the real fans had fought back in his defense, taking the name as a badge of honor. Ron had laughed at the online battle that never directly involved him, and gladly embraced the title. Though he never used it when referring to himself—even he didn't have that big an ego—Ron did enjoy the thought that his fans loved him and his work as if he were royalty.

"Ja'harrah" was another matter altogether. It was the most common religious phrase in *The Enduring*, and lots of fans used it. Some did it as a joke, some out of respect, but then there were some—like this one here—who chanted it because it held some kind of deeper meaning to them. Ron didn't know what that meaning was because it differed depending on the person. And, honestly, he didn't give a rat's ass. He hated those people. They were worse than the ones who argued plot points and story contradictions with him, because even though those types were annoying, they acted out of absolute love for his work. People could believe whatever spiritual thing they wanted, but Ron Lionel wasn't L. Ron Hubbard and *The Enduring* wasn't *Dianetics the Next Generation*. Believe what you want, but keep his creation out of it.

From her appearance and obvious desperation, Ron assumed she was the sort of fan who sat at home scouring his comics while concocting idiotic fan fiction. The stories invariably involved a damsel in distress (the writer) whom Dexter would screw somewhere in the Enchanted Woods of Mimmery.

Ron hated that, too—people taking his characters and making them do things against his will, especially when it came from social outcasts who basically regurgitated stories he'd already written and who didn't spell very well even with a spell-check program.

The only exception was if the fangirl was hot, or even vaguely cute, and Ron could flirt with her. That would lead to either a hook up, or finding himself in the pages of those fan magazines, where he would get to tap that same damsel's ass. In the first scenario, it was always better than his hand. In the second, even though the writing was never brilliant, the porn wasn't half bad and he could get off while reading it. He considered both cases a win.

Unfortunately, this one wasn't cute. She seemed truly odd—there was no better word for it. Like someone with a lazy eye whom you can never make eye contact with but you keep moving around like a cobra poised for attack, hoping you'll somehow connect with them. Only in this case, the connection felt more like a personality issue.

She freaked him out.

Ron turned and saw Sarah and the Weeble talking to a tubby dude in a suit who was probably the Expo president.

"Sorry, girl, I gotta go," he said and began striding over.

"It's Velma!" she shouted, her voice cracking like a cheap piece of Ikea glassware. Ron paused for a half-second, chose not to look back, and continued on. Stopping for this chick would only cause problems.

"Oh my God, you're Heidi!" the tubby guy said to Sarah as he walked up.

Everyone here's a fucking idiot.

Ron sighed and threw his arms around Sarah and the man he believed was the Weeble, ready to take on whatever came his way.

ISSUE #5

"A PERFECT STORM"

Comic Book Expo Opening Ceremony

Thursday, 8:55 a.m., Third-floor Lobby

First held on America's Finest Comic Book Expo's fifth anniversary, the opening ceremony is a time-honored tradition where a select group of attendees get to rub elbows with one of the industry's biggest stars. From comics creators to television icons, the CBE's special guest counts down to 9 a.m., when the Expo officially opens to the public. This year, that person is The Enduring *creator Ron Lionel.*

This event is limited to only 300 guests who enter a lottery to be among the lucky few; winners will be contacted one month before the event. An additional fee applies, and it does not count toward the entrance fee into America's Finest Comic Book Expo.

All moneys gathered from this event are donated to the San Diego Literacy Society and help underprivileged youth learn to read.

—From the Events section of America's Finest Comic Book Expo registration website

"It's nice to meet you, Mr. Lionel," Robert said, before turning back to Sarah in excited awe. "I can't believe it's really you."

Joe stared at him, stunned. Ron Lionel was the Expo's star guest. And Robert was never this dismissive, much less toward a professional whose work he admired. More shocking still, Robert seemed oblivious to the snub.

"Jesus tits, really?" Ron muttered.

"Lord Lionel," Xander jumped in, taking his hand to shake. "Xander Thompson, Comic Book Expo Fan of the Year..." He shrugged, laughing. "...again. Third year... I am so honored to meet you. It's just..." Xander slowed, as though he'd just realized who he was speaking to. "...amazing."

The younger man held Ron's hand longer than normal, and Joe could have sworn he saw a spark pass between them. Everyone knew Xander was gay; he'd started wearing feathered angel wings and short shorts to CBE when he was 14 and had since built a reputation for messing around with sexually fluid conventioneers. But Ron didn't strike Joe as being gay.

Nevertheless, he smiled at Xander like all the jocks and douchebags Joe saw hitting on women at the baseball games and concerts he managed with his Superior Staffers crew. As Ron stepped closer to Xander and was about to say something, Sarah interrupted.

"How old are you?" she asked, pulling away from Robert. Both Xander and Ron took small steps backward. She held out her hand. "ID. Now."

"You were Heidi the High School Witch!" Robert blurted out.

"Heidi the who?" Ron asked.

"The girl who flew into High School U. She'll put the hoodoo, voodoo, spell on you, too!" Robert recited.

"That was a lifetime ago," Sarah said dismissively as she turned back to Xander, all business.

"You were magnificent," Robert said, and Joe watched the hard features on Sarah's face soften slightly at the flattery.

Robert and Joe had started volunteering in the films department years ago, and when Joe moved into working with the security team, Robert went to programming. Over the years, they'd met hundreds of creators and celebrities, and Joe had never seen him geek out like this before. But clearly he'd grown up crushing on Heidi, and meeting the actress who'd played her was a long-delayed adolescent dream come true.

"I've wanted you to be a guest ever since I became Expo president, but we could never track you down. And I tried."

"I'm that good," Sarah joked dryly, waving her hand in a magical motion, now clearly enjoying the attention.

Robert clapped, delighted.

"What the hell!?" Ron snapped.

"I was a child actor. Don't be so surprised," Sarah said. "We've all got secrets in our pasts, I'm sure."

"It was a live action show, ran for seven seasons on Saturday mornings, and was top rated in its slot the entire time," Robert offered in rapid-fire fashion. "*TV Guide* called it the longest high school career in history, and a lot of TV networks tried to imitate it. They all failed." He finally took a breath. "I always thought there should be a reunion movie. Has anyone ever suggested it?"

"No," she replied, smiling. "But it's sweet of you to ask."

"You never told me," Ron said to Sarah. Joe could have sworn the man sounded hurt, and he turned to Pam and Zack to see if they'd heard it too. Their expressions said they had.

Sarah searched Ron's face, as if looking for something in his eyes, but then noticed everyone watching the exchange. She turned back to Robert, put one hand on his shoulder and the other on Ron's, and pushed them toward the stage. "Boys, you have a job to do."

Robert looked at his watch and was instantly all business. "Prepare for transformation in one minute, thirty-nine seconds," he yelled into his headset as he marched to the stage like a military commander. Bold morning sunlight flooded the area, and Joe couldn't help but smile at his friend's excitement.

Robert turned on the microphone, pulled the stand closer, and spoke. "Ladies and gentlemen, fans of all orientations, America's Finest Comic Book Expo presents to you, Ron Lionel!"

Applause erupted around the small stage, but they could hear the positive response outside the convention center where the audio was being broadcast as well. Usually the fans didn't care who the celebrity was, they were just thrilled to be getting inside, but in this case most attendees did know of Ron's reputation and eagerly wondered what might happen.

Ron pulled the microphone away from Robert. It squawked like an angry scavenger bird. He looked at Sarah, who nodded, then at Xander, and then at all the eagerly waiting fans. Ron's chest inflated like he'd just inhaled some kind of magical mist that imbued his pectoral muscles with superhuman confidence. He smoothly stood up straighter, his chin jutted out toward the assembled crowd, and he clenched the microphone like he was going to strangle it.

"Screw this ceremony bullshit," he said. Joe's eyes snapped from Ron to his agent, then to Robert, and finally to Pam. They looked stunned. "You guys want them to open these doors so you can have some fun, right?"

Cheers rose up from the crowd surrounding the stage. Joe immediately went on high alert, like he did at sporting events when hours of drinking combined with the home team's win could turn good people into riotous fools.

"I can't hear you bitches outside!" Ron yelled into the mic. His face grew red. The veins in his neck and forehead bulged. "You want me to do this stupid countdown, or do you want inside?"

Though they were high up in the convention center, separated from the outside world by glass, steel, and concrete, Joe could hear it in the distance: a long, dark roar like the Exogorth from *The Empire Strikes Back*, reaching up toward them, ready to crash into the building. He gave Pam a worried look, and quickly pushed his way through the crowd, hitting the "talk" button on his headset.

"All guards, we have a PITA situation," Joe said, using the acronym for "pain in the ass" that his staff knew all too well. He took the escalator down to the first floor, skipping every other step. "Attendees are pushing to get in. We've got to funnel that energy fast!"

Joe looked up and saw Ron fist-pumping the air. Fans had joined in. He couldn't see Robert, Pam, or any of the others. The Expo was expecting 30,000 people to enter during the opening hour—not in the opening minutes—and he needed to make sure no attendees got trampled or exhibitors' booths destroyed along the way.

"Exhibit Hall opening in thirty seconds," he announced. Voices from surprised team members started flooding back, but he yelled over them. "Time table has changed. It's out of our hands. Clear the floor immediately and prepare for attendees!"

Midway down the escalator, he saw the crowds through the glass, cheering and pushing toward the front doors. He needed to reduce that pressure.

"All outside door guards, open the glass doors now," he commanded. "Grey door operators for Halls A, B, C, and D, let attendees into the Exhibit Hall one at a time. Orderly. Control the flow but let them inside. No stopping.

"Grey door operators for Halls E, F, G, and H, funnel attendees up the escalators to the third floor. Tell them it's a shortcut.

"Third-floor guards, funnel attendees to the bayside. Bayside guards, open the doors completely and let everyone into the back of the Exhibit Hall."

Joe ran down the remaining steps and into the main lobby to see if his team at the front Exhibit Hall entrances needed help. He paused, and took all the stress out of his voice. "It's going to be a crazy thirty minutes, but you guys have got this. You. Have. Got. This."

"I hate Ron Lionel," Joe growled to Robert as they passed the gaming rooms, where players had begun their weekend-long campaigns to discover who was the greatest warrior in each of their respective universes. It was a relatively quiet area, since a lot of these people stayed in their meeting rooms, leaving only for food and bathroom breaks, which is why Joe and Robert often met here for a break. They stood, leaning against the wall while eating overly reheated slices of greasy cheese pizza.

"You and a hundred others..." Robert said, but he wasn't speaking for himself, Joe could tell. It was more of a general observation. He tore the crust from the back of the pizza and started eating it first, leaving the rest of his slice on the triangular cardboard plate.

"He's an invited guest," Joe argued. "And he talks like that? Talks to everyone like that?"

Robert gave him a surprised look. "You really don't know Ron Lionel?" Joe shook his head. "I was worried something worse would happen. And you handled the crowds really well. Kind of the best flow into the Expo we've ever had. We should look into what went on and see how we can replicate it for next year."

Joe stared in disbelief. "Why didn't you call him out on being late?"

"He wasn't," Robert said simply. "Almost, but not quite."

"But you didn't know where he was!" Joe snapped. "Neither did his agent or that weeble-looking publisher of his."

"He does look like a weeble, doesn't he?"

"Don't change the subject!" Joe said. Robert was two years older, and when they'd met in high school, Joe had quickly noticed how Robert used distraction tactics to keep the bullies from picking on him. It was part of what made him such a great president. He was ferociously smart, and lawful-good if you were looking at his D&D alignment, so he had a way of making the right choice for the Expo while at the same time making people think it was their decision. However, Robert wasn't one to start a fight, even when it was deserved, and that passivity sometimes pissed Joe off.

"What's going on with you?" Robert asked, finishing his crust and then picking up the cheesy section. Joe furrowed his brow. "There's a lot worse that happens here every year, and you normally roll with it."

"He just ruined the ceremony," Joe said. "And you love the ceremony. It's one of the few things you really look forward to every year. He ruined it for you." Joe truly believed that, but was surprised by how emotional the statement made him. He looked down at his pizza, put it back on its cardboard tray, and started to toss it out. Robert grabbed it before he could condemn the tasty triangle to the trash bin.

Joe pulled a paper napkin from his pocket and wiped his fingers, focusing on the orange grease that was staining them rather than look at Robert.

"Thanks," Robert said. "But something's wrong. You were a dick to Xander."

Joe wanted to say something but didn't know what. Instead, he sighed deeply, shook his head, and shrugged. A call came through their head pieces. Robert was needed in the Exhibit Hall; some exhibitor was unhappy because DC Comics' Bat Signal was hitting the side of his booth.

"How about dinner later?" Robert suggested. He shoved the rest of his pizza in his mouth as they rapidly moved down the hallway.

"What about Louise?" Joe asked, already knowing what the answer would be.

"She's not coming until Saturday," Robert said between chews. "You can be my date."

"Is Ron Lionel gay?" Joe asked.

"Haven't heard that he was, but who knows with the kids these days." He folded Joe's abandoned slice and shoved half of it in his mouth. "Mmwy?"

"Long story. I'll tell you over dinner."

"You should read some of his stuff," Robert said as he swallowed. "Might give you some ideas for your writing." Joe nodded but said nothing. The suggestion pissed him off and depressed him at the same time. "Seven at Morton's for steaks? I made reservations."

Joe nodded again and Robert waved before tossing out Joe's crust and heading down to the Exhibit Hall.

Joe stopped walking. He knew he should check on his team, but he also wanted to know: What *was* his problem? Why was Ron bothering him so much, and why had he been such a dick to Xander?

Two boys dressed as Rebel Alliance fighters went running past him.

"No running in the halls!" Joe yelled. The boys turned but continued on their path—right into a frumpy, dark-haired woman in an orange skirt and top holding a cell phone to her ear. She folded to the ground, dropping her phone and knocking over the two rolling suitcases at her side. The boys stopped for a moment, then took off running again.

"Selfish!" she screamed as she struggled onto her knees and up to her feet, obviously enraged. "SSSEEELLLFFFIIISSSHHH!"

Joe raced over to her and crouched down, putting his hand under her arm for support. She yanked it away from him.

"DON'T! YOU! DARE!" she screamed, scrambling on her hands and knees to grab the fallen phone.

Suddenly, with a swirl of fabric and light, Xander appeared by her side.

"Shh, sweetie, it's okay," he said calmly. "Let's get you over here and settled."

As Xander helped the woman onto her meaty legs, Joe reached for her suitcases. In a flash, she spun away from Xander and began slapping at him.

"Leave my things alone!" she screamed. "Someone help me!"

Joe tried to speak, to tell her who he was, but she just kept crying for help. Panic began to well in his chest. He raised his hands and froze in place. Xander stepped between him and the crazed woman, and he smiled at her, speaking slowly and calmly.

"Honey, it's okay," he said. "That's Joe. He works for the Expo. He runs security here." The woman stopped screaming, but still stared at Joe with suspicion. "I'll get your suitcases. You just sit here." Xander walked her to a bench, and she slumped down, slap-wiping some tears from her cheeks as he went to retrieve the bags. "Something's not right," Joe said to Xander. "Let me call First Aid."

They both looked at her. She was flattening down her hair, roughly. Some fans waved to Xander as they walked past, but he only nodded, focused on the woman.

"I think she's okay," Xander said. Joe resisted the urge to ask him when he became an authority on a person's physical and mental well-being. "She just seems shook up. Let me sit with her for a second, and if we need help, I'll call you." Xander started toward her with the bags, but as Joe began to follow, the young woman tensed up and glared.

Realizing he wasn't helping—and hating that realization the moment it hit—Joe stepped around the corner where he could keep an eye on things discreetly. He felt defeated, but knew he shouldn't leave in case things got worse.

"Now, then, better?" Xander asked as he rolled the suitcases to the woman's side. She bit her lip and looked up at him. "Somewhat?" She nodded. Xander plopped himself down next to her. "Xander Thompson," he said, extending his hand. "America's Finest Comic Book Expo Fan of the Year, three years running." No response. "And you are...?"

"Velma." She offered a dead fish handshake.

"Charmed, I'm sure," Xander replied. "Enjoying the event?"

She glowered: obviously not. Xander pointed to the phone in her hand.

"Were you calling someone?" Velma looked at the phone. "You want me to help you call them back?"

She shook her head. "I was trying to hear my mom," she said. "It's too noisy here."

"Is that what set such a sad frown upon such a glorious face?" Xander asked, but the compliment didn't improve her mood or appearance. "Come on, Velma," Xander finally said in his normal voice. "If you can't trust a queer at a comic book convention, then who can you trust?"

Velma perked up. "You're a free spirit?"

"That's one way of putting it, I suppose."

"Like Dexter has in *The Enduring*," she said. "He has a 'free spirit guide' named Whimsy! The Gods send Whimsy to help Dexter whenever he gets lost on his journey."

"And who are we to question the workings of the gods?" Xander nodded wisely. Velma looked at him with wide eyes. "Joking. I know the books well. I met Ron Lionel earlier today, in fact."

"Me too. Kind of. Not really." Velma stared intensely at Xander, and for a moment, Joe felt strange. He knew he shouldn't be spying, but there was something odd about this woman. And he was seeing a side of Xander he'd never witnessed before. Calmer. More ... normal. "What was he like?"

"Jesus tits, I'm fucking amazing!" Xander said, imitating Ron. Velma stared at him. "That was my Ron Lionel impression."

"That's not what he's like."

"Some people think so," Xander said weakly.

"That's not what he's like," she repeated. Joe couldn't help but laugh a little. "What was he like when you spoke to him today?"

Xander sighed, thought about it, and a small smile rose on one side of his mouth. "Not what I expected. But in a good way."

Velma nodded. "I came all the way here from Charleston, South Carolina," she told him. "My mother and I love his writing. We read it and reread it and try to figure out the clues together. We listen to podcasts and read articles and stuff. We figured out the secrets of the Rhyming Road before anyone else." She paused, then clenched her fists.

"You're upset about the Book of Revelation storyline," Xander said, nodding. "It's been the talk leading up to the Expo. You know he'll have to answer questions about it during his panel."

"It's why I came. I need to know—" Joe wondered what she'd intended to say, but Velma moved on, "Then I ran into him like Lady Fate had sent us both on the same path. And, Gods, when I heard his voice, it sounded like angels all yelling at once." Velma looked up at Xander. "I know this seems stupid, but we're his fans. And Dexter is his creation." She sounded wounded.

"So you spoke with him?" Xander asked.

"Not really," she looked at Xander, confusion written all over her face. "When I'm alone or with my mother, I can do whatever I imagine. I can talk, I can laugh, I can do anything. But my mother couldn't come to San Diego with me, and today…" Velma stopped, looking down at her thighs. "I just felt so stupid." She sounded lost, and as the tears slowly slipped from her eyes again, Joe felt uncomfortable. Half of him wanted to come out of the shadows and hug her, and the other half wanted to find a task that would get him away from her emotions.

"Girl, listen to me," Xander quietly instructed. "Stop those tears, because they aren't doing you or anyone else any good. And praying only gets half the job done. I mean, listen to yourself. When you were talking to me about coming out here just now, you lit up. But coming to San Diego was you taking hold of your life. Not any god or goddess doing anything. It was all you."

Velma stared at Xander as though his words were blasphemous. "But the Gods give us strength," she tentatively challenged.

"Did you ever consider that your gods simply helped you see the strength that you already possessed inside?"

Velma slowly sat up straighter. She smiled, and the dark cloud that had filled this corner of the convention center lifted.

"You know, I'm scared too," he said. Velma looked surprised. He stood up. "All the time. Anyone who wants to achieve a dream and isn't scared is both a fool and a failure. But my nana always said that the only way to overcome fear is to dive right into it." Xander looked deep into her eyes. "Miss Velma, you deserve to fulfill your destiny no matter what anyone else says, and that includes your doubting self! We might look like geeks out there in the mundane world, but we know who we are on the inside: strong, smart, and possessing the skills to do whatever we want! So to hell with the mundane world, and stop waiting for your gods to do your work for you. Make your own destiny happen!"

Velma wrapped her arms around him, causing his peacock-feathered hat to flutter off his head. He made a few half-hearted protests about not wrinkling his blouse and cape.

"Joe, come in!" came an urgent call over the headset. Pam. Joe backed away from Xander and Velma.

"You okay?" he asked, concerned. He could tell from the sound of her voice that there was a real problem.

"It's Ron Lionel," she said. "You have to get to the Sail Deck now!"

ISSUE #6

"THE CALL OF THE WILD"

"How can Myranda know what's going on with Majesty when she lost her powers two issues ago?" a nervous teenaged boy with a bad case of acne asked Ron Lionel during the Enduring panel I attended at WonderCon in California.

It was a question every fan wanted to ask. Every electronic device in the room clicked on in anticipation.

"Oh! Oh no, I've made a mistake!" Ron Lionel screeched like an English school girl, even though his British backstory had been debunked a month before at Project A-Kon in Dallas, Texas. "Who d'ya think you are, y'little wanker?" the fake Brit asked, leaning into his microphone as if to French kiss it. "I've laid out The Enduring with intricate care. I don't do things randomly so you can wet your pants thinking you caught me making a mistake. I don't make mistakes!" The boy slunk back to his seat. "Don't you sit down, y'little turd! Go home! Go home and beat off to pictures of Myranda and Majesty, y'fuckin' twit. That's why I make the boobs so big in the pictures!"

The boy grabbed his backpack and hurried from the room. His friends looked at one another, pretending they didn't know him.

"You lot, there!" Ron screamed at them. "I see you wettin' your pants wondering what to do. Well, I'll tell you: GET OUT! At least your friend had balls with hair on them, you useless sacks of flesh!"

Duly rebuked, the boys left. The audience exploded in applause; Lionel ate up the attention. No, they didn't get their answer. I don't think any of them expected they would. What they came for was the show—to be a part of that show—and they got it all in spades.

Whether you "get" the magic, mystery, or storytelling in The Enduring *is irrelevant. What matters most, and what I think will endure long after Dexter's adventures have faded away from the pages they were printed on, will be the legend of Ron Lionel that he himself created.*

—Excerpt from "My Day with an Asshole" by Shannon Spindler, originally published in *Vanity Fair*

"I hate comic books," Ron said to a fan as he signed her double-sized issue of *The Enduring* #50. The young woman had asked what comic books he read. Her mistake. "Hate them!"

This was true. Ron knew he should be doing bigger and better things—novels and screenplays like Tom Clancy, Stephen King, even Anne Rice. (Though he would freely admit to anyone, whether they asked or not, that he was never a fan of her Lestat books.)

"But you don't get to choose where life takes you," Ron said to the fangirl, making sure the Weeble, who was managing the autograph line, heard. The Weeble offered an uncomfortable smile to the girl, who looked confused. "I'm talking about.... Ugh, never mind."

Ron glanced past her and the Weeble, and down the long line of people waiting for autographs. The Sail Deck was an open-air section on the top floor of the convention center that housed food carts, giant round tables where visitors rested or ate, and an autograph signing area for guests whose lines would be too long for the Exhibit Hall. It had glass walls set between stone and metal pillars, which rose up high to beams that supported giant sections of draped metal shaped to look like sails. Hence, the name.

Ron sat at a long folding table, the kind used in banquet halls, conveniently draped in front with the same blue fabric as the makeshift curtain walls that divided his autograph section from the one to his right. That area was empty now, but in a couple hours it would house some has-been 90s TV action star whose current yearly income was derived from syndication payments and fans handing over $40 for an autographed head shot. It was a good thing no one was there, because Ron's line snaked around his section and spilled over in front of the other, blocking anyone interested in accessing that area.

Ron shook his right hand, sore from autographing for the past 45 minutes. He gently looked over his shoulder, careful not to move too much, to the glistening blue harbor just over the wall and out of reach. Far away to his right, looking like a picture postcard, was the famous Coronado Bridge, while lines of hotels, restaurants, and clubs snaked off to the left. Ron felt caged in his folding chair prison. But then the annoyance stopped, and Ron smiled as a wave of pleasurable warmth washed over him. He squirmed in his seat, suddenly feeling both relaxed and energized beyond belief. He finished his last signature and handed the fangirl her books.

"Have a great show," he said smoothly. Then, just as he was about to reach under the table and adjust some things, Sarah appeared in front of the next fan. He put his hands back on top of the table and interlaced his fingers. He smiled.

"Be nice to your publisher," Sarah said. "He's working hard for you." Ron's annoyance returned. "Promise me."

"This is nice for me," Ron replied, nodding to the fanboy who stepped in front of Sarah and held out a book. It was the kind of collected edition Ron hated most. "Ooh, paperback!"

The kid nodded eagerly, missing the sarcasm. Rob opened the

cheaply printed pages, wondering where he'd sign without cracking the spine or ripping the newsprint.

"Can you make it out to Hiroshi?" the boy asked. "H-I-R-O-S-H-I. And can you do a quick sketch of Ariel's eyes above the I? She's my fav—"

"No requests." Ron gestured to a foam core–mounted sign letting fans know what they could and couldn't get:

Three autographs only.

All autographs must be personalized.

No sketch requests.

Photos are acceptable, but no crossing the table.

No lengthy questions.

(*The Enduring* panel is Saturday at 11 a.m.)

Ron squirmed again, feeling very, very dirty in that moment. He may have hated comic books and known he should be doing something bigger with his life, but there were certainly some great perks.

"Sorry." He shrugged to Hiroshi. "I hate all these rules, but you know how fucked up convention organizers are. Loving their little moment of power." Hiroshi nodded eagerly. Fans loved it when Ron made them feel like he shared in their misery. He caught a glimpse of Sarah raising her eyebrow. "Get me a water, would you, please?" She turned just as Ron shifted suddenly in his seat. "No!" he shouted quickly.

Sarah stopped and looked at him, confused.

"Not you." He squeezed his legs in tightly and nodded to the Weeble. "You. Get me some water."

"I'm watching the line," the Weeble protested.

"Who's watching the booth?" Ron snapped. "Who's keeping everything safe and answering questions?"

"My staff and my wife..." the Weeble stopped, but it was too late.

"You're married?!" Ron looked up at him, then at Hiroshi, shocked. "See, there's someone for everyone." He shouted to the fans in line, "You guys'll behave, right, if he gets me a water?" They all cheered. Ron smiled at the Weeble. "Good. Go."

The Weeble hurried off, giving Sarah a look. Ron handed the book back to Hiroshi and smiled politely as the young man looked at the signature, thanked him for all his work, and walked away.

Sarah stepped in, holding her hand out so the next fan would wait. She leaned in and whispered, "I know you're disappointed about this morning's news." Ron started to object, but she held her finger up and he stopped himself. "I know you're bummed, and that's natural. But it's not the end of this story. We'll work it out." Ron tried again to speak. "However," she interrupted, "you've got three and a half days left of this Expo. If you're this pissy now, you're gonna royally screw up at the masquerade—by the way, you have a meeting for that tomorrow at three, don't forget—and have everyone hating you by Sunday. Including me *and* yourself. And even you won't be able to fix that."

Ron met her eyes. She was right. He'd been in a great mood after the opening ceremony. Sure, he'd been thrown by finding out that Sarah—who knew everything about him—had never told him such an important detail about her past. But he still felt it had gone well, and afterward he'd made a quick stop in the restroom for another two bumps.

From there, things were in sync. He was on! Sarah had escorted him to the Ragnarök booth, and on the way, he'd met fans (including celebrities from TV shows) who loved his work. A couple of big name comics creators—Frank Svengsouk and Michele Miller—had invited him to a private dinner that evening, and they'd dropped hints about collaborating on "a fun little project" if he was willing to discuss the option. He'd actually meant it when he told them he'd be thrilled to join them. And whenever Sarah had taken a bathroom break, or answered a call, email, or text that took her focus away from him, he'd flirted with fans. He'd met some cute ones, a few hot ones—and of course the girl under the table, who was both hot and dirty.

Yes, Thursday at America's Finest Comic Book Expo was looking to be a good day, despite how it had started. And he knew he should be enjoying everything right now: the great weather, meeting people who loved him and his work, the sultry sensations that occasionally slunk through his entire body. But the coke was wearing off, and with that came frustrated boredom. The muscles in his jaw tensed up, and his neck shivered involuntarily.

He clamped his teeth and nodded. Sarah nodded back.

"That pizza smell is killing me," she finally said. "You want anything?"

This time Ron shook his head, and she walked away toward one of the food carts.

As Ron sat back and opened his legs to allow the girl to continue, he noticed a woman—one of the staff from the opening ceremony—looking at him. She turned away when she saw him looking at her, but she didn't leave. Clearly she was interested in what he had going on. Ron admired her tight body and guessed she was in her 30s. She looked like she took care of herself. But there was something else about her that made Ron take notice.

"She's sexy, huh?" Ron asked the fanboy who had just handed him three first-issue first editions to autograph. The boy turned and looked. "The one in the grey slacks and that clingy red top."

She looked toward him again. She was too far away to hear him (even if she had been nearby, the din of chatting fans roaming the Sail Deck made conversations difficult), but she had looked over; perhaps there was some bigger connection she was sensing between them. Ron liked that idea.

Sexy Convention Lady turned away once more, acting like she was checking out the fliers on a nearby freebie table.

"She looks like my mom," the fanboy said, uncomfortable. Ron didn't care. He liked it when people looked at him like that.

"How old are you?" he asked.

"Thirteen…"

"Son, let me school you," Ron said. "That woman isn't an actress or a model or anything like that. She's good looking, and when she does herself up, I bet she's pretty great. But the difference between her and a lot of other people in the world is that she knows how to embrace the sexy."

The boy stared at the woman, then back at him, confused. Ron realized she was staring at him again, this time without any embarrassment.

Ron gave her a nod and a slight smile, and she sharply turned away. *Caught!* Ron smiled. This was definitely going somewhere.

"There are a lot of attractive people in the world, and a lot of dogs. Look at me. I'm not your typical Hollywood type, but I know myself. I know what I got here…" He pointed to his head. "…here…" He pointed to his heart. "…and right here between my legs." Ron smiled, pleased with himself. "But even a dog can score the best ass ever if he knows it. Has confidence. Mark my words on that."

Ron looked down, signed the three books he'd laid out in a row, and handed them back to the boy.

"I would have written something like, 'Stay sexy, stud,' but my agent would freak out. We'll keep this talk between us bros, right?" The boy nodded, took his books, and warily opened them to check the signatures. "Okay, move along…"

Ron slid one hand under the table to make adjustments, then looked across the Sail Deck for Sexy Convention Lady. She seemed to have disappeared.

"Sorry, signing's over. You guys will have to come back tomorrow," said a middle-aged guy in a dark blue polo shirt who'd suddenly popped up next to the autograph area.

"What the hell d'ya think you're doing?" Ron shouted, pissed, but Blue Polo Shirt and another random dude in a black trench coat ignored him. Instead of answering, they grabbed the weighted-down poles holding the curtained wall between them and the empty cubicle next door. Ron slammed his hands on the table—but didn't stand up—as they dragged the poles, their heavy metal bases scraping into the concrete floor with a horrible grinding noise that cut through the talking on the Sail Deck. Within seconds, Ron was boxed within a curtained cage, hidden from the fans outside.

He read "Joe Cotter, Expo Security" on Blue Polo Shirt's badge, and vaguely remembered that he and Black Trench Coat were both at the opening ceremony.

Suddenly, Sexy Convention Lady threw open the curtained wall and Sarah stormed inside. Before she could say anything, Sexy Convention Lady and Black Trench Coat went back out to make sure no fans would see what was about to happen. That's when Ron realized two things. One: Sarah was more pissed than he'd ever seen her in his life. And two: He'd been caught.

Sarah gave a hard, swift kick to the drape covering the table in front of Ron. A sharp pain stabbed into his dick.

"Ow!" screamed a muffled voice.

"Christ!" Ron snapped, jumping back in his seat. "Watch the..." he started to say "teeth," but stopped himself. The curtain whipped open again, and the Weeble raced inside. He stopped when he saw Ron's hard dick, and the girl trying to stand up from under the table. The Weeble made an "Okay, then..." face and quickly backed out, pulling the drape tightly closed behind him. Ron started buttoning up his pants.

"You pervert," Joe hissed, low enough that the fans outside wouldn't hear. He pulled up the tablecloth so Sarah could drag out the girl. "Between your half-mast eyes and the drapes moving, it's no wonder everyone in the damn convention center didn't know what was going on."

"Don't be mad," Blowjob Girl said. "He's Ron Lionel. He created *The Enduring*."

"So that means you should act like a cheap tramp?" Sarah snapped, grabbing the girl's wallet out of her pocket.

"Give that back!" the girl shrieked, clawing for it. Sarah grabbed the girl's wrists with her free hand and shoved her up onto the table, as though possessed with Wonder Woman's strength. The girl thunked down, stunned, her spit-covered cheek smearing the table top.

"She's legal." Sarah let her go with a sigh, and held the ID out.

The girl snatched it back.

"Consenting adults!" the girl said, pissed. "We can do what we want."

"Not at an all-ages show you can't," Joe said. He grabbed her Expo badge from around her neck. "Pam?" he called, and Sexy Convention Lady came back in. "I need a woman with me when I escort her off the property."

"You can't!" Blowjob Girl started crying. "That's a four-hundred-dollar badge!"

"You should have thought of that before you decided to whore yourself out in public," Sarah said.

"Don't you slut shame me, bitch!" the girl spat through clenched teeth.

Joe and Sexy Convention Lady—Pam—escorted her to the back curtains so the fans up front wouldn't see. Joe looked back at Ron.

"We'll figure out how to deal with you when I get back."

Ron scoffed at him and stood up as the trio disappeared out the back. It felt hollow. He was about to shrug at Sarah—no big deal—but the look on her face stopped him cold. She stood rigid, shaking with anger. Her jaw muscles were clenched, but her lip quivered slightly. Her eyes were filled with rage and tears and disappointment.

Ron stopped breathing. Guilt wrapped tightly around his neck and engulfed his body from back to front. His hands shook. His tummy twisted. He needed to pee. He thought about the coke in his pocket. He wished he hadn't brought it. He wanted to cry. He wanted Sarah to hold him. He didn't want to feel what he was feeling.

"I didn't think it..."

SMACK! Sarah's palm made such quick contact with Ron's cheek that he didn't see it coming. It stung madly. And for a second, Ron felt good again. Right. Normal. But then Sarah threw open the side curtain and stormed out, leaving him standing there alone. The guilt returned and engulfed him once more.

Sarah had been partially right: she hated him, and a part of him hated himself, too. But it didn't take until Sunday to make it happen.

ISSUE #7

"PRIDE AND PREJUDICE"

SAN DIEGO UNION-TRIBUNE: How was the transition from the end of this year's Expo to preparing for the Republican National Convention?

JOE COTTER: *A piece of cake.*

That's it? You only had four days.

Sorry, I'm really tired. (He takes a deep breath, trying to focus through obvious exhaustion.)

It's been a busy week going from one event to the next, and dealing with all the security restrictions and stuff. But we've been doing this for 35 years, and I've been the head of their security team for three. Plus, I've been working at Superior Staffers since I was 18. So everything went pretty smoothly.

We'd heard there was some confusion with the Expo's exhibitors moving out last Sunday night while the RNC's security team came in to secure the location.

(He pauses, clearly selecting his words carefully.) *There may have been some hiccups at first with the RNC's team, but those are misunderstandings that always happen with big events like this one. We worked them out, and their convention is safe, secure, and ready for tomorrow's big launch.*

Some members of the city council seemed worried about a fan group like America's Finest Comic Book Expo holding their event right before a big political gathering.

(He laughs cynically.) *Of course they did. They've always seen us as just a group of geeks with our Spock ears and weird costumes running around the city for four days. And no matter how long we host this event, and no matter how many visitors we bring into the city—last year almost a quarter of a million, thank you—and no matter how much money we bring to the local restaurants, tourist attractions, and hotels—which all sell out, every single year—they will always see us that way. They will sit in their big offices, look down their noses at us the same way they looked down on the nerds in school, and happily take the tax dollars we bring into this city, all the while making jokes about us behind our backs. So, no, I'm not surprised some of them "seemed worried," but if they ever came down to America's Finest, they'd see that there's nothing to worry about.*

—From the first, and last, interview Joe Cotter ever gave on behalf of America's Finest Comic Book Expo and Superior Staffers

"No one's seen Ron since the incident?" Robert asked the "Operation: Blowjob Breakup" team. Zack, Pam, and Joe shook their heads. They had assembled in the candlelit dining room at Morton's, where Robert had originally made dinner reservations for himself and Joe. Unfortunately, their relaxing evening had turned into a brisk strategy meeting. Amy was also there. Joe needed someone from his team to help keep an eye out for Ron, someone trustworthy. Besides, she'd been the one to name the incident Operation: Blowjob Breakup, and Joe felt some levity was required during the crisis.

"We checked all the social media channels and prominent sites," Joe said to the motley crew, who looked out of place in their rumpled clothes. "No one's talking about it, not even the girl who was caught doing it."

"She's probably too embarrassed," said Pam. "And scared. If we kick Ron out of the Expo and word gets out on why it happened..."

"And he'd definitely let the world know what happened," Joe said, still pissed. And hungry.

"...she'll get the blame." Pam finished. "She's going to be 'the whore' in everyone's eyes, and he'll just be a dog, but no one will fault him for it."

"Come on..." Robert started.

"What man turns down a blowjob?" Amy asked. "Under any circumstances?"

Joe looked at Robert and Zack. None of them wanted to argue.

"No, people believe it's the woman's job to say no, and even though it takes two to do it, she'll get the blame and the shame," Amy concluded.

"Truth," Zack nodded thoughtfully, though Joe wasn't quite sure he actually agreed.

"And even if they both stay quiet, the CCK could be dangerous," Robert added, staring into his drink with concerned eyes.

Joe and Zack nodded. Pam and Amy looked confused.

"Comic Convention Karma," Joe explained. "It's the closest thing

Robert has to a religion—which is a lot to say, considering he was raised by agnostic parents."

"It's just karma, karma, right?" Amy asked. "One bad action can eventually come back and bite you in the ass."

"It's more complex than that," Robert said solemnly, leaning in. The others did the same. "Within the walkways, meeting rooms, exhibit halls, and waiting areas of CBE, you have celebrities, industry professionals, exhibitors, volunteers, and fans all crossing paths and exchanging money, words, thoughts, barbs, advice, and so on. Big meetings happen here. You could be replaced as soon as your contract is up."

"Sooner if the sales on your comic have been lower than expected," Zack added.

Joe nodded. "People are here to celebrate comics and pop culture, but I think ninety percent of the working professionals are worried they're going to be fired at any moment."

"Why? For low-selling books?" Pam asked.

"Low-selling books, a hot younger writer or artist, you posting something on social media that pissed off someone in the legal department. Who knows?" Joe said. "The job security our grandparents always talked about is gone these days, but I don't know that it ever really existed in the creative arts."

Robert continued, "So you have a paranoid creator who thinks an editor has dissed him—even though the guy may just need coffee, or he had a bad breakfast, or he got a call about his sick child. The 'why' doesn't matter, because now that artist's panel presentation is horrible, and that impacts three thousand or more attendees. They talk about it—in the halls, online—and now people wonder if that artist is even relevant anymore. That can hurt the artist or editor in the long run, or it could simply piss off a woman in the audience whose boyfriend told her this panel would be 'awesome' and convinced her to miss an anime screening she wanted to attend."

"Which shows her that he's really a selfish guy, and so she breaks up with him," Zack tossed in.

Joe sipped his whiskey and avoided looking at Pam.

"Seriously?" Amy asked in disbelief. "You seriously think it's that intense."

"The paranoid creator scenario is allegedly what got the Five Young Turks at Marvel fired in the eighties," Zack said. "It's also why Michaels and Chabon wouldn't work together for years; they both thought the editor liked the other better after a comment he made at an opening night cocktail mixer in 1973."

"It supposedly caused a redo of the Hong Kong Disney parade last year when a former Imagineer laughed at something that execs believed to be the parade concept," Joe said. "And I know three couples who broke up because of panels that turned out bad."

"The *Babylon 5* versus *Dr. Who* panel of 2010?" Zack asked.

"*BSG* reunion versus *Grimm* and *Outlander* in 2017," Joe added.

"The point," Robert interrupted, "is that everything at this show feeds off everything else—a world of karma in one tiny four-day microcosm. And I refuse to let one man's urges ruin the Expo for everyone else. Because it could. I know it could."

"It's just so stupid," Joe said, his anger rising again. "Hell, Ron Lionel should be less desperate. He's got women *and* men throwing themselves at him. He could wait until he got back to his hotel room, for God's sake."

Robert waved his hand to get them all back on topic. "So he's not at his hotel?"

"If he is, he's not answering his door," Amy said before sipping her martini.

"You went there?" Robert asked, surprised.

"We both did," Joe said, taking some sourdough bread from the basket on the table. It was still warm. "I figured if he saw her when he looked through the peep hole, he'd be more likely to open the door." Zack raised his martini glass and nodded with approval. Joe smiled, but then it struck him that he'd never seen Zack drink a martini before. The grimacing face he made every time he took a sip made Joe think it wasn't common practice.

"Did you get hotel security to open it up for you?" Pam asked, pulling Joe back into the conversation. "Make sure everything was okay?"

"No," Joe said as he brought the bread to his nose and inhaled. "To do that, we would've had to tell them we thought something was wrong. At this stage, we don't want to raise any red flags. If he doesn't show up tomorrow, then we'll do it." He brought the bread to his mouth, paused, and asked, "Does anyone need to order? I'm starving."

The others shook their heads, as if this Ron Lionel situation was so desperate that it had robbed them of their appetites. Joe understood the stakes involved, but he also knew how irritable he got when his blood sugar was low. So did Pam. She slid the plate of butter to him.

"What about his agent?" she asked.

"Sarah's livid," Robert said. "She took one of my calls. She didn't even ask me to cover for him, or let him stay at the show. And I don't know if she's staying or leaving." Robert was clearly bummed at the possibility that she might go. "Anyway, she hasn't heard from him either, but thinks we should wait until tomorrow as well. Ron's known for disappearing with fans at these events."

"So, we kick him out tomorrow, right?" Joe said between bites.

"He broke the law," Zack agreed, holding up his index finger.

"That could mean refunds to any fan who says they specifically came because of him," Pam pointed out.

"And they can wait until the end of Saturday to ask for it," Zack threw in. "They could legitimately argue that they didn't know he'd been kicked out until his panel."

"At that point, we won't be able to sell on-site admissions to make up for the loss," Pam said. "In theory, if they were really litigious, they could extend that to their hotel rooms, flights, all that stuff."

"Class-action lawsuit," Robert said, and Joe could see the sweat forming in large ovals under his armpits. "And then all the negative press."

"He got a blowjob on the Sail Deck!" Joe snapped, too loudly.

Pam hit him in the arm. A couple gliding past (he in a black suit, she in a short dress with plunging back) glanced at Joe but moved on without any reaction, as though they didn't even speak his language.

"He broke the law," Joe whispered. "How are we at fault?"

"You're 'The Man.' You're always at fault," Amy said simply. The men stared at her, confused, but Pam seemed to understand. "Guys, I hear it all the livelong day. People are always complaining that the show's greedy, that you charge too much for entry..."

"We're competitive," Robert argued. "I did a cost analysis, and if you look at our programming—"

"Blah, blah, blah," Amy interrupted. "You're forgetting how it used to be, before you had fancy jobs and were running things. For these guys who work at low-paying jobs, who have a limited budget and would rather be spending their money on books and toys and crap, paying a couple hundred bucks for admission is a lot. And not everyone does the twenty-four-hour programming, or they think the event's not as cool as 'the old days,' or they say it's 'too Hollywood' now and you don't feature comic books enough anymore..."

"More than seventy-five percent of our programming is comics focused," Robert interjected.

"And none of them care, Robert, because you went from being the geeks to being the big guys on campus," Amy said sympathetically, touching his arm. Robert blushed. "Just like that girl, you guys are going to be positioned as the bad guys because you ruined the fans' weekend. I don't know that it'll damage the event too much, but it won't make your lives easier."

"Should we loop Danielle and the marketing team in on what's been happening?" Zack asked.

Robert ignored him. "If New York or Chicago gets Ron for their conventions this year, things could get even worse."

Joe could see how the various scenarios were playing out in his friend's mind, slowly driving him crazy. It was like when they were young and getting picked on—the frustration they would feel at not being able to do anything against the bigger kids because they were smarter, faster, or stronger.

"Okay, so let's do nothing for tonight," Joe suggested. "We all need food and sleep, and we need to see how Ron responds."

Everyone at the table nodded, offering up a collective sigh. They were all as emotionally exhausted as he was. And it was only the first day.

A server approached in smart black pants and a white shirt. Morton's would be considered very formal by most CBE attendees, but both Robert and Joe had matured in their tastes. Besides, this had been a serious business meeting, and no one on the America's Finest Board of Directors would argue the meal receipt.

Joe looked up. "We'll be set to order in a couple minutes, but could you bring out maybe a large Caesar salad for the table?" He looked around, but everyone except Robert was standing up and making their apologies: Zack had the Marvel party, Amy was already late to her mom's birthday dinner, and Pam was meeting friends up in Hillcrest.

Joe looked back at the server and fumbled. "Sorry, give us a minute to figure it out."

When it was just Robert and Joe, they ordered more drinks and their meals—salad, filet mignon, potatoes, mac and cheese, and grilled asparagus so they didn't feel guilty.

As the server walked away and the two men sat back with drinks in hand, Robert smiled. "Thanks for that." He nodded to the empty chairs. "This whole thing has been a lot..."

"A *lot*," Joe agreed. "It'd make for a good book." Robert tensed. "I'm kidding!" Joe threw his napkin at Robert, who tried catching it but missed. He picked it up off the table, tossed it back. The black cloth landed in the chair next to Joe. "Number one, I'd never betray the

Expo, and number two, no one would buy a book about a comic convention, anyway."

"How is the writing going?" Robert asked.

Joe smiled, started to speak, then exhaled. "It's not, really." Earlier, when Zack had asked, he'd felt tense and defensive, but with Robert it was different. "I'm just not feeling it anymore."

"No one cares about Robotech fighters battling alongside Voltron?" Robert asked.

"Just the same ten people who have stuck with me since I started." Joe laughed. Robert didn't, exposing the hollow feeling inside Joe's chest. "I want to write something else."

"So write something else," Robert said, as if Joe could just snap his fingers and make it happen.

"It's..." Joe stopped, unsure of what to say. He sipped his whiskey and shrugged. "It was easy. I could imagine stories and scenes and come up with episodes in my head and it would just flow, you know? But now it's like I'm too old to be writing make-believe stories."

Joe looked down at the brown liquid in his drink, feeling guilty for having said it.

"Why don't you write something original?" Robert asked. "You have the skill—and I know I've told you this—to do all this complex research and put it into a format that makes it easy to understand. I hate reading some science fiction authors because they get too caught up in the technical minutia. It's like the writer's trying to impress you with how much he knows. But you make it really organic. I mean, the way you hypothesized how the 'Mirror, Mirror' universe couldn't exist in these new *Star Trek* movies because of how they dealt with time anomalies was brilliant, and I don't think other writers could do it as well."

"But that's *Star Trek*," Joe said, deflecting the compliment.

"Which is why I said you should do something original. It's been years since I've seen any of your writing that wasn't based on a TV show or movie."

Joe wanted to. He did. He just didn't know how. And for one second—two, three, four, five seconds—he stared into his drink, lost in the golden brown ribbons swirling around the glass. Then he realized Robert's eyes were on him, so he looked up and smiled.

"I should!" he nodded, smiling with excitement he didn't feel. He leaned in and whispered, "I seriously almost busted out some melodramatic line like Zack would've done. About the writer's journey, and how I took the road less traveled." He tossed back the rest of his whiskey. "Maybe I should stick with wine for the meal." Robert smiled back at him, but Joe wasn't sure if he would let the subject drop. "This is like old times, huh?" he said. "Only we'd be at The Old Spaghetti Factory with cheap wine, noodles with meat sauce, garlic bread…"

"I loved that garlic bread," Robert said defensively.

"And figuring out whether or not we had enough money for one more glass of wine and a decent tip for the waitress."

"Whom you would try to flirt with," Robert added.

"It never worked." Joe laughed. "I was thinking about that years later when I made management at Superior Staffers. I notice it all the time now: drunk guys at events trying to be players with the cute waitress who's paying her way through college."

"Or still in high school."

"Right? And have you ever thought about how many of those cute waitresses get hit on by customers, all thinking they're the guy who's going to get her? That she's going to say yes to them. Not thinking about the fact that she's got a story of her own, and the chances of her story matching up to your story and your needs and wants are so slim."

"I don't think most guys our age understand that, much less when they're in their twenties."

"Twenty-one," Joe said, laughing. "We were just legal enough to drink. And I thought I was so slick ordering merlot."

"That merlot came from a box," Robert added, and the two laughed again. He drained the last of his Manhattan and looked over at Joe. "What's happening with Pam?"

"Nothing." Joe sighed. He didn't like the heavy turn the conversation had taken. "You know that."

"There was something at the opening ceremony today. Before the chaos."

He saw that. Of course he saw that.

"I still like her," Joe said. Robert gave him the Vulcan eyebrow. "Okay, I love her. Nothing's changed. But when we went to New York, it was clear that she wanted one thing and I wanted something else." Robert's stare filled him with a strange mix of anger and embarrassment. "What?"

"After two and a half years of dating, she wanted to discuss marriage," Robert said thoughtfully, as though laying out the pieces of a complex mystery.

"No, she wanted to *get married*," Joe countered sharply. "There's a difference."

"And you didn't. And that's that. End of story," Robert continued, calmly sounding out the beats, which frustrated Joe even more.

"And that just doesn't make sense to me. You've never once said that you didn't want to get married, or that you don't believe in the institution of marriage, or that you think it's a stupid idea. And you like Pam—you're *into* Pam—more than I've ever seen you be into anyone else."

"Because you know me so well," Joe said flippantly. He raised his glass to take another sip, but he was out.

"Yes," Robert said simply, in his plain, logical way, divorcing emotion from the discussion. "I do know you. Better than anyone, I think. And I'm worried about you."

The two men stared at one another. They had been friends for 25 years. They'd lived most of their major life moments together. They'd shared laughs over Joe's many first dates with many bad girlfriends, and helped one another face the fears and triumphs of moving away to college (Joe to UCSD for English, Robert to UCLA for undergrad and then business school). Robert had attended every one of Joe's fan-fic panels at CBE, and Joe had nominated Robert for a seat on the America's Finest Board of Directors—a move which had given Robert a chance to show the "old guard" how smart he was, and laid the groundwork for where he was today. Robert had been there for Joe when his mom had died suddenly one summer of a blood clot no one knew about. Joe had toasted Robert long-distance when he'd finally lost his virginity as a college freshman, and then he'd driven three hours to Robert's dorm room, pizza in hand, when Robert had found out the girl didn't want anything to do with him the next week. Joe had called Robert when he thought he'd gotten his first college girlfriend pregnant, called him back when he found out it was a false alarm, and called him again because he needed to tell someone that the whole experience had scared the shit out of him. Joe had been the first of Robert's friends to meet Louise, who at the time was a recent graduate from UCLA med school, and whom Robert had somehow found the nerve to speak to in the campus cafeteria. And Joe did his best to like Louise, because he could see that she made Robert happy.

And even though the two men considered themselves brothers, they'd never spoken to one another with the blunt honesty Robert used in that moment. Joe didn't know what to say.

"Pam is wonderful," Robert said. "You are wonderful. I've never seen you be more you—the you that I know—than when you're with her. She makes you happy the way Louise makes me happy." Joe shook his head, then stopped himself. But it was too late. "I know you don't like her that much. Louise, I mean," Robert said softly.

"I do..."

"I'm not the guy you can lie to," Robert said, simply. Joe stayed silent, because everything Robert said was the truth. "Some people just don't mesh. I get that. I wish it was different, but..." He shrugged. "You want her to like comics. To enjoy Expo more. To be more like me. But I never wanted to date me or marry me. I'm boring. I'm really good at some things—numbers and money and interest rates and investments—and I know that, but I also know I'm boring. And when I was getting spit balls shot in my hair in high school, or found strange crap smeared on my locker, or got punched in the head on the bus on the way to grad night, I always dreamed of fun adventures. With a woman. A smart woman. And Louise is that woman."

Joe's eyes stung. He'd hurt Robert.

"I'm happy. Now," Robert said. "And that's why I work for the Expo; to do what I can to make every one of those attendees happy. They deserve to be happy, too. At least during the four days we're open." Robert paused, and Joe could see the red around his eyes. "You deserve to be happy, too. Now. And I can tell that you're not. Not really."

A hundred pounds of pressure on Joe's chest lifted, as though yanked away by a common man with super strength. He inhaled deeply.

"Robert!" came a woman's voice, and both men turned to see Louise hurrying to the table. Joe had to admit that she was beautiful—tall and thin, with long red hair and toned arms from all her Pilates classes.

With a nod of acknowledgment to Joe, Louise leaned in and hugged Robert, then kissed his cheek. She looked thin next to his large frame, but the hug she gave him was strong, powerful. Robert must have told her about Ron.

Louise took Robert's face in her hands and kissed his lips. It was brief but potent, and Joe saw an immediate transformation. Like a young cripple picking up the mighty hammer of Thor, an everyday nerd being struck by the electrifying Speed Force, or Mother Earth granting an inner-city girl the power of the elements, Robert changed. With Louise's kiss, his body rose up. He looked stronger. Braver. Wiser. And as she slid herself into the seat next to him, patting his thigh reassuringly, Joe realized just how much of a man Robert had become over the years. And he also saw what he, himself, was missing.

Joe pushed back from the table and stood. Both Robert and Louise looked up, confused.

"I'm gonna head back to my room," he said.

"I didn't mean to interrupt anything..." Louise started, clearly worried she'd offended Joe in some way. And in that moment, he finally understood something: Louise knew her presence had changed Robert's relationship to Joe, and it bothered her. It was as if she wished the three of them could enjoy hanging out together just as much as Joe wished it.

"No, you... you're great," he said, moving around the table. He meant what he said. "Robert's just given me a lot to think about." Joe impulsively leaned in and hugged them both. "Thanks."

Robert wasn't a hugger, especially with guys, and stiffened for a second. Louise reacted the same way, not because she wasn't a hugger—she was, in fact, a huge hugger—but because Joe had given some not-so-subtle hints in the past that her generous embraces bugged him. But in that instant, it felt right, and after that initial awkwardness, they both relaxed. Finally, Joe let go.

"But what about the filet and mac and cheese?" Robert asked.

Joe just smiled, waved, and walked away. He needed to find Pam. He didn't know what he was going to say, but for the first time in a long while he felt excited, and he needed to see her before that feeling faded.

ISSUE #8

"CLASH OF THE TITANS"

There have long been rumors of underground tunnels below the city of San Diego. Caves off Ocean Beach allegedly helped Mexican smugglers bring liquor into the city during Prohibition. Abandoned passageways under El Cajon Boulevard once allowed citizens to cross under busy intersections without risk of harm. Tunnels were supposedly dug between city hall and various hotels and office buildings so that elected officials could evacuate in an emergency—such as if the Navy or Marines bases were ever attacked.

The most interesting twist to the downtown tunnels story is that city officials were said to have used them to conduct extramarital affairs, sneaking into and out of local hotels where prostitution was still active before the redevelopment of downtown. However, official sources deny that these secret passages ever existed, and say that if they did exist, any that were used for illegal practices would have been blocked off or destroyed years ago.

If you're exploring any of San Diego's beach caves or historic neighborhoods, you're advised to only visit well-lit, accessible areas that are *designated for the public. The risk associated with sneaking into off-limits areas is too great.*

—From the *Exploring Forgotten San Diego* visitor's guide

"This is going to be huge," Frank Svengsouk said in a hushed voice as he led Ron through the streets of downtown. Frank was thin and nimble, and Ron had trouble keeping up as they wove between grid-locked cars and throngs of fans meandering down the sidewalks. Ron focused on Frank's denim Looney Tunes button-down as they crossed Broadway, where the honking cars, ringing pedicabs, and boisterous crowds forced Frank to raise his voice slightly.

"I'm talking Siegel and Shuster creating Superman huge. Stan Lee and Jack Kirby huge." Frank glanced around, presumably to make sure they weren't being followed, yanked open a side door to the U.S. Grant Hotel, and led Ron inside.

This clandestine behavior had been going on since Frank showed up at Ron's hotel room. He'd made sure Ron wasn't wearing his Expo badge, then led him through side streets to the Horton Plaza outdoor mall, obviously trying to avoid fans who might recognize the two of them together.

Frank had made a name for himself as the creator of the Marvel Alternates Universe, which had made so much money that the company eventually folded it back into their main line of comics in hopes of bolstering overall sales. It worked. Kind of. But rumor had it that the move, which took away much of Frank's creative control, had pissed him off so much that he was looking for work elsewhere. Being seen in public with Ron Lionel—who never socialized with comics creators even though he kept up on industry gossip—would have piqued the curiosity of many.

Ron was adrift. Sarah hadn't returned any of his calls or texts, hadn't answered the door of her hotel room, and her two assistants in LA said they had no idea where she was. *Liars.* They hadn't taken his suggestion of calling the police seriously, so they clearly did know where she was.

She just didn't want him to know.

And now, as he slowly realized that Frank and Michele had some bigger business plan in mind, he was nervous. This was Sarah's territory. She'd know what to say, or if even meeting with these people was in breach of his contract with Ragnarök. But as he followed Frank over the hotel's gorgeous red and gold carpet, past ornate, original-construction marble pillars from the early 1900s, all under gloriously huge crystal chandeliers, he didn't know how to back out.

"No one will spot us here," Frank said as he darted down a small service staircase, taking the steps two at a time. "Rumor has it that, back in the day, the U.S. Grant had a lot of secret rooms where city officials and businessmen could come and have rendezvous without anyone knowing. I've even heard there were underground tunnels from city hall—which is only a couple blocks over." Frank hit the bottom landing, which was unlike the rest of the hotel with its plain tan carpeting and artless walls.

"Sorry for all the cloak and dagger," he said before knocking twice on what looked like a supply closet door. "But we can't let anyone from DC, Marvel, or the others find out about this. Not yet." Someone opened the door, and Ron followed Frank into a small, speakeasy-style lounge, complete with leather couches and dark wood tables topped with glittering candles in red glasses. Michele Miller and three others stood staring at him. A waiter—the man who had opened the door— held out a glass of champagne.

"Don't worry about him," Frank said. "He signed an NDA." He paused, then added, "Non-disclosure agreement."

"Yeah, I got that." Ron nodded, taking the flute and then a deep sip. "So what is this?"

"The birth of Visionary Comics," Frank said, the excitement practically exploding from his tiny pores. "We're starting a new company that's going to blow up and take on the competition."

"A comic imprint?" Ron asked, boredom accidentally leaking into his voice.

"A media brand," Frank replied, unfazed. Ron suppressed the urge to roll his eyes. "DC, Marvel, Image, IDW, Archie—those brands are old school, stuck in their history. We're the new, fresh vision. The vision of what comics fans today will want tomorrow. And it's not just comics. We're talking TV, movies, games, novels—all done our way—with creators in mind."

"And readers," Michele chimed in.

"Because we will own these properties entirely," Frank said, very seriously. "Not a major corporation with faceless board members and stockholders taking all the profits. Us."

Ron looked around the group. "I know these two," he said, nodding to Michele and Frank. "Who's the rest of this dream team?"

Frank introduced them, and Ron immediately forgot their names. But he did learn their roles. Frank was clearly the leader, fueled by a raging anger at a major entertainment company that constantly reminded him that they owned the sandbox within which he was only allowed to play with their superhero toys. If they didn't like what he was doing, he was stuck. A talent forced to play by the bully's rules.

Opposite Frank was Breasty LaRue, the artist behind DC comics' entire line re-launch from two re-launches ago. (Ron vaguely remembered when that happened, and thought her name might be Marianne, but all he could focus on was her boobs.) She still got work, but that re-launch hadn't been as successful as DC or their parent company, Warner Bros., had wanted. The blame had fallen on her, the artist, as it often does in a visual medium. And even though she produced solid work, she'd never made the successful jump to TV or movie properties; "Where the real money is," she told them all knowingly.

Michele, meanwhile, was a well-known indie writer and artist.

Her work was flowery, elegant, and far too beautiful for comic books in Ron's mind. It looked like a cross between luscious Haight-Ashbury psychedelic posters and darkly delicious Edward Gorey pieces. She was very well respected, written about in academic circles, but her work focused on minority themes and wasn't mainstream enough to make a name (or a living) for herself in major comics. She gave the group a respectability that Frank and Breasty did not.

That was it for the actual comics creators. The other two were Peachfuzz and Earth Mother Jones. Peachfuzz was probably 21 and trying to make himself look older with a beard, except it grew in light-colored wispy patches, like a boy who's just hit puberty and hasn't yet shaved his facial hair. He was the social media guru, an "influencer" in the world of pop culture—with nearly a million followers due to connections within the industry. Rumor had it that Disney had hired him to talk shit about Warner's comic book movies. Ron didn't buy it. Movies were movies and social media could only do so much to fix or harm that. But he did have to admit that if a new media company was going to take off, they would need a kid who could create excitement among a target audience where none currently existed. Especially when that excitement involved a bunch of people in their mid-to-late 30s who may or may not have a future as "media" creators ahead of them.

"But I also have some stories of my own I want to create," Peachfuzz said. "Marianne likes them and will be the artist." (*Ahh, so her name is Marianne*, Ron thought.) The stories were all comics for people of color, set within a world where people of color were the majority and whites the minority. Given that this was an untapped market, it seemed like a good idea. On paper.

And then there was Earth Mother Jones. She was introduced as a "thought leader."

"And what does a 'thought leader' do?" Ron asked as he finished off his glass. "Besides think, of course."

Frank and Peachfuzz politely laughed, but Michele and Breasty didn't.

"Don't be a dick," Michele warned. "I'm putting up with you staring at Marianne's boobs right now. So don't push it."

For a moment, Ron felt like she'd punched him; he wasn't used to that kind of confrontation from someone in the industry. He wanted to tell her to fuck off. At the same time, he respected the fact that she'd called him out on what he'd assumed she hadn't noticed. But Earth Mother Jones, with her flowing robe dress and abalone jewelry, just smiled.

"Ron's question is fair," she said, waving the waiter over to refill his champagne glass. "I spot the trends before they happen. I see the pop culture buzz that people like him are generating..." Ron looked to Peachfuzz, wishing he'd paid attention to the guy's name. "...and see where it's going. It's half data, half gut. I'm a voracious consumer of media. I'm reading something in print or online while I stream videos, TV, whatever is out there. And with all that consumption, combined with hard analytics from what's worked in the past, I can see where things are going." She stepped up to Ron, her flowy robe brushing against his leg. "I'm Saydi, by the way. Saydi Staud. You'd forgotten my name already, hadn't you?"

He nodded, taken by her authority. "It's fine. First meeting."

Earth Mother Staud stepped back and gestured at the group. "They're talented, all of them. But what are they missing, Ron?"

"An asshole," he said without hesitation. The others looked surprised, but Saydi nodded knowingly.

"I would have phrased it more as a 'devil's advocate,' but 'asshole' will do," she said. "It's why I asked you here."

"We didn't think you'd come," Frank chimed in. "You're so outside of our world that we didn't think you'd want to be bothered."

And why had he come? Sarah. She'd encouraged it, said it would be a good idea for him to have other friends in the industry. Ron knew she was right. Out there at these conventions, he was a celebrity—which wasn't saying much given the competition. But here, in this room, he was needed. In an instant, it created a new feeling in Ron, a sense of pride in himself and what he owned on the inside, capital he'd earned through years of experience and forging his own path.

"So what do you think?" Saydi asked, her voice a mixture of smugness at knowing she was right and excitement at what he might say. "About the group," she continued. "What are the chances of Visionary Comics being more than a dream?"

Ron could have shot them all down. In fact, three years ago he probably would have delighted in telling these major players in the industry that they were fools—not for setting out on their own, but for the way they were planning on doing it. But all of them except Peachfuzz were close to his age, and he felt a certain envy. For one reason or another, they were each trying to reinvent themselves and their careers. He respected that. And as Ron recognized that, he didn't snap, mock, or criticize. Instead, he said what he really thought.

"You have amazing ideas," Ron offered. Then, as their faces lit up—and he knew that joy was because of him, specifically—a chill ran up his back and down his arms. He had goose bumps, even though he was totally sober. "Your problem is that you're still all thinking as individuals." He looked at Peachfuzz. "You have probably the freshest idea—people of color in comics. Huge market that hasn't been successfully tapped by any mainstream brand because the big guys get nervous when sales slump, so they shrink back to their old classic characters rather than investing more in that new audience. And it's a large, growing audience with money. You want that, you need that, and it could work. The downfall? You guys want to make a separate universe."

He turned to Michele. "I bet you had the same idea for your feminist themes." Her eyes widened, probably in surprise that Ron knew about her work. "That sounds like a noble idea, but that shit only works in a college minority studies classes. In the real world, you need to sell books and toys and everything else. By putting your characters in their own universes, you're saying they can't exist in the mainstream, and the truth is that people of color, and women, *are* the mainstream. It's self-imposed oppression: viewing yourself as the old white male majority does, like they don't or can't coexist alongside the heroes that Frank or Marianne create. That's not okay. It's character segregation. You need to create one universe, where a black Superman archetype is as important as an entirely female Fantastic Four, as a Native American Captain America, as a black Elemental."

"Yes, yes!" Michele agreed enthusiastically. "We've been having these discussions, but they've been too polite." She looked at the others. "Look, I don't care what kind of dog he is with women, he's right about this. We need to be realistic and blunt and argue about this stuff."

Ron saw a mixture of discomfort and excitement on Peachfuzz's face, like the kid didn't know if he should be excited or worried about the impending arguments.

"Look, kid, fights are gonna happen." Ron said, buzzing from the sudden thrill of being really heard by people who actually cared about his opinion. "Things are going to be said and feelings will be hurt, but at the end of the day, if the product is better than it was before—and if you can see that it's better than it would have been without everyone's contributions—you win." Then, without thinking, he added, "It's one of my biggest problems."

The others looked at him, surprised, waiting for more. Ron paused, thinking about what he'd just said. The truth had slipped out. He shrugged. "I've got an ego." They laughed. "Everyone knows that."

"We need that ego," Frank said. "It's part of the plan." He went around the room, pointing to each person. "Marianne and I have the mainstream experience that can help us compete with the big guys. Michele gives us indie cred, and will keep us honest about both our stories and our mission to bring new voices to the table. Anthony will have readers buzzing about everything we do, *and* he's got some killer ideas. And with Saydi, we have a strategist helping us develop new ideas and keeping us on the cutting edge."

"And I'm the asshole." Ron lifted his glass. "I suppose you want me to bring *The Enduring* over with me. Don't legally know if I can."

"*The Enduring* is yesterday," said Marianne. Ron started to bristle until she added, "You're more than that. Everyone knows it and wants to see what's next. And the insider buzz is that your publisher doesn't know how to help you get it out. We will."

Ron loved that idea.

"And you're the missing link," Frank said. "Hollywood."

Ron looked at them, confused.

"All three of us have had projects optioned," Marianne said, indicating herself, Frank, and Michele. "We all got screwed in the end—not respected for our work, and not compensated properly, either. You're the only one who's won the fight, who knows how to navigate that world. You also have a powerhouse agent."

"If the studios don't want me writing my own script, I'd happily let you write it," Frank said, and the others nodded. "That's the point, right? We build a trust with one another, covering all our bases, and we retain more control. See our real visions come to light."

Sweat broke out on Ron's forehead and temples. The basement's air conditioning was making his clothes and skin cool, but the sweat kept coming.

"And if I'm honest, I'd be happy to sign over Visionary to your agent at Creative Artists," Marianne said. "My agent didn't do anything for me."

"Sarah doesn't rep companies," Ron offered feebly as his heart beat faster and faster. He hadn't done any coke since the afternoon fiasco, but he suddenly worried he'd done too much over the years, and with all the excitement, his heart was going to give out. Now. Of all times.

"Of course not, but your agency does rep companies," Saydi said, seemingly understanding the anxiety that Ron was sure he was displaying all over his face. "But we don't have to go down that road if it puts you in an awkward position."

"Why would it be awkward?" Michele asked. "We're all big talents, and together we're a force in pop culture. We bring big value to the agency. I'd be willing to leave my guy at United."

"Me too," Frank said. "We're all in it to make this succeed—and I know I can speak for the others when I say if you're in, there's really no stopping us."

Ron smiled, but he felt nauseous. It was them—this group of truly talented creators staring at him, eyes brimming with hope, excitement, aspirations, and anticipation. He couldn't take it.

"Okay, let me think on it," he said, putting his glass down on one of the low wooden tables. He moved too quickly, and some liquid sloshed out onto a candle, dousing it. "That's not a sign or foreshadowing or anything," he quipped, feeling like an idiot.

"Don't go. We ordered dinner," Frank said.

"I wish I could," he said quickly, while the mantra *Don't blow it! Don't blow it!* echoed through his head. "But the studio has notes on what I can and can't say to fans this weekend, and I fucked up today..." Ron stopped. He'd been trying to forget about the afternoon, but it kept creeping into his mind. He couldn't believe he'd almost told them. They were nice, honest people. But they weren't his friends. They weren't people he could trust. Not yet, at least.

"Anyway, there's some damage control that needs doing," he said. The others smiled, nodding as if they understood. They couldn't. It was sweet of them to try, but they couldn't.

Then Ron saw Saydi eyeing him suspiciously. "Can we talk more tomorrow?" he asked. "The studio has me doing a round-table interview around one, but then I'll be at the Ragnarök booth in the afternoon."

"We'll be there," Saydi said, and Ron bolted out of the room.

As he hustled up the stairs two at a time, he took deep, welcome inhales of air; the room had been cool—he knew that—but something had made it seem suffocatingly hot. When he reached the top landing, he paused for one last deep breath.

"Lord Lionel?" said a woman's raspy voice. Ron turned and saw someone he recognized. A small, roundish, dark cloud of a woman with dark, greasy hair, wearing an ill-fitting skirt. "I would seek an audience with you."

"You were at the opening ceremony, right?" Ron asked. *The mouth breather*, he thought. She nodded, and he noticed her clutching a rare hardbound first edition of issues #1–12; only a couple hundred were produced because the printer had gone bankrupt. It was one of the few times the Weeble wasn't to blame for a production error, and it added to *The Enduring's* collectible mystique. "How did you find me here?"

"I met my Whimsy," she said. "My free spirit guide, and he encouraged me to follow my path. So I sent my intention to the Whispering Winds, just as Ariel taught Dexter, and there you were crossing Broadway." She smiled with a look of wonderment. "It works, Lord Lionel. I mean, my mother and I always joked about it. She'd say things like, 'Faerie Queen, full of Grace, help us find a parking space' when we were driving around downtown Charleston. And it would work, but we would just think we were pretending. Or when the winds pick up and you can feel a storm coming, we'd say things like, "I wonder what message the Whispering Winds are bringing today?' Mom thought it was just in good fun, but I would look for signs. I couldn't decipher them, but I'd write them down and try to study them. I'd try..." She stopped and fell into awkward silence, clutching her book.

Ron was stunned. He'd met serious fans before—people who got tattoos of *The Enduring* artwork, cosplayers who wanted him to settle arguments about whose outfit was more authentic to the book, and even a few Wiccans who believed the ceremonies in the books were based on ancient texts and wanted to find out how he'd learned the rituals. But he'd never met someone like this—who actually believed that what he'd written was real—and he wasn't quite sure if he should burst her bubble or not.

"Look, I need to get someplace," he said. "What's your name?" he added, remembering Sarah's coaching on how to deal with fans.

"Velma," she said sternly. "I told you that this morning."

"Forgive me, *Velma*," he said with a bite. She looked shocked, then lowered her eyes. Pleased that he had put her in her place, he continued, "There's a small VIP signing tomorrow at the Ragnarök booth in the afternoon. I can get you in, and I might have some time to answer a question or two. If not, the big panel is on Saturday at eleven and you can ask then."

Ron turned, but Velma's hand shot out and clutched his wrist, her scraggly fingernails scratching his flesh.

"I would have a word!" she snapped, her eyes washing between rage and worry, wet with tears that never leaked out. "I need answers to the twist, to the secret of the Faerie Queen!"

"Jesus fucking Christ!" Ron yelled as he yanked his arm away from her grip. "What the fuck is wrong with you?" Velma stepped back, her eyes down. "That's not how you talk to people. You don't fucking grab people. Didn't your mother teach you anything?"

Velma looked up, shock, fear, and sadness dancing in her eyes. She clutched the book and took off running down the hall and out the side exit to the street.

Ron turned, alone in the empty hallway. He thought about taking out his phone and calling Sarah, but then changed his mind. He knew she wouldn't pick up.

ISSUE #9

"REALITY BITES"

People who attend America's Finest Comic Book Expo on Thursday are die-hard fans looking to purchase rare or exclusive merchandise that will sell quickly and become unavailable the rest of the weekend. Saturday is the busiest day, crowded with attendees who can't get time off work during the week. It's also the busiest day for programming, with every major comic company or Hollywood studio bringing in big name talent for their presentations. Sunday is known for bargain shopping, with exhibitors offering tremendous discounts so they don't have to haul extra merchandise home.

This makes Friday the slowest, calmest, and most enjoyable day (in our opinion) of this four-day event.

**—San Diego Tourism Society's write-up on
America's Finest Comic Book Expo**

An exhausted Joe stood at the coffee station in the skybox, filling his insulated stainless-steel coffee mug and praying Friday would go smoother than Thursday had. He'd tried to make something happen after leaving Robert and Louise at the steak house, but instead his plans had fallen flat. Logically, he knew that was the kind of thing that happened when you have a big idea but don't involve the other person in it until it's happening, but that didn't help him feel any better.

It was 30 minutes before the show opened to the public, so he and other Expo staffers were trying to grab a bite before they lost all sense of time. Unfortunately, Joe was already dealing with a new crisis.

"I think Xander did it," he said to Anna Marie Van Aken, CEO of the San Diego Convention Center and the woman who managed day-to-day operations on behalf of the city.

She looked from Joe to Robert and finally to Louise (who had decided to stay for moral support), clearly confused.

"Xander is one of the attendees," Robert explained to Anna as he perused the food spread. Then, to Joe, he added, "And no, Xander didn't do it."

"You don't even know the full story," Joe replied. He let the knob on the large metal carafe rise back up, shutting off the flow of dark liquid energy. "Are you sure it was a woman and not a guy dressed as a woman?" He gave Louise a small nod when she held out the creamer carton to him, and she poured some in his mug.

"Well he—the person..." Anna started.

Suddenly, the door exploded open and five vampires raced into the room screaming, knives drawn, and with what looked like fresh blood covering their teeth and lips.

Louise jumped back, splashing creamer all over Joe's face and blue shirt. Robert, Anna, and the handful of staffers sitting elsewhere in the room just stared, donuts, breakfast sandwiches, and fruit skewers half in their mouths.

"LARP is in room G1," Robert told the vampires before looking back down at the food and selecting a cheese Danish. He then explained to Louise, "Live action role-playing."

"We're vampires," one of them said simply, a hint of disappointment in his voice, presumably from having wasted a perfectly good attack entrance.

"Room G4," said Joe, grabbing far too many napkins to dab his clothes and wipe away the cream clinging to his eyelashes and cheeks. The vampires turned to the entrance and began to ready themselves.

"I'm so sorry," Louise said to Joe, trying to stifle a laugh as she cleaned up the spill on the coffee table.

"They used to startle me, too," Anna said sympathetically, grabbing for more napkins to help.

Robert looked over and finally saw his friend's predicament. He laughed out loud. It *was* funny, Joe assumed, but he could still feel his ears burning.

There was a collective inhale from the vampires, and another "Aaaahhhhhhhh!" as they raced out toward the gaming rooms down the hall. Louise jumped again, but this time Anna steadied her. Just then, Pam walked in.

"How fun!" she said, and Joe grinned at her enthusiasm. In this world of oddities where no one blinked at such incidents, Pam's reaction was very cute. She noticed Louise and lit up. "Hey!"

Joe watched as Pam and Louise hugged. Neither were the type who would normally attend CBE, so they always bonded over their outsider status. Pam looked over and saw Joe's wet shirt and pants.

"The vampires scared the hell out of me," Louise explained. Then, to Joe, "Sorry again."

"Start over," Joe told Anna. "You'll want to hear this," he said to Pam.

Anna nodded. "It was just after seven this morning, and I was the first person in the office. I always get here early for big shows."

"And we appreciate that," Robert said.

Louise raised her eyebrow in a "don't interrupt" expression, which annoyed Joe even though he agreed with her.

"This young person came into the center's offices wearing an Expo badge. She... Look, I really think it was a woman." Joe and Robert both nodded for her to continue. "She was short, with short black hair, and she was wearing a baggy purple sweatshirt, thick Buddy Holly glasses, and white jeans that looked soiled." Anna glanced uncomfortably around the group. She whispered, "When she walked, her pants made this kind of *swick, swick, swicking* sound. You know, when her thighs rubbed together."

"The person had thick legs?" Robert asked.

"And she kind of smelled like sour milk," Anna added.

"No way that was Xander in drag," Robert said definitively.

"Could've been one of his social media followers," Joe said. "Go on."

"She came into the administration offices wheezing, red faced, and sweating. Then her eyes rolled up into her head and she sort of plopped onto the waiting room couch and clutched her chest. I thought she was having a heart attack or something, so I told her to stay there and ran out to get the on-site EMT." Anna paused, visibly upset. Pam rubbed a comforting hand on her shoulder. "Anyway, we got back maybe two minutes later and it looked like she was searching through her backpack. I don't know if I mentioned that before. She had a backpack. It was one of those old JanSport ones, like the kind I had in high school. It was pink, but also really dirty, like this woman had owned it for years. And when the paramedic got to her, she said, 'Found it,' and showed us an asthma inhaler.

"She then stood up, grabbed her bag, and marched out of the office. The paramedic told her to sit down, but she sprayed him in the eyes with her inhaler and took off running. He stumbled back and fell to the ground. I think it startled him more than anything else, but I stopped to see if he was okay."

"Did you see where she went?" Joe asked.

"No," Anna said regretfully. "All I could hear was the *swick, swick, swicking* of her thighs as she got further and further away from the office."

"So this girl was rude, but can we do anything to her for spraying an EMT in the face with her asthma inhaler?" Pam asked.

"I'm not sure that's all she did," Anna said. Joe gave Pam and Robert an "I told you so" look. "When I went back into my office, I saw that a binder was missing: the one detailing the convention center's expansion from two years ago."

"It contains blueprints and maps for the entire structure," Joe explained to Pam and Louise, who wouldn't understand the significance. "It's a maze in the back corridors if you don't know where you're going, but someone with this info could have the run of the place. Xander would value bypassing the regular routes."

"That doesn't seem like him," Pam said. "And he already knows his way around, so why would he need these maps?" Joe started to object, but Pam cut him off. "Just stop," she said, and the sharpness in her voice made Joe do just that. "You don't like Xander, that's fine, but you of all people should know better than to accuse someone of a crime without having the facts."

She was right. Joe felt stupid. He stayed silent.

"I've called my team to see if anyone took it for some reason," Anna said. "But since she had a badge on and kind of looked like one of your attendees, I thought you should know. If no one on my team knows about the binder, I'll have to call the police right away."

Anna exited the room, but before anyone could start discussing the situation, Joe leaned in to Pam. "Hey, can we talk for a second?"

"What, about the binder?" Pam asked, matching the surprise on Louise's face.

"Until Anna talks to her people, we can't do anything," Joe said. "And, no, I don't think Xander did it." As an afterthought he added, "But I'm not taking him off the list, either."

Pam shrugged, grabbed a paper cup, and started filling it with coffee. She was ignoring him. Joe deliberately avoided looking at Robert or Louise, which only made the situation more obvious. The room suddenly felt cold.

"Let me show you the Exhibit Hall from up here," Robert suggested to Louise. He hooked his left arm, which held the cheese Danish, around Louise's elbow, being careful not to spill the coffee in his other hand. She picked up her fruit plate, gave Pam a knowing look, and went with Robert, clearly uninterested in which comic book dealers were positioned where.

"You didn't come back to your hotel room last night," Joe said, then quickly added, "I know that sounds creepy, but it's not. I mean, we dated." Pam looked up at him, then back at the two Sugar-in-the-Raw packets in her hand. She ripped them open, dumped the dark crystals into her drink, and swirled the contents around with a wooden stir stick. "Did you ... have fun last night?"

"Just ask me the question," she commanded. Joe wished she'd keep her voice down in front of the assembled staff, most of whom knew their history.

"Were you with someone?"

"I stayed at my apartment," she said, putting the coffee down with some force. "What were *you* doing last night? Calling me, hanging outside my hotel room until midnight?" Joe was stunned. She'd never come back, so how did she know? "I had dinner with Matt and Andreas, and I saw all your texts and voicemails," she explained, "but you couldn't even say what it was really about. You could only talk around the subject, which was ridiculous."

"I wanted to talk in person," Joe replied, following her down the table as she added fruit to her plate.

"I know, because I did come back to my room last night. And when I did, I saw you there, half passed out in front of my hotel door," she said, putting two mini muffins atop her fruit.

"I wasn't passed out drunk," he whispered, frustration leaking into his voice. "I was just tired from the whole day."

"Well, so was I, so I went home and stayed at my place."

"Why?"

"Because I didn't want to talk to you!" Pam snapped, immediately hushing the other conversations in the room. Joe saw her face melt into marked control, a skill she'd acquired growing up around parents who'd constantly argued, embarrassing her in public. Joe knew she was done with this conversation, especially here in front of the others. She put the plate down and a lone muffin rolled off into the pile of leftover powdered sugar on the donut plate. Pam ignored it, picking up her coffee and walking to the exit. Joe followed her, down the stairs and out the heavy grey door leading to the Exhibit Hall.

"I came to apologize," he said in a whisper. "I was scared in New York. And I kind of am now, but I think we can make this work…"

Pam stopped and turned to face him. She didn't look angry, just sad.

"You weren't scared, Joe," she said. "You were ashamed."

"What?" Joe felt as though she'd slapped him. "Pam, I've never cared about anyone more than you."

"You're ashamed of yourself," she said, stopping him cold. "This is why I didn't want to talk to you last night, because I knew it would eventually happen. That you'd have some major event or disappointment shake you up so bad that you'd come back to me, hoping to make everything better in your life. But it won't. It's just going to hurt me all over again."

Joe instinctively reached out to take Pam's hand, but she pulled away.

"I've thought about this a lot, you know," she said. "When we went to New York, and you made everything so special. You got us that gorgeous suite, we played tourist, you kissed me at the Statue of Liberty in front of people for God's sake! I had never felt more beautiful." She stopped, her voice cracking slightly. Joe's chest was heavy. "Two and a half years we'd been together, and when we went to that oyster bar on our last night in the city, I thought, *This is so us!* Great food, classic location, wonderful and kind of weird." She laughed sadly. "It wasn't a fancy dinner—it didn't need to be—because that place was all the things we loved." A tear leaked out of her left eye. "And you never asked."

"I wasn't ready to make that jump," he said. "I explained that when you finally told me what was pissing you off."

"I know..."

"And you said we were good," he pointed out logically. "What, did you want me to go against what I knew was right for me?"

"Of course not..."

"I didn't think I was misleading you," he said.

"We'd talked about marriage before!" she said.

"We'd talked about living together," he corrected.

"Fuck!" she snapped. "We talked about having a future together, and for me that meant marriage. And kids. And you know that, so don't play word games with me right now!" Joe had never seen her this upset before—not even when they'd broken up on the flight back to San Diego. Nearby, exhibitors who were preparing for the day's onslaught watched out of the corner of their eyes. "I have dreams, too, just like you."

"I know..."

"But I'm thirty-four," she said. "And I can't spend my best years dreaming dreams." Joe stared at her, his heart beating faster as sweat welled up between his shoulder blades and ran down his back. "You would say things to me like, 'When I sell that manuscript,' or 'One day I'm going to write that comic book.' And the implication is that 'one day,' when any of those things happen, everything is going to change for the better. We all do it. 'One day' I'll go to college and get away from my annoying parents. 'One day' I'll get promoted, or get a better job, and not have so many bills to worry about. 'One day' I'll meet a great guy—not through a blind date or a stupid app where I'll have to play games to figure out if he really likes me or if he's just biding his time until he finds someone hotter or cooler or whatever the hell he thinks he wants.

"But what if this is it?" she asked, tears glistening on the edge of her lids. "What if 'one day' is now, and you're an exec at a security company who never became a professional writer, but who can maybe write for fun on the side and find enjoyment in that? And what if I'm just an accountant for a comic book convention, and that's it? What if 'one day' is now, and this is it?" Fear clutched at Joe's heart. "I can live with that reality, Joe. I'd love it," she admitted sadly. "But I don't think you can."

Joe stayed silent. He couldn't argue. She was right.

And with nothing else to say, Pam walked away.

The morning announcement blared over the PA system, letting everyone know the Exhibit Hall was now open to the public. Friday at America's Finest Comic Book Expo was about to begin.

ISSUE #10

"CROSSING THE THRESHOLD"

What Is Cosplay?

The word "cosplay" is said to be a contraction of the words "costume" and "play." According to Fandom Wiki, Nobuyuki Takahashi of Studio Hard invented the term while attending the 1984 World Science Fiction Convention in Los Angeles, and it took off after that. However, since you can't always rely on Fandom Wiki, the best way to find out the truth is by asking a cosplayer!

Cosplayers are the men and women who dress as costumed characters from anime, comics, science fiction, video games, and related pop culture, and they definitely help create part of the fun fan spirit at America's Finest Comic Book Expo. While some of their outfits are elaborate pieces of art, others are simpler—a wig and face paint, street clothes inspired by a favorite character, poor in execution but funny in concept, or of the "costume in a bag" variety. Cosplayers are a friendly bunch who love it when people dress up, so put on those tights and capes and have fun!

**—From the FAQ section of the America's Finest
Comic Book Expo registration website**

"Aw, what's the little baby gonna do, start crying?" a pimply redheaded teenager jeered. His two raggedy buddies laughed. They were taunting three younger kids in line for Cartoon Network's Fall TV Preview.

"Shut up," said the young boy dressed like Robin. His friend was painted green like the superhero Beast Boy, and the little girl wore a blue cape like Raven. Together the trio made a mini version of the Teen Titans, a cartoon Ron loved watching in repeats.

"Ooh," mocked Pimply Red. "Robin told me off!" He and his friends laughed some more.

Ron was standing outside the Media Room, where industry professionals did interviews with members of the press. Some areas were sectioned off for on-camera tapings, so bigger actors could promote a Hollywood movie or TV show. Others would be smaller round-table meetings, where a professional would sit opposite nine journalists from various publications and websites, answering questions for a given time period. That was what Ron was here for, but he was early, so he took a water from Homely Volunteer Girl and stepped into the hallway to see if he could get Sarah on the phone.

He'd had a lot to think about after last night's meeting. He liked the idea of teaming up, which wasn't his normal response. But as he'd considered the offer, he'd had to admit that it was exciting—and not just because they respected his insight and honesty, but because he actually thought he could learn from them, too. Maybe the reason his *Enduring* script hadn't worked wasn't because he didn't technically know how to write it, but because something was missing from the writing.

He'd just assumed he could tackle it on his own. He was Ron Lionel; he could do anything—especially when it came to *The Enduring*. But as throngs of fans walked past to their various workshops and panels, he shook his head, embarrassed. *Maybe*, he thought, *if I'd had a team of collaborators, they would have had the insight I needed to make it work.*

Tingles shot up Ron's arm, and he instinctively reached down to feel the cocaine bullet in his pocket. The rush felt like a fresh bump, though he'd been totally clean since the blowjob incident.

Ron took a big gulp of bitter-tasting water. He wondered if it had been left in the sun too long, but then realized it was probably just remnants from the cocaine drip. He took another sip, hoping to clear his throat. It didn't work.

Ron looked at his phone again. He really wanted to tell Sarah about what had happened with the Visionary Comics people. Hell, he wanted to tell anyone. But there was no one to call.

"Where'd you get your costume, Robin?" asked Pimply Red, pulling Ron from his thoughts.

"My mom made them," Robin answered warily.

"At the homeless shelter?"

As the older boys laughed, rage ripped through Ron's entire body. He'd grown up wearing secondhand jeans and shirts. He knew what it was like to wear dirty clothes to school, either because they couldn't afford laundry soap until his mom's next payday, or because neither of his parents thought about taking care of Ron like that. They'd had bigger deals in the works, and they'd taught him to take care of himself, anyway. But all of that independence had meant nothing when the guys at school told him he smelled, or the pretty girls whispered about him as he walked by, or when people laughed at something he assumed they'd said about him.

"And why's this guy dressed like Raven?" Pimply Red pointed to the girl hiding behind Robin and Beast Boy.

"That's my sister!" Robin yelled, his face burning red. Ron saw that he wanted to hit the older boy, to defend the sister he loved, but the kid was too scared. He looked like he might cry.

"What a pussy!" Pimply Red laughed, shoving Robin back. It was mean, sharp.

Ron threw his bottled water, narrowly missing Pimply Red's face. The acne-ridden teen turned in shock, and Ron shoved him into the wall. His two friends were suddenly frozen with fear.

"What the hell?" squeak-yelled Pimply Red.

"What? You're not such big shit now when there's someone bigger than you?"

"Hey!" Pimply Red screeched. "Someone help us!"

People paused, but Ron shoved the kid again and he stopped talking.

"They're just little kids, and you threatened to beat them up!" Ron yelled, drawing more attention from the passing fans, who had already started to gather around the scene.

"I'm sorry," the boy stammered.

"No you're not," Ron said, shoving his arm into the kid's chest again. "You're just scared, and now you're trying to save your ass." Ron leaned in, whispering low so that only the three boys could hear. "Bitch, I've seen the inside of a jail, and you do *not* scare me!" To be fair, it had been for a DUI, but they didn't need to know that.

Pimply Red started crying, and that shook Ron. He'd never been violent like this before—those were just fantasies he'd play out in the comics. But he knew better than to back down when facing a punk, so instead he said loudly, "Don't let me ever catch you little scrubs doing this shit to any kid again! Hear me?" They nodded, terrified. "Get lost!" Ron dropped Pimply Red and the boys ran like their lives depended on it.

Ron felt panic rise in his chest. He'd just assaulted three minors. Shoved them into the wall. The blowjob was one thing, but this could get him arrested and seriously destroy everything.

Then, just as Ron was about to run into the Media Room in a blind panic, three sets of arms grabbed him around the waist in a huge hug and the hallway erupted in applause. Ron hugged the children back.

He looked up at face after face, and slowly it dawned on him: These people had been picked on as kids, and had never had a Ron Lionel to defend them. He smiled, his eyes starting to burn with tears. He blinked them back as he crouched down to the trio.

"You guys okay?" The Teen Titans nodded, wiping away tears as the applause continued. Ron smiled at them, adding, "You guys look sharp. Don't let stupid people bug you, okay?" They nodded as if Superman himself had just delivered the message.

Someone recognized him and chants of "Ron! Ron! Ron!" echoed among those gathered in the hallway. And that's when he saw Sarah standing in their midst. She walked toward him, a mixture of pride and annoyance written all over her face.

"I'm going to have to clean that mess up, huh?" she asked with a laugh. He hugged her. Tight. Fans walking past patted his shoulders and back, and Homely Volunteer Girl appeared by his side, handing him a fresh water.

Sarah bent down and got the kids' numbers, saying she wanted to call their moms later and check in. Ron knew she was also getting insurance in case Pimply Red and his friends wanted to press charges or sue. She was watching his back. Again. Like she always did. But the fact that she was doing this, after the way he'd disappointed her the day before, filled Ron with a love he hadn't quite acknowledged before. She stood up.

"I was on coke," he blurted out in a hushed voice. Sarah paused a moment, looking at him. "Yesterday."

She studied his face, then glanced at the passing fans and pulled him into the Media Room, where only professionals and credentialed members of the press could enter. They moved to a side wall, away from everyone.

"Are you high now?"

"No," he said, smiling.

"Are you holding?"

"No," he lied instantly. "I left it in my hotel room after yesterday."

Sarah looked at him a moment, sadness mixing with understanding. Then, in an instant, the stoic business woman came back into focus. "We'll finish the day, go back, and I'll flush it. Creative Artists will pay for your rehab. We can get you into Simpson House in Malibu, and no one needs to know unless you want them to know." She waved her hand as if a gnat had flown past her face. She smiled reassuringly.

"Whatever, we'll figure that out later. First thing is to get you into rehab right after this weekend, and you can work on a next draft there."

"The studio doesn't want me," Ron said. "We both know that."

"Fuck the studio," Sarah said. "Without you, they don't have anything. There's a way we can—"

"I need to learn what they want," Ron interrupted. Sarah looked more shocked about this than the cocaine. "I had that dinner with the comics guys last night, and they want to make me a partner in a new venture. But they also helped me see some stuff—like what I don't know."

Ron stopped as he smelled something: Homely Volunteer Girl had appeared next to him again.

"Sir, your roundtable is ready to start," she said, waiting for him.

"After this, we can figure everything out," Ron said. He didn't want to flush the coke. He didn't have a problem. He only did it now and then for fun, as a boost to make things better, or when he'd had a drink while writing. A toot now and then, but that was it. He'd stopped plenty of times when "the day after" had been rough and he recognized that he'd pushed himself too far. And yesterday, he was just being an idiot, reacting to the news about his script.

But he'd needed to tell Sarah something. He owed her that.

Ron nodded to Homely Volunteer Girl. "One sec."

She paused, giving him a confused look, as if she didn't know what a "sec" was, and Ron realized he'd said it more like "scheck."

"I'll be there in just a moment," he clarified. As she moved away, he turned back to Sarah. "I didn't think you'd come back. I was really fucking scared, I gotta say."

"Who'd watch out for you if not me?" she joked, but the look in her eyes told him how much she cared. She put her hands on his shoulders and gave them a gentle squeeze. "We'll kick the coke's ass," she said. "Trust me on that one."

Ron smiled, nodded, and walked to the table where the press waited. With Sarah on his side, he knew he could handle anything that came his way.

ISSUE #11

"INTO THE TRASH COMPACTOR"

To all our visiting journalists, bloggers, and social influencers: Welcome to America's Finest Comic Book Expo!

Room 7G is the official Expo Media Room—with free wireless Internet access! Here you will find a quiet space for writing articles, recording stories for broadcast, or just escaping the general hubbub of the CBE floor. One member of the Expo publicity team will always be on hand to answer questions and make sure interviews start and stop on time.

PLEASE NOTE #1: Due to the size of America's Finest Comic Book Expo, all scheduled interviews must start and end on time. There will be no exceptions.

PLEASE NOTE #2: All round-table or on-camera interviews must be arranged through the publicist for that given project or company. The publicity team has no control over these schedules and cannot "squeeze you in" no matter what outlet you work for. If you are late, it is up to the *interviewee or publicist as to whether or not you can join an interview in progress.*

PLEASE NOTE #3: *There are pitchers of water, coffee, and tea available for press. Snacks, in the form of chips and trail mix, will be set out in bowls throughout the day. Please do not attempt to eat or drink items from the professional station behind the blue-curtained holding area. These bottles of soda and water, along with coffee, tea, catered sandwiches, and snacks are supplied for our invited guests only. Thank you for understanding.*

—America's Finest Comic Book Expo
media welcome letter

"That damn Bat Signal is still a nuisance!"

For Joe and Robert, those words could only mean one thing: problems in the Exhibit Hall.

The moment Pam had left, Robert and Louise had come racing out of the skybox exit like lead characters in a sitcom. Clearly they'd been listening. Joe didn't care. He was wiped. Everything Pam had said was true—at least to some extent. He may have never admitted it to himself, but when she said it, he couldn't refute it. And now he needed time to process.

The problem was that there was no time; he had a major event to watch over.

Making matters worse, Joe, Robert, and Louise now faced Maxine and Max Stone, the mother/son team who owned #1 Comics in Fresno. Every year, they packed their dented, off-white, decommissioned AT&T technician van with dusty publications dating from present day back to the 50s and 60s, and drove down for the Expo. Their booth was never fancy, just tables with long rows of white, acid-free boxes loaded with bagged comics, and a snap-together metal display wall featuring some prime first editions and a bunch of tweaked and creased promotional posters they would try to make an extra buck off of. The Stones had been with CBE from the beginning, since before Max was even born. So of course Robert felt an obligation to them—and the ever-ornery retailers agreed.

Without exaggeration (or trying to be mean), Joe had long ago observed that Maxine resembled a mini Tolkien troll. She stood no taller than five feet and sported a horribly thinning perm. Her short, meaty arms poked from the sleeves of a housedress (her standard uniform), which usually featured a dingy grey ring around her protruding belly where it continually rubbed against the soiled boxes. The apple didn't fall far from the tree. Though Max was younger than Joe, he had thinning, curly hair like his mother, perched atop a wider face. He always wore tan cargo shorts with numerous pockets to hold his cash and calculator (#1 Comics was the only booth that didn't accept credit cards due to bank processing fees), and on this day he sported an extra-large black Hulk T-shirt.

The two were obsessed with comics and scoured swap meets, garage sales, and the Internet for books they knew customers would love. Lucky fans could walk up, find a rare item at a great price, and leave both happy and unscathed. But the dealers also had a habit of shouting at one another at any given moment. Experienced CBE attendees like Joe and Robert knew they weren't necessarily angry; it was just how they spoke. But new shoppers were often stunned by the behavior and tried to politely remove themselves from the lively dialogue by averting their eyes to the ground. That's where they witnessed the real horror: Maxine and Max's feet always featured toenails that could slice bread, and flaky patches of dry skin accented by rings of brownish dirt running around the edges of their flip-flop straps, toes, and soles. At that point most folks just took off, which caused a real argument over whose fault it was.

Sadly—because they did have some genuinely great merchandise for sale—the Stones never understood what the problem was.

"Tell him what it's hitting!" Maxine shouted, returning Joe's attention to the situation at hand—the offending Bat Signal.

"I will, Ma! Jesus Christ!" Max responded, then turned back to Robert. "It's hitting our posters of Elemental and The Mystery! Again! Like it was doing when we called you yesterday!"

"Illuminating them?" Robert asked, obviously trying to spin this into a positive.

"No!" Max snapped, causing Louise to take a slight step backward. "Elemental and The Mystery are not published by DC!" Robert knew this, and opted for silence. "Everyone is laughing at us!" Joe doubted it, but he also thought it was wise to stay quiet. "Now, my father started selling at this convention years ago..."

"Back when you were nothing!" Maxine yelled over her son's shoulder.

"I just said that!" Max snapped at his mother.

"No, you didn't!" she countered.

"It's tantamount to the same thing!"

"No, it's not! Don't get defensive..."

"Tantamount!" Max snapped back. "Tantamount! Tantamount! Tantamount!"

Passersby were staring. Wide-eyed. So was Louise.

"Maxine, Max," Robert said calmly, trying to focus them. "Who's manning your booth?"

They stopped and stared at one another. Then Max screamed, "I told you to stay at the booth!"

"I'm not your damn slave, you know!" she shouted back. "And I needed to make sure you really talked to him instead of saying you had when you hadn't! I know you! I know how you are!"

Robert leaned in and said, "Why don't we head back there and see what's happening? I can then ask DC about the signal. It won't be a problem."

"It better not be!" shouted Max as they turned around into Louise. She stood with her arms crossed—an immovable object if there ever was one—but with the sweetest face Joe had ever seen on her.

"The phrase 'thank you' is comprised of two simple, easy-to-use words," she said with a lilt. "You should try it sometime."

For the first time that day, Joe laughed. He stopped when the dingy duo glared at him. They headed off down the hall, bobbing left and right as they waded quickly through the crowd.

Louise turned to Robert. "You shouldn't let people bully you, Robert."

"I've been dealing with Max and Maxine for years."

"That doesn't make their behavior right," Louise countered. She stopped as she and Robert realized Joe wasn't joining them.

"I can't handle them right now," Joe said. "I'll say something I shouldn't."

"Get some air on the bayside terrace," Robert said. "Or just take the day off. We can handle it with Amy. It's only Friday."

"Are you coming?" shouted Max, who had somehow popped up in front of Robert without anyone noticing. Both he and Louise jumped back slightly.

"Go," Joe said. "I'll text you when I figure out what I'm doing." Louise and Max started off, but Robert paused again to shoot Joe a concerned look. Joe nodded reassuringly, knowing full well that Robert could see through the façade. Joe turned and walked toward the bayside entrance to the Exhibit Hall. He thought about heading back to his hotel suite at the Hyatt. It was a spacious, beautiful room with enormous windows that overlooked the city—a perk that he never actually enjoyed because of all the time he spent at the Expo itself. Joe knew that lying down in a cool, quiet room, closing his eyes and just breathing for a moment would be good for his mind, so he changed direction and headed toward the front entrance. That's when he got a call on his cell.

"Lionel just caused more trouble," Amy said the second he picked up. "I've got three kids and a pissed-off parent at the security desk. I guess he shoved them into a wall or threatened them or something." The fire rose in Joe, pushing down the sadness and exhaustion he'd felt seconds before. "He was outside 7G."

"Media Room," Joe said. It was the best place to start his search and possibly get some witness information. "I'm on my way to 7G now," he said, changing direction once more. "Get the kids' statements separate from one another if you can. I don't want them building the story bigger than it is." Joe didn't like Ron, but he also didn't want anyone taking advantage of his celebrity and exaggerating the details for a bigger payout if the families sued.

As Joe left the Exhibit Hall for the back staircase, Robert called on the walkie-talkie. "Our problem child is messed up."

"Tell me something I don't know," Joe replied. "Amy just called me about it."

"His agent just called me," Robert said.

"Did she see the alleged altercation with the kids?" Joe asked.

"What kids?" Robert asked back. "She said he was drunk or something and she needed help. She's not sure what's up—said he was normal when she talked to him before the interview—but the volunteer from the publicity department isn't doing anything to stop him, and I can't reach anyone on their team. I can tell she's worried."

Joe took the stairs two at a time to the second floor. On the way, he explained what Amy had told him, carefully choosing his words over the open walkie-talkie line.

"I'm still dealing with the Bat Signal," Robert said. "I know you were on your way out, but I need you." The blood coursed through Joe's veins as he quickened his pace. He felt good again. "As soon as I'm done, Louise and I will get there."

Joe signed off, turning down the back hallway and into the unmarked side entrance to room 7G. Ron Lionel sat at a table with journalists. He was clearly a mess, trying to answer questions as his head drooped to the side and then sprang back to attention, like a drunk trying to convince everyone he's more sober than he actually is.

"Security to the bridge!" Ron shouted as he pointed at Joe. This caused the nine reporters and a few stragglers to turn and look; some even snapped photos, in case this was important.

"There's the beeatch who ... did that thing to me yesterday," Ron shouted.

Sarah appeared from behind the blue-curtained holding area, looking relieved to see Joe. She immediately led him to the press table, all business once more.

"Sorry, everyone, but clearly Mr. Lionel isn't feeling well," she said.

"This is Sarah, everyone!" Ron said happily. "Everyone say, 'Hi, Sarah...'"

And like good reporters who are also fans, they did. In unison.

Joe hurried over, took one of Ron's arms, and nodded for Sarah to follow his lead. He noticed a girl in a red Expo polo shirt (indicating that she was from the publicity department) putting some of the PR department's water bottles into a backpack. Joe assumed she was one of the poorer volunteers who snagged extra snacks here and there to help defray the cost of her Expo weekend. If she wasn't cash-strapped, she certainly looked homely: her polo was too long, like she'd taken a man's shirt by accident, and she wore a tattered red cosplay wig and off-white slacks that seemed to squeeze in her thick legs like undercooked sausage casings. Normally the Expo PR team had their people looking more professional when dealing with the press, but that was an issue for another time.

"Is he drunk?" asked one of the reporters.

"No, but I could use a bump right about now," Ron said, and Sarah smacked him in the face.

"Enough of this!" she yelled. Joe could hear the worried anger in her voice.

"I'm not a fucking child!" Ron snarled back, pulling away from a shocked Sarah.

Joe struggled to hold Ron up and keep him moving toward a nearby exit leading to the off-limits service halls that convention center employees used to quickly move through the building.

"I demand some respect," Ron continued, blearily looking at the homely girl from PR. "Like the respect she gives me." Joe impatiently nodded at the girl to take Sarah's place and help him. That's when Ron brushed her breast with his hand. "She knows respect!" he said, then did it a second time. "Respect..." A third time. "Res..."

Both Joe and Sarah grabbed for Ron's hand, but Joe caught it and pulled it behind Ron's back so he could gain full control and escort him out like a criminal. Ron let out a pained moan, but the time for being discreet was over. The press were snapping photos, the news would be out within seconds, and if the PR girl had any brains, she would have lawsuits against both Ron and the Expo without much effort. Although, given the fact that she hadn't done anything to stop what was happening, and was now staring at Ron with a mixture of fangirl adoration and nervous fear, Joe wasn't sure what her brain power actually was.

Without warning, a woman from the 70s sci-fi series *21st Century* passed out at her table. Joe looked at her, started to reach for his walkie-talkie to call Amy for help, but Ron slumped down again. As Joe lifted him back up, he saw the teen cast from an MTV werewolf series laughing hysterically. Out of control. The press room seemed to be falling into chaos, and Joe now knew what was happening.

"I've seen you before," Ron said to the volunteer.

"I escorted you to the table, Lord Lionel," she said with the kind of respect Joe didn't think was necessary right now.

"Did he ask you to give him something?" Sarah whispered to the girl. She shook her head. "Well, what did he take before I got here?"

"I don't know," the girl barked back impatiently.

"Get the door," Joe hissed, and Sarah hurried to open it. They led Ron into the concrete-lined, fluorescent-lit hallway just before he collapsed in a heap, unseen by the journalists. Sarah crouched down in her power suit, lifting Ron's face up so she could look him in the eye.

"What did you take?" she demanded. No answer. "Sweetie, you have to tell me so we can get you help." Again, nothing.

"He didn't take anything," Joe told her. Sarah looked like she was about to say something, but then her gaze landed on the volunteer kneeling next to her. "Someone roofied something in the Media Room," Joe said. He'd worked enough events to know when people were drunk or drugged up—but that kind of thing didn't happen at CBE; alcohol wasn't even served until the evening parties. "I could see it hitting all of the pros."

"Who the hell would do that?" Sarah asked.

"We should get a wheelchair!" the volunteer shouted. "We can wheel him to the loading dock and into a limo to the hospital without anyone knowing."

This, Joe realized, was actually a good idea. "Do you have the number for First Aid?" he asked as a whiff of something sour crossed his nose—most likely from the dumpsters outside in the summer sun. Or worse, the spoiled cream that Louise had spilled on him that morning.

"No," she said and looked at Ron with worry. Joe sighed and pulled out his phone. There was no service in the back halls.

"God d..." Joe muttered, then bit his tongue. He turned back to the girl. "Run down to the programming offices and call First Aid from there."

"I don't know where that is," she said, examining Ron's face.

"What-the-fuck-good *are* you?" Sarah asked, voicing the sentiment Joe would not. The girl shrank back from the verbal attack. Joe needed to handle this.

"I'll go," he told Sarah. "Do you have a car service that can go around back to the loading dock? We can get him out unseen." Sarah nodded and grabbed her phone. He turned to the volunteer. "You stay with him, and if he wakes up, don't let him leave. We want to keep what's left of his reputation intact."

The girl stood straight and saluted, her hand drawing an infinity symbol. Joe shrugged, then he and Sarah hurried past her and around the corner.

"Once we get into the main convention center hallway, you should be able to get a signal," Joe said. Sarah nodded and kept pace, concern written all over her face. "He'll be okay."

She looked at him, but said nothing. They both knew there was no predicting how this would end.

Joe slammed open the service door into the hallway, not caring if they startled a fan on the other side—only to have Zack McCullock jump in their way, the base of his black trench coat swirling around his legs to meet the rest of his body.

"Oh! Hey, Joe," Zack said in surprise. "I thought it was some fans sneaking into the service hallways." He nodded to Sarah but continued talking to Joe. "You know, I have a military background and was thinking I'd be more useful in your department than running Industry Registration. I'm getting burned out..." Sarah pushed past him and lifted her phone to her ear.

"Not now, Zack," Joe said, just as someone dressed in a giant Bart Simpson costume followed by a bunch of fans raced past them. "No running in the halls!" Joe yelled. A scent from one of the fans hit him. It was like the sour trash/spoiled milk smell he'd gotten a whiff of moments before.

Joe suddenly realized that nothing from the past ten minutes made sense.

"Why does the PR department have a homely volunteer on staff?" Joe asked.

"Ooh, is this a riddle?!" Zack asked.

"And why would she be taking bottled waters when it's free from the tap?" he continued.

"Was it sparkling or flat?"

Joe ignored Zack, recognizing a logic flaw. Forget about the girl's inability to handle a crisis. Joe now wondered why the PR department would have anyone who couldn't communicate very well and was obviously a die-hard fangirl acting as the point person for the Expo's most important on-site press conference. The answer was simple: they wouldn't.

"Call the police. Have them come up to 7G," Joe commanded Zack. "Now!" Zack and Sarah looked at him, suddenly worried. "Ron Lionel's in trouble."

Joe yanked open the service door and was half a hallway away before he heard Sarah come through behind him. He rounded the corner and raced back toward the passage behind the press area, where he found the volunteer pushing a cart loaded with convention center linens away from him. She turned, saw Joe, and the race was on.

BAM! She slammed the cart through another set of grey double doors. Joe sped up, lungs burning. He didn't think, didn't wonder what he'd do when he caught her; he just acted. There was no other choice. He crashed through the doors moments behind her and blinked at the harsh sunlight flooding the loading dock.

"Hold it!" Joe yelled as he cut her off, stepping between the cart and the loading ramp. They were on the far side of the building, where food and supply orders for the convention center restaurants were delivered in the early morning hours. This time of day, the area was completely deserted.

"Where is Ron Lionel?" Joe asked, his voice deepening noticeably. The girl glanced toward the linen cart—just as he'd worried she would.

Joe was so horrified that for an instant he didn't know what to do. He had met obsessive fans. He had dealt with crazy creators. Hell, stopping a girl from giving a guy a blowjob was the wildest thing he'd ever seen at the Expo. Until now. Joe lifted the top tablecloth and found Ron sleeping blissfully underneath.

The girl shoved the cart into him and Joe stumbled backward. He pushed his foot down to stop himself, but there was no floor. In an instant that felt like forever, Joe knew he was falling off the loading dock.

There was a THUNK—hard, solid, the precursor to pain Joe knew would come. But that pain didn't hit. Instead, there were lights, blinking stars. Dizziness. And then darkness.

"Ja'harrah!" he heard in the blackness, as the smell of sour milk filled his nose.

"THE NEUTRAL ZONE"

There is a strong argument to be made that comic book readers, and people considered "loners," are actually more intelligent than their peers.

Dan Hurley, who was considered "slow" while growing up in the 1960s, saw his life change after discovering a Spider-Man *comic. "By age 11, I was getting straight As," he wrote in* The Guardian. *"Later in my teens, I took a college admissions course in the US, and scored the equivalent of 136 on an IQ test."*

Hurley spent three years interviewing psychologists and neuroscientists about the subject. He found that reading increases a person's "crystallized intelligence" (the knowledge that helps you "navigate and thrive in the world"), "fluid intelligence" (ability to solve problems), and "emotional intelligence" (ability to accurately read and respond to people's feelings). Adding to this concept are Satoshi Kanazawa of the London School of Economics and Political Science, and Norman Li of Singapore Management University. The duo surveyed 15,000 people, 18–28 years old, using 100 as a ranking of baseline intelligence, and 140 as genius level. Kanazawa and Li found that intelligent people often needed more alone time.

"The findings suggest—and it is no surprise—that those with more intelligence and the capacity to use it ... are less likely to spend as much time socializing because they are focused on some other longer term objective," noted Carol Graham of The Brookings Institution in Tech Times.

So before you turn your noses up at the women and men who write, draw, ink, and letter those comic books you disdain in the classroom— know that they are helping to make this country smarter. Thank you.

—Saydi Staud, Thought Leader and Education Advocate, Speaking at the National Education Alliance's Literary Symposium

Joe's skull ached, and he hadn't been drinking. It was these two slow understandings that made him awaken suddenly and throw his head back—right into something hard. A piercing pain stabbed through his head.

"Ughh, God—" He bit back a curse.

"Fucking A!" yelled a man's voice at the same time.

Ron Lionel. Joe realized he was tied to a chair and had banged into the back of Ron's head. Looking down and to the side he could see that the back of his seat was tied to Ron's with rope.

That's when Joe noticed the dull, eye-drying heat and funky scent: stale cigarettes and car exhaust mingling with dust that was slowly smoldering inside a barely functioning, metal-coil wall heater. The space was decorated in French Quarter-chic from many decades past. It both looked and felt incredibly drab, everything covered in a film of

Hepatitis yellow—sagging curtains, dingy walls, and stained rug. Joe knew where they were.

"This is the San Diego Hotel," he announced. Ron grunted. This had been the host hotel for America's Finest Comic Book Expo when it first started, and at that time it was considered a fancy establishment. When Joe had joined the Expo 25 years ago, it was still being used for a couple of after-hours events, mostly late-night movie screenings for nostalgia reasons. But as downtown San Diego gentrified and newer hotels and businesses came into the area, it had transformed into an hourly-rate hotel. Needless to say, it was no longer on the list of approved accommodations.

"Great," Ron said. "Now that we know where we are, how do we get out?"

"You don't!" barked a loud voice. Joe and Ron jumped, thumping heads again in their surprise. A woman slid her legs off the edge of the bed next to where they sat. It was hidden in shadows, and in his disoriented state, Joe hadn't noticed it or her.

Sinister music kicked in as she approached, her thighs *swick-swick-swicking* as she slowly moved toward them. Joe realized the sinister music was playing on her phone, and he'd only heard it once she pulled the headphones from her ears. She silenced the device.

"When one begins the journey toward self-unity, things always fall into place," the woman said with a spirit of enlightened excitement. She sidestepped over to Ron. "You said so yourself in issue seven, didn't you, Lord Lionel?"

"I did, indeed. So, now that we've got that covered, you can let me go," Ron said flippantly.

Joe gritted his teeth and tensed. This was a serious situation. He had no idea what this woman wanted, but he knew it wasn't funny, it wasn't a game, and he needed Ron to work with him if they were going to figure out how to escape safely.

"I cannot," she said softly. "I need answers." She bent down, and Joe could feel her hands behind his head, gently playing with Ron's hair. Even though they weren't directly touching, Joe could sense Ron stiffen under her touch.

"What's your name?" Joe asked. He hadn't been trained in hostage negotiation, but he knew that knowledge could potentially help them. Plus, he'd seen it done on countless TV shows.

"Velma," she said calmly, continuing to stroke Ron's hair. Something snapped into place in Joe's mind, and he remembered where he'd seen this woman. With Xander. Right before Operation: Blowjob Breakup on Thursday. He'd recognized she was odd then, but "odd" is relative at CBE so he hadn't paid much attention.

And if he was honest, he'd been more concerned that Xander was the person she'd turned to in her time of need, that she had angrily pushed him away. Now Joe wished he'd paid more attention to her.

"What kind of answers are you looking for, Velma?" he asked, turning his head to try and make eye contact.

"They don't concern you," she said softly. "Just Lord Lionel."

"Can you..." Ron fidgeted behind Joe, leaning away from Velma's hand. "...please stop with the touching?"

Velma stepped back and looked at Ron. She tilted her head, studying him. "Are you above the people, Lord Lionel?" she asked.

Joe didn't like where this conversation could go, especially with what he knew of Ron's abrasive manner. "I think he's more curious. We're not far from the convention center. Maybe ten blocks."

"How did you get us here without being seen?" Ron asked, playing along.

Velma smiled and spun around in a circle like a pleased little girl. She flopped onto the bed gleefully.

"I'm smarter than they think," she said, and her voice took on a slight growl as she added, "I'm smarter than you thought last night."

"I didn't think you were dumb," Ron said defensively. "I'd just had a very bad day and..." Joe swore he felt the nervous heat coming off Ron's head and neck. "I'm sorry if I slighted you."

Joe held back a sigh of relief. He recalled chasing Velma through the service tunnels and seeing Ron passed out inside the trash cart. He remembered falling and banging his head. But even using the cart, Velma would have somehow needed to get them into a vehicle and to this hotel, unload them again, and get them up to the room without anyone noticing. It wasn't like she could walk all the way here from the convention center, could she?

"Oh, wow," Joe said as he figured it out.

"Wow, what? I'm being honest here!" Ron snapped, but he didn't sound sincere.

"Before we moved to the current convention center on Front Street, and before the Convention and Performing Arts Center on C Street..."

"I don't know what the fuck you're talking about!" Ron yelled.

"We held the Expo in hotel ballrooms and meeting rooms," Joe snapped back, losing patience. "We used this hotel back then, when it was still nice. I was in the films department, and one night at about three a.m., I fell asleep against a wall and it opened."

"What, like a secret passage?" Ron asked. Velma sat forward, clapping her hands with glee.

"It was too cool to not check out," Joe continued. "So I went exploring. It led to service tunnels throughout this hotel and down under the city streets, but I was too nervous to check them out. It turned out a lot of the original Expo staff knew about them, and we'd go exploring on weekends. But we never went too deep because of rats, and the smells, and water that would rise up in there."

"Water?" Ron asked.

"Much of downtown San Diego is below sea level," Velma said, clearly enjoying her moment of superiority. "Supposedly there were some homeless people that used to live down there, too."

"I thought all the passages would have been cut off when they built Horton Plaza..." Joe said, realizing a scary truth: Velma had taken this path, so there was a slim chance that anyone had seen her. "*You* stole the plans from the convention center, didn't you?"

Velma hopped off the bed and bent forward in front of Joe. He noticed the fingerprint smudges on her black-rimmed glasses, her oily forehead, the way her hair looked like it had been rough-chopped with kitchen scissors. She smiled.

"You are very bright." She tapped him four times on the nose, once with each word, then moved away.

"So what is it you want to know?" Joe asked. "Ron is right here. He'll tell you anything you want."

Velma stopped her spirited movements.

"You like the book," Ron said. Then, nervously, "Right?"

"I've heard the hymns of Mount Morenou in my sleep, and walked to the Tavern of Lyre in my waking dreams," she replied. "When I was lost, *The Enduring* helped me find my way home." Velma's phone sounded off an alert, and her sad mood instantly changed. "Mother!" She put her thumb on the screen. "Ja'harrah!" she said into the phone, and walked into the bathroom.

"Do we call for help?" Ron whispered.

"No! This place is an hourly-rate dump for hookers and dealers," Joe whispered back. Word on the street was that the owner hadn't put anything into the building since he paid it off in the 70s, and he'd made more money from the residents' seedy dealings than he would if the property and land was sold as a tear-down for developers. "No one will call the cops."

Joe's eyes darted around the room, fear and panic growing inside him. But he pounced on those feelings and transformed them into anger. He'd allowed himself to be scared once, long ago, when a strange man had forced him into the back of a van. He was thirteen—old enough to walk home from school by himself—but when the man came at him, he'd frozen. Joe was shoved into the van, and that's when instinct took over. He'd kicked and screamed like a terrified animal, and he'd been able to get away. The man was never caught.

To this day, Joe believed that if he had just conquered his fears, he could have stopped that guy—gotten a better look, memorized the van's license plate. Was the van off-white or light blue? Joe still didn't know.

So later, whenever he started to feel nervous—whether it be from a bully at school or drunk frat guys at a Padres game—he would grab that energy, embrace it, even let it overtake him slightly. Then he would get angry and use that to his advantage.

"Can you move your feet?" he whispered to Ron.

"Yeah, so?"

"If we move at the same time, we can make small hops toward the door," he explained.

"Are you shitting me?"

"You will listen to me!" Joe commanded. "She could kill us, and I refuse to die because of you."

Silence. He felt Ron slump slightly in the chair. "Alright. You lead."

"Okay," Joe whispered, adrenaline pumping. "Okay, on three. One, two ... three!"

The duo hopped ... in a circle.

They both froze. Joe looked nervously toward the bathroom but could see Velma's block-like silhouette. She was still absorbed in her conversation.

"You have to jump left," Joe instructed, keeping his voice low and trying to stay patient. "You went right."

"I went left!" Ron hissed.

"You went right or it wouldn't've happened!" Joe whisper-yelled, wishing he was alone. He could probably save himself. "Okay," he said, refocusing them. "Move in the same direction one more time so we're even with the door again. One, two..." They jumped again, turning so they were now in the reverse position from where they'd started. "Okay, good," Joe said excitedly. "Okay, we do it again, only you jump right this time and I jump left and we move toward the door." Ron grunted in agreement. Joe inhaled. "One, two..."

They moved an inch toward the door and paused. Velma made a noise and Joe looked to the bathroom, but she had just bent down to pick up something from the floor.

"One, two, three..." Joe whispered, and they jumped. Again and again until they reached the door. They were centered with it, but Joe couldn't reach the knob. "Scoot toward you," he instructed. "One, two..."

They made two small hops in Ron's direction until the line of their backs was even with the doorjamb.

"Now what?" Ron asked.

"Gimme a second here," Joe said, nausea threatening to overtake him as he contemplated his next, unavoidable move. "When the door opens, shove the back of your head in."

"What sort of idiotic—" THUD! Joe slammed his head into Ron's.

"Dammit!" Ron whisper-screamed. "Alright! Christ!"

The move had hurt Joe too, sending a painful, blinding light into his skull, but it also distracted him from what came next. He turned his face toward the door and clamped his mouth on the old brass knob, his lower teeth sinking into a ring of greenish, greasy dirt on the underside. Then, trying not to lick it, he quickly turned his head downward and pulled the door open.

Ron grumbled as the edge of his head went into the opening. "Brilliant!" Ron whispered. "Got part of my shoulder in there, too. But you have to rotate your side toward the room now."

"You lead," Joe whispered back as he involuntarily licked the film on the inside of his bottom teeth. Ron counted down and Joe hopped away from the door.

The hallway light started edging its way into the room as Joe continued hopping and Ron popped more of his body and chair out.

"There's a window at the end of the hallway!" Ron whispered. "We can yell to someone on the street!"

Joe saw Velma through a crack in the bathroom door, shutting off the phone.

"Move!" Joe whisper-yelled, and without any counting, he and Ron began madly hopping into the empty hallway. Velma yanked open the bathroom door, looked at Joe in shock, and raced at him just as the two men hopped out of the room. "She's coming!"

"HELP!" Ron yelled as they hop-raced toward the window that was only two doors away. "A woman kidnapped us!"

"Someone help!" Joe screamed. "Call the cops! Someone call the cops!"

Velma emerged into the hall, kicking off her shoes and pulling down her socks as she trudged toward them.

"Almost there!" Ron yelled. "Faster!"

Joe shoved his feet into the floor and kicked hard. They popped down, further than before. A rush filled his chest as he realized they might actually make it, so he tried again. And again.

But on the next move, either Joe kicked too hard or Ron's timing was off—Joe didn't know which—because they were suddenly listing. And in an instant, they came crashing down onto their sides.

Velma was on them, quickly shoving one sock into Joe's mouth and the other into Ron's. She bent down, dug her heels into the peeling carpet, and used her meaty legs to drag the two men back to the room. They tried to yell, but their voices were muffled. And, even if they were heard, Joe knew no one would come to their aid in the San Diego Hotel.

ELEMENTAL
Episode #55

"Say 'Nope' to Dope"

Written by

Jase Peeples

FADE IN

EXT: DOWNTOWN DETROIT - NIGHT

A rented panel truck races through abandoned streets. Lasers
from the passenger side fire up at Elemental, who dodges left
and right to avoid the blasts.

After a close miss, she uses her hurricane-force winds to fly
in front of the truck, then lays down a wall of fire.

INT: PANEL TRUCK - NIGHT

The GUNMAN looks back where the four GLORY GIRLS are tied up
on top of wooden crates marked with names like "Marijuana,"
"Black Tar," and "Snow."

Suddenly, the DRIVER sees the fire wall and hits the brakes.
The Gunman is thrown back and accidentally shoots the drug
crates. A fire breaks out, and the four Glory Girls scream.

EXT: DOWNTOWN DETROIT - NIGHT

                    ELEMENTAL
                 (hearing them)
            My girls are in there!

At lightning speed, Elemental rips off the roof of the truck,
uses her winds to pull everyone out, and disarms the Driver
and Gunman with water blasts. Just as she binds the two men
in an ice cage, the truck explodes.

                                        FADE TO:

EXT. DOWNTOWN DETROIT - MORNING, NEXT DAY

MACK MCMURRAY stands by Elemental and the Glory Girls as his
government agents take the Gunman and Driver into custody.

                    MACK
            Where was Ms. Carter through all
            this? She should be supervising you
            orphans.

                    ELEMENTAL
            She was the one who contacted me,
            Mack. She's too much of a mouse to
            take on a band of drug dealers by
            herself.

Elemental gives a sly wink to the audience. DOMINIQUE tugs on Elemental's flowing sleeve.

                    DOMINIQUE
          Sorry we acted like a bunch of jive
          turkeys and didn't listen to you
          and Ms. Carter, Elemental.

                    AYASHA
          We never should have gone off the
          reservation like that and taken
          matters into our own hands.

                    BAH NEE
          It doesn't even take a math genius
          like me to calculate how bad our
          odds would have been.

                    ELEMENTAL
          If you ever suspect trouble, girls,
          you should always find an adult --
          like myself or Mr. McMurray.
               (to Leti)
          And what did you learn from all
          this, Leti?

                    LETI
          To never try black tar -- or ANY
          drug -- ever again. Even if the
          people you think are cool say it's
          okay.

                    ELEMENTAL
          And if you're not sure, ask a
          family member.

                    LETI
          Like how you, Ms. Carter, Mr.
          McMurray, and the Glory Girls are
          my family?

Elemental nods, pulling the girls into a big hug.

                                        FADE OUT.

ISSUE #13

"UNMASKED"

"What is this?" demanded a voice. A woman's voice. He knew that voice.

Something smelled. His face. His upper lip. Like nail polish remover mixed with model glue mixed with cum. No. Not cum. It smelled like poppers, kind of, and that made him think of cum.

That voice. *Velma.* He'd been kidnapped.

Ron opened his eyes and saw a blurry figure standing nearby.

Velma. Looking at someone. Not him. Joe, the security guy.

Ron felt dizzy. He closed his eyes. Forced them open. Velma held stuff in her hands—a white bag and large cup in one, something small in the other. Ron smelled greasy food. He realized he was starving. And that he wanted to puke.

Joe mumbled. He was gagged—cloth in his mouth and duct tape over his lips. Still tied to the chair. Now with zip ties. Not rope. The chair was tied to the nightstand. With the rope.

Ron realized he was also gagged, and tied spread-eagle to the bed. Wearing only his boxer briefs. Ron pulled at the bonds on his wrists and ankles. More zip ties. He felt sick again.

"Tell me the truth, or no McMuffin for you!" Velma commanded Joe. He nodded.

She thundered over to Ron, put a large soda cup on the nightstand next to the bed, and dropped the bag on the floor; McDonald's, Ron realized. She looked at him with confused anger—not unlike Sarah when he'd been caught on Thursday.

Thursday. That had happened Thursday. Velma had grabbed him Friday.

Ron turned his head and saw morning light coming in through the dirty window. It was Saturday now.

Velma turned back to Joe. She bent down and picked up something large from the floor. A sword. The Sword of Mount Morenou. Not the real one, obviously, or even an authorized one—because the Weeble hadn't tried to broker any deals for *The Enduring* before the comic had been optioned, and now that it had, all merchandising rights were controlled by the studio. What Velma held was one of those fan recreations Ron hated because it wasn't really accurate to what he'd envisioned. And he didn't make any money from the sale.

"If you scream, I will use this," Velma warned. Joe nodded. She ripped the tape off his lips and pulled a wet sock from his mouth, then bent down and picked up something small from next to the McDonald's bag. She held it in Joe's face. "What is this?"

Shock was written all over his face. "Where did you get that?" Joe asked, and his eyes slid toward Ron.

Ron squinted, stared, and realized what Velma held and where she'd found it. It was the glass vial of coke.

"His pants," she said, nodding toward Ron. Then, off Joe's questioning look, she added, "I wanted to buy you both breakfast, so I took his cash."

Joe gave Ron a wary look, and Velma smacked him in the side of the head. "WHAT IS IT?" she shrieked.

She knew what it was. Ron knew she knew, or at least suspected. But she needed to hear it from someone else.

"What did you give us?" Joe asked, his eyes moving around, desperately trying to focus. Ron blinked rapidly, assuming he looked the same way. "You dragged us in here and put rags over our mouths. That's all I remember."

Ron wanted to scream. This guy was always looking for answers, always asking random questions.

"Did you use chloroform on us?" Velma still said nothing. Whatever she'd used, it had to be the cause of his headache and nausea. "You can't just get that anywhere. Did you look it up online, or...?"

Velma hit him again. Ron could see the anger springing in Joe's limbs, and for a moment, he hoped the guy would rip off his bonds and beat the shit out of her. But he couldn't. Joe was tied tight.

"I've warned you," she said. "One more time. Answer the question."

"Let me smell it," Joe said warily. "But not too close." She waved it under his nose. "I think it's cocaine."

Velma threw the vial down at Joe's feet, and for an instant Ron felt his heart clench at the thought of the glass breaking over the filthy carpet. But then she stomped to the end of the bed and he saw tears streaming down her face.

She sob-asked, "C..." She couldn't even say the word. "How could you?"

"Velma, please," Joe said gently. "*The Enduring* is just a comic book. Ron is just a normal guy. A lot of people suffer from addiction."

Ron tensed. He was not an addict. He did coke now and then, sure, but not all the time. And it wasn't crystal meth or heroin. He could be doing a lot worse—like a lot of other people he'd known.

Velma took a deep breath, slowly picked up the bag of food, and patiently focused on Joe.

"If I'd heard you say that about Lord Lionel two months ago, I would have thought you were one of the Simple," she said. "Someone on your first or second cycle in the realm. And as someone on her fifth cycle who can see with clear eyes, I would have pitied you." She turned to Ron. "But I guess we were all fooled, weren't we?"

Joe looked at her. Then to Ron. "Translate, please."

Velma stomped over to Ron and yanked off his gag, but she held the sword high and near as a warning. He moved his jaw to try and massage the sore muscles in his face, then took a deep breath.

"In the books, it says we're born into this world on the highest strata of society—we're babies to the universe so we need it easy, okay? And with each reincarnation, we come back in a lower societal level," he summarized. "That makes your spirit stronger, and by the fifth cycle you're as spiritually evolved as possible."

Velma dropped the fast-food bag in Joe's lap. Ron's stomach groaned. "And that's when we have the depth to see the world for what it is, and take that step to the left of normal, into the land of the Enduring." She bent down in front of Joe so they were eye to eye. "Ja'harrah!" It sounded sad and lonely. "For so long I would've given anything to be like you," she said to Joe. "Like everyone else. But my spirit wouldn't allow it. And eventually, I realized I didn't need it."

"What changed?" Joe asked.

"Mother discovered *The Enduring* and shared it with me. I realized those 'curses' I thought I had in life were blessings. I just couldn't see the world's paradoxes yet."

"What ... paradoxes?" Joe asked carefully.

Ron knew he was trying to buy time, but that just frustrated him more. Buying time for what? They couldn't get out, they couldn't scream, and she obviously had no intention of becoming a normal, sane human being any time soon. What could he be hoping for?

"We're told to look a certain way and ignore how our bodies are really made," Velma explained. "We're told to make money even if it's over someone else's suffering. Be thin even if our spirit craves something else. Be ashamed of sex and our bodies even if that's the only pleasure you have. None of it adds up unless you realize it's all an illusion to the beyond."

That's when Ron lost all patience. "There is no 'beyond,' you idiot!" He could hear his words, sharp and anger-filled, as if he were watching the scene from above. "I made all that up. It's a fucking comic book."

"There is wisdom in those pages!" Velma spat back. "I believed it, and so do all those people who came to this convention to see you."

"Yes, I believed those concepts when I wrote them, but only as concepts." Ron sighed. He didn't have the energy to maintain his anger. "They're not a shit-ton different from what I learned in my college World Religions class." Ron looked at Velma. He couldn't read her, not like he could normally read people. So he tried to appeal to her reasonable side. "There's no land of the Enduring, Velma."

"I know that," she whispered.

"So just let us go," Ron pleaded.

"I can't..." she whimpered.

"What do you want from Ron?" Joe asked.

"Stay out of this," Ron snapped. He had things under control.

"You are not a nice man," Velma said to Ron, a dark anger filling her eyes. "Why did you create the world? Did you want to be popular? Did you want to fool your fans? Do you laugh at us?"

"I don't get why the fuck you're so pissed!"

Velma threw the sword to the ground, clenched her fists tightly, and appeared to flex every muscle in her body. Her mouth and nose and eyes scrunched up into a ball, and she stomped her feet in place over and over again. Ron looked to Joe, who seemed genuinely worried. Ron wondered if he'd gone too far.

Suddenly, Velma lunged at him, straddling him. She shoved her face within a millimeter of his and screamed. She raised her fists up to strike. Ron pulled on his bonds and pushed his head back into the mattress as though he could escape—but Velma punched herself in the face. Once! Twice! Three times! Then collapsed on top of him.

Ron felt her heavy body, her thick thighs resting between his open legs, her huge breasts pressing into his chest as she breathed heavily.

He thought of his cock under her—he couldn't help it—and there was a small stirring. But before anything more could happen, Velma obliviously planted her elbow in his chest and pushed off him. He gasped for air as she rolled off the bed.

"I need Mother," she mumbled as she took the sword and her phone and walked into the bathroom, this time leaving the door fully open.

"You need to calm down," Joe whispered.

"Don't you fucking tell me..."

"She's crazy," Joe snapped. "Emotionally unstable."

"A fucking retard could see that," Ron said. He looked at Joe and pointedly added, "Clearly."

"We may be able to use that against her," Joe said, keeping one eye on the bathroom. "No one knows where we are. We are the only people who can save us."

"Sarah's probably freaking out. She was the last person to see us." Joe looked at him, skeptical. "I also have a panel this morning. When I don't show up for that, she's going to know something's wrong for sure. And, knowing her, she'll get the fucking US Navy and Marines to come looking for me." Ron was confident in his logic. Sarah had always watched out for him, always protected him. But Joe was looking at him as if he was the biggest idiot on the planet. "What?"

"She doesn't know we were kidnapped; she just knows we disappeared. No one will believe her."

"She'll make them believe."

"Believe what?" Joe snapped. "That some drug-addicted, misogynistic bisexual who makes people give him blowjobs in public at an all-ages convention is in danger and hasn't just gone on some bender?"

"You're bisexual?" Velma asked. She stood just outside the bathroom, sword in one hand, phone in the other, and she looked stunned.

"I'm not..." Ron started. Velma seemed confused. Joe clearly thought he was lying. "Do I like getting attention from guys and girls? Absolutely.

Have I messed around with guys and girls? Sure, whatever. I like it when a guy gives me head because they know what a guy wants and they know how to give it. But then they always want me to give it back, and I don't like dick enough to do that. And please, God, don't kiss me after we've done stuff. That's just shit." Both Velma and Joe were staring at him, dumbfounded. "The point is that I'm not gay or bi or whatever label you feel the need to lay on people so you can put them in your tidy little Puritan box."

Joe flinched as if he'd been hit. Ron liked that.

"Why do you do drugs?" Velma asked, innocent as a child.

Ron's immediate reaction was to lie and tell her he didn't do drugs, but she'd found the coke. No one had ever found his drugs before. He'd never been "caught," and he'd never been asked why.

"Drugs are bad," she said.

"They are..." Ron nodded.

"Drugs ruin lives," she said.

"They can..." he acknowledged.

"Why do you do them?"

"Because I like it," he answered truthfully.

"So you *are* an addict..." Her eyes widened.

"No," he said. "It's only coke, and I don't do it all the time. Just now and then. Very rarely."

"Then why did you have it at the Expo?" she asked, her voice quiet and confused.

Ron sighed. "I don't know, Velma." It was the truth.

She looked at him, contemplating his answers. Everyone was silent for a long, uncomfortable moment. Finally, Velma nodded.

In an instant, she opened one of her suitcases, reached in, and pulled out a laptop and some tech Ron didn't recognize. She opened the laptop on the desk opposite the bed and did some rapid-fire clicking. Ron looked to Joe, who was also trying to see what she was doing. No luck. Finally, she turned around.

"You are a disappointment," she scolded him as if he were a bad doll she'd invited to an afternoon tea party. "I'm going to show you what that means. How it hurts people."

Ron felt the scream rising up, but Velma was on him before he could make a sound. She returned the sock to his mouth, shoving it in deeply before covering his lips with the tape again.

"What are you planning, Velma?" Joe asked, the worry evident in his voice.

"I've locked the keyboard so you can't send messages," she replied. "Please don't unplug it or damage it. Mother just bought it for us." She shoved the other sock in his mouth, taped his lips closed, then spun around looking for things. She pulled more tech from her suitcase, shoved it into a backpack with Ron's cash, and grabbed the sword. She then stopped, picked up the vial of coke, and added it to the bag.

"Ja'harrah!" Velma said, waving her clawed hand in an infinity symbol. She grabbed the food bag and walked out, leaving behind the faint smell of Egg McMuffin.

ISSUE #14

"WHAT ARE YOU WEARING?"

If you are visiting or staying at one of the official hotels that have partnered with America's Finest Comic Book Expo, please behave appropriately.

While we understand that many of you look to save money and share rooms during the event, there is a limit on how many people can safely inhabit a hotel room. Please adhere to the policies set down by the property. For example, don't try cramming ten people into a room that was designed for four.

Likewise, loud parties of any kind will not be tolerated—whether the noise was created due to excessive drinking, excitement leading to the masquerade, or any other legal adult activity.

Please also be aware that our partner hotels function independently of the Expo. If you and your friends are ejected from a property due to inappropriate behavior, there is nothing we can do to rectify the situation.

**—From the Hotel Information section of the
America's Finest Comic Book Expo
registration website**

Joe looked over at Ron, hoping to make a visual connection—not because he liked the guy, but just to experience some kind of human interaction in this insane situation. Fear was scraping at the back of Joe's brain, and he was worried that if he didn't have something to focus on it would take over.

But Ron was staring at the ceiling, probably reeling from the fact that his status as God on Earth wasn't as infallible as he'd believed. Joe's eyes wandered over the younger guy's toned body and he slumped in his chair. He felt soft. Logically, he knew he was in better shape than many guys his age. He'd been trained in self-defense and could disarm someone if necessary. He technically knew how to fight (even though he didn't spar much anymore). But that didn't change this feeling. Because when he looked down, he realized his stomach, crotch, and thighs were like a shapeless mass of Silly Putty squished into khaki pants.

Enough. This wasn't getting them anywhere. Joe had a small window of opportunity with Velma gone, and he had to take it. He had to save them. He could hit the gym later.

A thrilling rush flooded through Joe's tingling hands, feet, and exhausted body as he performed a status check: Velma had covered their mouths tightly, and Joe was sure their muffled screams couldn't penetrate the walls. Plus, if no one had come the last time they'd screamed, he doubted anyone would right now. He pulled at his bonds again, hoping something would loosen. No luck. Velma had used zip ties. She was smart. Probably smarter than anyone had ever assumed. He would need a knife or something seriously sharp to cut them.

He looked around the seedy space for anything that could be

broken, but other than the wall-mounted light, a cheap plastic phone, and a cup of soda on the nightstand, there wasn't much. Velma's suitcase was too far away, and Joe was tied to the nightstand. He looked down to see if there was a way to break it, but even though the stand was old, it looked solid.

Of course there's nothing to use! Joe realized. Velma was a fan. Like him, she'd probably spent her entire life figuring out plot twists in books, movies, and TV shows. She'd probably spent so much time researching by herself or talking about plots with her mother (who seemed to be her one and only friend) that she knew how to do all kinds of crazy things. She'd figured out how to kidnap Ron easily enough, used the Internet and the blueprints to access the underground tunnels, and knocked them out using a homemade solution.

Hell, she could probably make a dirty bomb or other explosive if she wanted. Joe's heart froze. It was a huge, drastic, and dangerous move, but not impossible. It would get Velma endless attention, show the world how truly angry she was at Ron ... for whatever it was he'd done. Joe wasn't sure. In fact, he was confused by her anger; Velma clearly adored the universe Ron had created. But she didn't seem like the type who would kill herself. Not fanatical enough. Brave enough. Velma was the kind of person who'd had some crappy things happen in life, but rather than find solutions, she sat in a pool of pity.

Joe took in a sad, surprised breath. He wasn't like Velma (he didn't think), but he knew that pool. He'd swam in it before, and not just recently because of the way things had worked out with Pam. He'd also done it with his job. His dreams of being a big-time writer hadn't panned out, and for so long he'd been bitter about the cards life had handed him, and quietly envious of people like Ron.

And that's when it hit him. Velma didn't see herself as a righteous villain or hero. She saw herself as a victim, which made Ron a kind of arch enemy. And if that was the case, she'd want everyone to see him the way she saw him. So, yes, an attack may be in the works, but Velma wouldn't sacrifice herself.

She'd sacrifice others and somehow blame Ron for it, he thought, his eyes growing wide. *That's how I'd do it, so that I could become a hero. Because in a world of mere mortals, at the largest comic book event in the United States, what would a fanboy or fangirl really want? To be the superhero who catches the bad guy!*

Joe's mind flashed over everyone he knew at CBE, from volunteers he only saw once a year, to minor annoyances like Xander and Zack, to people who really held a place in his heart—Robert, Pam, even Louise. Any of them could be hurt or killed if she was planning what he thought. And the Expo itself, which brought such joy and community to so many, would be irrevocably damaged.

Joe shook the chair in frustrated panic. Ron looked over, saw something, and tried to sit up as he let out a muffled warning. Joe stopped, realizing something was wrong. But it was too late: the cup of cold, watery soda came crashing down into his lap.

Ron laid his head back down and sighed; clearly he thought Joe was an idiot.

Joe growled, his anger directed at everything in the room. Ron lifted his head once more. His eyes widened as Joe furiously yanked at the bonds, rocking the nightstand and bed as the plastic cut into the flesh of his wrists and his sock-covered ankles.

Ron tried to yell again, and Joe once again stopped his rocking. The phone was about to slide off the nightstand and into Ron's head. Ron saw Joe see the phone and smiled in thanks, then winced in pain as the tape pulled.

A light bulb went off in Joe's head, and he started shaking the nightstand with even more enthusiasm. Ron saw the phone sliding, his eyes widened further, and he yelled as loudly as he could through the gag, but Joe didn't stop.

The phone fell, bashing into Ron's skull.

Ron's muffled swearing started immediately, then grew more forceful as the pain hit and a small stream of blood leaked out from a tiny cut on his forehead. Joe didn't care. He smiled at Ron and indicated the phone with his head. It was next to Ron, on the bed, and off the hook.

Ron didn't understand, so Joe darted his eyes from Ron to the phone. He then moved his head in a circle. Ron looked at Joe like he was crazy. Finally, after a minute of this, Joe let out a frustrated scream.

How could he be so stupid? Had he never seen any action show at any time during his entire life? No, what Joe had in mind might not work given the hotel's sordid history, but maybe the operator would send someone to investigate. Drug deals and prostitution are one thing, but no property owner wants dead bodies in his rooms.

Joe tried again—eyes darting to the phone, head circling in an "O" as in "Operator"—until Ron finally looked over and saw the receiver cord wrapping around his ear. Ron craned his neck and looked to the side. The phone was half on his bare shoulder, half on the bed, the cradle up next to his ear. Ron finally realized what Joe was suggesting. He stuck his neck out and lifted his shoulder to tilt the phone in his direction. Joe nodded and moaned a muffled, "Yes! Yes! Yes!" Ron scrunched his head, focused, and tried using his chin to hit the keys; the phone was too far away.

"NNNN!" Joe shouted through the tape. Ron looked at him. Joe twitched his nose back and forth like Elizabeth Montgomery in *Bewitched*.

Ron nodded, and instead of reaching out with his chin, he tucked it into his chest so that his nose stuck out. He stretched as far as he could, then adjusted his right shoulder to see if that would give him even a millimeter more. It did.

Ron hit the zero and they both heard ringing on the speaker. Ron smiled and excitedly nodded to Joe. For a moment, Joe felt he'd earned the man's respect.

"Front desk," came a bored, possibly stoned voice.

Ron and Joe yelled as loudly as they could, over and over. They couldn't say specific words, but maybe the moaning would make the guy think they were in trouble.

"God!" the operator said with obvious aggravation. "Just 'cause I work here doesn't mean I'm into this crap."

"HHH?" Ron asked in a moan, then began gasping for breath through his nose. Joe kept screaming.

"Wait a sec," the operator said, curiosity wrapping his voice. "Are there two of you?"

"YYY!" Ron yelled. Joe joined him, making as much noise as possible, rocking his chair and shaking the nightstand and bed. The headboard hit the walls, and the tired mattress under Ron squeaked like a monkey being murdered.

"You're a dirty couple, huh?" the operator said as he clicked away on a keyboard. "Room 665? Is that Velma I hear?"

As soon as he said the name, Ron's screams became even more frantic. Joe, however, stopped.

Ron doesn't sound like a girl, he thought. *Does he think I'm Velma? Do I sound like a girl?* He felt like he was back in sixth grade, and some kid had made fun of his prepubescent voice.

"She likes that, huh?" said the operator. "She likes me listening to you plow her? Yeah! Well, I got my junk right here, buddy, so hit it! Hit it like you mean it! I'm right here with you guys!"

Ron stopped, shocked. Joe looked at him, equally shocked but also insulted, and tried grunting deep and loud as he shook the nightstand and bed more, trying to make himself sound more like a guy. Ron looked at Joe, confused, and made a high-pitched sound under the gag.

"Yes, yes, yes..." said the excited operator. "Give it to her hard!"

Just then, a board under the mattress snapped and Ron screamed as he fell slightly. Joe screamed too, startled by the sudden snap.

"Yeah, buddy!" yelled the operator as the phone slipped away from Ron's reach. "Yeah! Me too! Me... Oh, God! Oh my God...! Tell her I'm gonna..."

The operator made some more grunts as he orgasmed. Then, silence. Ron moved his head away from the receiver.

"Thanks, man," the operator said in a hushed voice. "I'm here tomorrow. Call me if you want." The line went dead.

Before Joe could register any sense of defeat, the laptop monitor came to life and Velma's face appeared. A green light on the screen indicated that the laptop's camera was now active as well.

"Ready to watch the chaos?" she asked, her eyes gleaming behind those smudged glasses.

ISSUE #15

"MIRROR, MIRROR"

Due to the overwhelming popularity of programs in Hall H, there are few safety rules:

1. Enter and exit the room in an orderly manner.

2. No rushing the stage.

3. Do not throw anything at the stage.

4. No standing on chairs or yelling at panelists.

5. For Q&A sessions, you must submit your written question to the Programming Committee prior to the panel. Your question will be reviewed in advance. If you divert from your written question, the microphone will be cut off.

6. Do not ask stupid questions. (Just kidding. But please be polite and respectful to our invited guests.)

7. No eating stinky/noisy food in the room; if your lunch or snacks bother other attendees, you'll be asked to leave.

8. Only drinks with screw tops are allowed; if you spill your drink, you will be asked to clean it up, and then asked to leave.

9. If you are asked to leave the room, you will need to get back in line behind the other waiting attendees.

10. You can leave to use the restroom and return, provided:
• Someone inside saves your seat for you.
• You take a restroom pass upon exiting.
• You return to the meeting room through the designated restroom exit door.

11. You may not leave to get food or drinks and then expect to return to your seat.
• Do not say you are going to the restroom, take a restroom pass, and then attempt to smuggle food into the meeting room. We will find out the truth from other hungry fans, and you will be asked to leave and consume your food outside.
• Please see rule #7 about stinky food.

12. No camping. Once programming ends for the night, you will be asked to leave the building.

**—From the Programming Information section of
the America's Finest Comic Book Expo
registration website**

Ron was hungry, thirsty, and had a headache. His wrists and ankles were seriously chafed. The rest of his skin was dry-warm from the old heater, and sweat occasionally dripped down his armpits and behind his knees. Then there was his back, throbbing under his shoulder blades from the sudden fall when the bed broke, which had jerked his arms away from his body. His hands and feet were still secured to the bed frame, but now they hovered slightly above his head. His fingers and toes tingled. His throat was hoarse from yelling into the sock, and it was hard to breath in this position.

But Ron didn't care about any of that. He just wanted to beat the shit out of Velma.

This, Ron realized, was exactly why he hated horror movies. Not because they scared him, or because of the gore, or even because he thought they were silly and a waste of time. He hated horror films because they pissed him off.

Thinking of their plots logically—as Ron did, and as he thought every person should do when watching any kind of movie—the characters should know their time was up. The facts are that someone is trying to kill some people, some of their friends have already been wiped out in stunning fashions, and the odds are not in their favor. With that very practical information in mind, what's the wisest course of action? Run upstairs where there's no escape route? Hide, when it's been shown that the killer is pretty damn clever and can probably outthink you? Or do you just say to yourself, "This is it. My time is up. But if I'm going to die—which is the most logical outcome here—then I might as well pick up the best weapon I can find and try to hurt that motherfucker as much as I can before he murders me."

Not that Ron believed he was going to die. And he didn't want to kill Velma. He just wanted to hurt her. A lot. Like she'd hurt him. Who was she—this social outcast, someone who didn't have any friends except her mother (that bitch was probably the one who fucked her up in the first place), a girl who had clearly found great pleasure in his stories—to treat him this way?

Ron let out as much of a scream as he could, given the gag and his sore throat. Velma stared back at him on the laptop screen, but it was unclear whether or not she could see the broken bed and fallen phone. Ron doubted it.

She thinks she's going to humiliate me? Make me look like a fool? Ruin my reputation? He scoffed. *She's fucking crazy if she thinks she can do that. I've done more to ruin my reputation than any other person could...*

"When I hook up this cord," Velma whispered into the mic, showing the two men a computer cable, "it will all be over for you."

Ron squinted and recognized a familiar grey room with blue drapery behind Velma as she positioned her phone on a tripod to give them a better view. He saw what looked like his name on a giant screen in the distance.

She's at the convention center? Realization dawned. *At* my *panel?*

Ron's fiery temper blazed brighter at the thought of Velma trying to steal his thunder. He would turn this into an epic Ron Lionel melt-down™ after he got out of this rancid hotel, painting himself as the victim of a crazed lunatic fan.

For a second, Ron's heart leapt with excitement. His eyes darted around the room. He wanted something. A weapon, something he could use against her. He craned his neck to look on the nightstand for a pen or a paperclip. If he could hide something in his hand, he could stab her when she got close, maybe slash her face so she knocked into Joe and he could help in some way.

Ron's mind darted through scenarios, seeing Velma accidentally freeing Joe, who would free him. Joe would get help while Ron kept her there, using something to beat her down. But what? The desk drawer? A chair leg if he could break it off?

No. The laptop! He would yank the laptop from the wall and smash it into her head, knocking her into that wall heater. Some of her oily hair would catch fire, causing her to panic. But Ron wouldn't let her burn; he'd smash the laptop into her head over and over again until the fire was extinguished and she was down on the ground in a heap. Then he would take the power cord and tie her up, tightly, and enjoy the look of the black wire digging into her purply-pale flesh.

"You can't do that to a girl!" Joe would whine. Fucking fanboy.

"Save your PC bullshit!" Ron would shout. *"She's not a girl. This bitch is a fucking bitch!"* Ron could imagine the spit flying from his mouth, the veins on his neck straining as he yelled, *"As soon as you kidnap someone, hurt them, and humiliate them, all gender rules go out the fucking window!"*

A sweet voice snapped Ron's attention back to the present. And the laptop monitor.

"Hello, America's Finest Comic Book Expo!" she said.

The camera jerked right, then left, then finally focused on the person speaking. It was Sexy Convention Lady—Pam. Ron looked over at Joe, who seemed stunned. The crowd cheered with excitement.

"And now, the moment you've all been waiting for!"

Ron's heart stopped. He didn't understand what was going on. Maybe this wasn't his panel after all.

"Please give a warm welcome to Comic Book Expo's featured guest." She beamed. Ron's blood went cold. "That creator of contro-versy and *The Enduring* comic series..." The audience cheered and laughed, eating up every second of her introduction. "...the indomitable..."

"Shut up, y'stupid cunt!" came a harsh British accent from backstage.

Pam looked genuinely shocked, like she'd been physically slapped across the face. Ron felt like he'd been slapped, too. He'd never call a woman he thought was sexy a C-U-Next-Tuesday. Ron turned his head toward Joe, who was leaning forward as if to get a better look.

"What's going on?" Ron heard a nervous Velma say behind the camera.

Pam turned to the backstage area, where the unseen speaker was. "What did you just say?"

"Y'heard me, you lame bitch!" said a voice that sounded frighteningly like Ron's. He shivered involuntarily.

"Now wait just a minute," Pam said. "I don't care how much I like you, that is inappropriate and..."

"Like I give a fuck, you bleedin' cow!" the voice yelled back. "Why the hell do I care what you or any of those fuckers think?"

Joe gave what sounded like a choked laugh. Ron didn't know how, but from the look on Joe's face, he knew what was going on. Ron desperately wanted the gags off so Joe could explain. Instead he jerked at his bonds, hoping something would give.

Just then, the Expo president ran up onto the stage and grabbed Pam. She looked ready for a fight, but he managed to drag her into the audience and down by the tech board.

"That's right, run, you stinkin' bastards!" the man yelled as he stumbled out onto the stage, his back to the audience. He seemed drunk. The crowd jumped to its feet, applauding and cheering.

That's not me... Ron thought sadly. Then, just as quickly, it warped into anger. *THAT'S NOT ME!*

"This convention is bullshit!" the fake Ron Lionel screamed before walking backstage again. "Making me whore myself out..." Banging. Crashing. Unintelligible statements. "I created *The* motherfucking *Enduring!*"

The audience screamed for more. Chants of "Ron! Ron! Ron!" thundered out, causing the microphone to crackle.

Velma's face appeared in front of the camera and she squinted at Ron and Joe. She turned around as soon as "Lord Lionel" stumbled back out from behind the curtain with a half empty bottle of scotch in hand. He took a long pull.

Ron watched as Velma looked from the phone to the stage, worry washing over her face. She looked up and Ron's eyes followed hers: the screens that were used to broadcast the stage panels to the back of the room were now blank. Fans in the audience were climbing onto their chairs to look over the other attendees.

"Why are the screens off?" Velma hissed. She looked into the phone, and her eyes grew wide with realization. "I have to get them back on!"

Ron looked away as the camera, still aimed more or less at the stage, bobbed and weaved through the crowd like a low-budget thrill ride for *Cloverfield* or *The Blair Witch Project*. He looked from the screen to Joe, back and forth, trying to watch what Velma was doing without getting motion sickness.

"I want to know about Myranda!" the fake Ron yelled, mocking the fans, who had started to quiet down. "When will August finally make the crossing?"

Idiot! Ron thought, and grew giddy at his double's mistake. One of his fans would say something now.

"August already made the crossing..." yelled a confused guy in the front row.

Whoever this imposter was, he did look like Ron from a distance, but if he paused or spoke too long, the fans would figure out the truth. Ron didn't want Velma to succeed in whatever it was she'd been planning, but he also hated thinking that he could be replaced by some guy in designer jeans with messy hair and an uncanny accent so easily.

"FUCK YOU, you stupid wanker," Fake Ron yelled. "My pubic hair is smarter than that!"

That's a good one, Ron acknowledged. *Makes no sense, but it's good...*

The imposter tripped, fumbling the scotch toward the back of the stage. He stumbled toward the gushing bottle, away from the audience.

"You're a freakin' bunch'a idiots reading and buying whatever I throw out because you don't know crap, and now you're tryin' to tell me what I wrote?"

Sarah rushed on stage, picked up the scotch, and tried to help Fake Ron stand. A small shred of him was relieved to see her, still trying to protect him and his brand.

"I don't need your fucking help!" the man spat, shoving past Sarah and running backstage. The camera lowered as Velma approached the tech board next to the stage.

"I'm sorry, but clearly Mr. Lionel isn't well right now," Sarah's voice said over the microphone. She sounded so close to Velma. Ron wanted to scream out to her, hoping she would somehow hear him over the laughing and cheering fans—like a mother who can pick out her child's voice in a crowded carnival.

Suddenly, a man appeared in front of Velma's phone, blocking Ron and Joe's view.

"Ma'am, what are you doing?" he asked.

"We need to turn those monitors on!" Velma said. They could see her trying to push past him.

In the background, Sarah said, "I'm afraid we'll have to postpone today's panel, but you can..."

"Ma'am, this is a union house," the tech guy said. "We can't have you touching the equipment."

Fake Ron's voice boomed out on the hall speakers. "You're not canceling this panel! This is my fucking panel!" The audience roared with excitement. "Are you gonna let them shut me down?" He screamed to the audience. "I've got shit to hand out!"

"That's not him!" Velma yelled, aiming her phone up at Union Tech Man's face, then at the stage, where Fake Ron emerged with a stack of comic books.

"That's not Ron Lionel! You have to let me plug my phone into the monitors and I can prove it!"

"How?" asked a woman's voice. The view changed again, and both Pam and the Expo president were standing next to Union Tech Man.

Ron's heart jumped with excitement. *Get this bitch.*

"You're in on it," Velma said, fear and panic gripping each word.

The camera quickly turned and Velma raced away.

"Wait!" a man commanded, and the camera jerked backward a few times, as if Velma was being grabbed. But seconds later there was no resistance, and she was running down an aisle.

"Look at this crap!" Fake Ron screamed. The real Ron caught glimpses of him tossing shirts and comic books out to the crowd. "You'll beat off on anything I touch, won't you, y'bastards!"

Suddenly, the camera froze as Velma stopped herself from plowing into a woman who had jumped onto a chair in front of her.

"Ron Lionel touched that!" the woman screamed. "I want it! That's mine!"

Chaos erupted as fans surged from the back of the 5,000-seat room and rushed the stage. A swarm of people shoved into Velma and she fell, losing her phone in the process. Ron and Joe looked at one another as feet kicked it along the carpeted floor. The two men instinctively ducked their heads as sneaker-clad feet knocked it under chairs and into backpacks. They could hear Velma's desperate shrieks of "My phone! I need my phone!" above the raging crowd.

Finally, a chubby hand grabbed hold, but was immediately knocked away again. A paper of some kind covered the lens, and Ron hoped Velma wouldn't be able to find it. If someone else turned it in, they might be able to use it to find him. He didn't know how, but clearly these people were brighter than he'd believed.

A hand picked up the phone and ripped the paper away. Velma's panting filled the audio. Ron saw both Sarah and the Weeble grabbing the imposter Ron and hustling him backstage. Security guards appeared to block fans from following, but they didn't stop the crowd from grabbing up the loot left behind.

As Velma picked up her bag and shut off the camera, Ron and Joe shared a smile. Their side had won that tiny battle.

ISSUE #16

"CAMP KHITOMER"

...which brings us back to the question that people who don't attend fan conventions always ask: Why do these women and men willingly volunteer to subject themselves to such horrible working conditions? Why do they use their precious vacation time from their regular jobs to perform unpaid, hard work for multiple days—battling constant hunger, sore feet, and sleep deprivation—just to make sure these events happen?

Sure, they get into the conventions for free. But that's too simplistic an answer. For me, it comes down to their "love of the tribe."

My father was in the Marines and served in multiple combat zones. And not to diminish what he or any other service member has sacrificed, but there is a similarity between the bond he and his brothers-in-arms experienced, and what these convention volunteers share. They sacrifice their own comforts for what they see as the greater good, and they derive great enjoyment from being able to tell "war stories" in the evening about encountering unruly fans or meeting an idol.

But, I think the most important reason is that they know what these events meant to them when they were growing up, and they want to give that same sense of safety, joy, and fun to younger members of the tribe.

It's that sensibility, if properly harnessed, that could help any business achieve greatness.

—Saydi Staud, Thought Leader and Business Optimization Consultant, Speaking at Fortune 500 Business Symposium

Joe smiled to himself, his eyes closed. He still sat in Velma's stagnant room at the San Diego Hotel. The laptop had gone dark hours ago, and the evening sun was fading outside the soot-smudged windows. Velma hadn't been back to the room all day, and both he and Ron had given up on trying to free themselves.

Joe could no longer feel the pain in his chafed wrists. The hunger had curled in on itself inside his stomach. He was desperate for a drink of water, and periodically bit into the sock clogging his mouth, hoping to squeeze out enough spit to swallow and pretend it was a sip of something refreshing. Even the fear in his chest was now a nervous flutter he could ignore if he didn't think about his situation too much.

To keep from thinking about the present, Joe allowed himself to drift in and out of a waking sleep. He thought about when he was 15 and a third-level magic user. Back then he used a staff of healing, carried a vial of holy water to handle undead creatures, and was incredible when it came to hitting an enemy with magic missiles.

Robert, 17, was a chaotic-good thief with a magic shield he'd stolen from an elf camp. He didn't like talking his way out of battles; he preferred using his two-handed broadsword. He also had a killer saving throw.

Robert had first approached Joe when he was reading a D&D manual during S.U.R. (Silent, Uninterrupted Reading). The school-wide class mixed students of every grade level and required that they all read *something* for 20 minutes. That class changed Joe and Robert's lives forever. They met in September, and soon Robert was telling Joe about a magical place he'd visited the past three summers: America's Finest Comic Book Expo.

Back when they first met, Joe had been secretly happy to have a friend like Robert who understood why he enjoyed cartoons, comics, and other things you were supposed to outgrow ("secretly," because even though Robert was older, he was mostly an unknown on campus, whereas Joe had a pretty solid group of friends and was hesitant to be seen hanging out with the nerdy guy from the library).

But that next July, they donned grey cloaks, black breeches, and white blouses Joe's mother had sewn for them, and black leather boots and belts they'd bought at the Purple Heart Thrift Store with money saved from their part-time jobs. Robert also carried the coolest triangular metal shield they'd ever seen, which his dad had made (with a mechanic buddy of his) and painted to match the design Robert had crafted for his D&D character. They hopped into Robert's mom's Toyota Cressida and headed for the Civic Center on B Street. There, they went straight for the gaming room ... only to discover that the D&D campaigns at America's Finest Comic Book Expo were too advanced for beginners like them. But the DM said he would be happy to host one for beginning levels later in the day, so the two went exploring.

"Wassup...?" asked one of three boys Joe recognized from school—recently graduated seniors like Robert. They were the type who announced to anyone who'd listen that they were above "the bullshit" of high school. They smoked cigarettes (and Joe assumed pot), knew music, hung out with girls, and got laid. Joe thought they were cool.

"We won tickets from KGB-FM, so we figured we'd shit away a couple hours downtown," the leader of the pack explained. "Maybe see if we can slip into a tittie bar downtown later on." The idea thrilled Joe. "We were about to check out the dealers' room. Want to go? Cool costumes," he added.

Robert was less enamored, but Joe jumped at the chance,

convinced that Robert would tag along. Robert was painfully intro-
verted back then, but as their friendship had grown, Joe had taken it
upon himself to get him out into the world. He'd convinced Robert to
drive them to *Rocky Horror* at The Ken, explore Balboa Park on weekends, and spend a day at the Del Mar Fair where they'd met some girls
from Orange County and danced to old songs from some band they
were sure their parents would have loved. Robert had enjoyed all those
things, so Joe assumed this would be no different.

Robert didn't follow. *Screw him, then!* Joe thought. But when he
and the boys entered the Exhibit Hall, his emotions whirled. There was
merchandise he'd never seen before from beloved TV programs and
movies—from British science fiction series to exotic animation from
Japan that he couldn't understand but enjoyed watching anyway—and
rows of comic books and novels just waiting to be absorbed. It was
everything Joe loved, and he wanted to be sharing it with Robert.

"Check this shit out," one of the follower boys laughed at a booth in
front of them. (Joe couldn't remember their names now, and he
doubted Robert would be able to either, but vowed to ask him when
they got out.) In retrospect, Joe knew that laugh. It was deep and dirty,
a mixture of insecurity, horniness, and fear of potential trouble. He'd
heard it often from guys his age back then, and it usually involved girls.

The boy slid aside a collected edition of *Elfquest* comics to reveal
Penthouse, *Juggs*, and *Club* magazines hidden underneath. There was a
box at the far end of the booth clearly marked "Adults Only," so Joe
assumed the magazines belonged there. Everything was such a disorga-
nized mess that it was no surprise they had gotten shuffled over to this
side. In the CBE's early days, organizers didn't always notice (or care) if
adult material was being sold in an area that was open to the general
public.

As if they shared a telepathic link, two boys moved simultaneously
to one side of the table, blocking the dealer's view of their leader as he
shoved the magazines up his shirt.

"You can't do that," Joe whispered.

"Be cool," the leader whispered. "I'm over eighteen."

That wasn't Joe's point. He didn't care about the porn. (He had a couple *Penthouse* magazines hidden in the back of his dad's shed at home.) What bothered him was that they were stealing. And that went against everything he believed, tainting this wonderful new place he'd discovered. No, this wonderful new place Robert had introduced him to. Robert, who had read these three better than Joe ever could.

"Those boys are stealing from you!" Joe blurted out to the dealer. Everyone in the aisle stopped to look, and the boy quickly dropped the magazines. He and the other two ran.

"Thanks," said a small, gentle-looking man with a quiet voice and a soft smile. He walked over and picked up the magazines from the ground. "They were your friends?"

"Not really," Joe responded, feeling guilty about Robert and worried he'd have to report the guys from school.

The man just nodded and smiled. "You know, I was talking to my friends who help run the Expo. They were saying they could use trustworthy volunteers. You should try it. Gets you in free, and I think it's fun. At least, it looks fun."

"Cool," Joe said, for the first time realizing that the event didn't simply spring to life on its own.

"You like comic books?" the man asked. A confused Joe said he preferred regular books, so the dealer turned to his dusty folding shelf and pulled down Robert Heinlein's *Stranger in a Strange Land*. "Read this yet?"

Joe shook his head. "It's a favorite. Take it." Joe stared at him. "You did a good thing today. You deserve a little thanks."

"Artemis J. Stone!" yelled a woman. "What do you think you're doing?!"

In the hotel room, Joe choked back a laugh, remembering that first time meeting Maxine, and how he'd immediately thought she looked like a creature Ray Harryhausen might have created for a film.

"He's giving away stuff!" screamed a smaller, cracking voice.

Max. Joe remembered seeing him step out from behind his mother, his unruly hair and pale moon face a vision of things to come. "Whoa!" Max said, looking at the magazines in his father's arms. "*Juggs!*"

Maxine spotted the magazines too. "What the hell are you waving those things around for?!" She looked at Joe, then back at her husband. "Put them away, you idiot! He's a minor! Max is a minor!"

"I've seen those already," Max said with a wave of his hand.

"YOU WHAT?!" Maxine yelled.

As the arguing ensued, Artemis smiled at Joe and nodded for him to leave. Joe found Robert—who hadn't moved from where they'd last seen one another—and brought him to the volunteer desk. The two signed up to work in the films department for the rest of the Expo. It was the highlight of Joe's year.

Joe had never told Robert he was sorry for ditching him back then. He felt guilty about it now.

The hotel room door whooshed open, and Velma hurriedly stumbled in. She dropped her bag and sword, looked back out the door, then shut it and clicked both the chain and deadbolt into place.

"Who was that?" she demanded, barging over to Ron. She ripped the duct tape from his mouth and yanked the sock out, oblivious to the spit that oozed off the fabric and down her hand and wrist before she tossed it aside. Ron tried to say something. It was strangled and hard to hear, but Joe could clearly see his disdain for Velma. She saw it, too, because she climbed on top of him, straddled his nearly nude body, and banged both of her hands against the headboard above him. "Do not play dumb! You are not dumb!" she raged. "I demand to know WHO THAT WAS ON THAT STAGE!"

Ron looked at Joe and nodded. "He knows..." he choked out.

"How do *you* know?" Velma asked, her head snapping to Joe.

She rolled off Ron, stumbled slightly as her foot hit the ground, then regained her balance.

Joe pulled back his head, worried Velma would hit him. But then he saw Ron behind her, looking at his left arm. He could now move it up and down the headboard bar, which had been loosened by Velma's enraged punching. Just as Joe processed that information, Velma grabbed the corner of the tape and pulled. Hard.

Tears burned in Joe's eyes as he felt the plucking sensation of tiny hairs being yanked out of his face, all the way down to the roots. He blinked rapidly, not letting the tears fall. Velma's spit-covered fingers reached into his mouth and pulled the sock out.

"Do you know?" Joe nodded. "Who?"

"I think that was Xander..." Joe laughed, at first just a short, small explosion that grew as he noticed the looks on Ron and Velma's faces: his a mask of indignant rage, and hers like a petulant child who didn't get her way and was about to explode. "He studied voice at Stella Adler and starred in the Christian Community Theatre's productions of *Jesus Christ Superstar*, *Darn Yankees*, and *Godspell*—where he learned American Sign Language." Joe doubled over as much as his restraints would allow, laughing even harder as he recited the speech he'd heard Xander give any person who'd ever asked about his acting. "I never thought much of him before," Joe admitted, then nodded to Ron. "But he did a pretty good you."

"Fuck..." Ron shook his head in disbelief.

"Oh!" Joe realized. "You guys were hitting on each other before the opening ceremony."

"That guy?" Ron asked, incredulous. "The Ren Faire twink with the muscles?" Joe nodded. "He's a foot shorter and has a bubble butt! I look NOTHING like him!"

Joe's laughter exploded again, sending a sharp but almost pleasant pain through his chest. He wondered who had come up with the plan. Certainly not Xander, because it would have taken too much behind-the-scenes work for even him to pull off alone. Maybe Sarah? But she didn't know how the CBE really worked. If Joe had to make a bet, it would have been on Robert. He was far smarter than anyone ever gave him credit for, and he engendered a lot of loyalty at the Expo. He'd be the best person to get everyone involved—including Louise, who had jumped up on the chair in front of Velma and screamed about wanting the comics, causing them to shut down the room. And security had been prepared, which could only mean Amy was in the wings and ready to send them out. It was all a huge risk, but well-orchestrated. Joe didn't know why they'd done it, but he was intensely proud.

Velma slowly backed up and sat on the edge of the bed, defeat written all over her face. She pulled the cell phone out of her pocket and stared at it, mumbling something to herself. Joe's laughter calmed as both he and Ron watched her.

"For Christ's sake, let us go," Ron said, his attitude softening slightly.

"Velma, murder goes against everything Ron writes about in *The Enduring*, right?" Joe asked, looking to Ron for support; he nodded. "Hurting us or people at the Expo is just wrong. You know that." Ron's eyes went wide, and Joe realized the idea of them being killed hadn't crossed his mind until that moment.

"It is," Ron said, suddenly. "It does. I mean, think about Myranda's banishment to the netherworlds. She was condemned because she killed the Faerie Prince even though it was an accident. I made that quite clear."

"It wasn't murder," Velma gently explained to Joe. "Not really. The cycle brings us all back, better than before."

"It's a fucking fantasy story," Ron said, and Joe fumed at his inability to grasp just how dangerous their situation was.

"You know it's a fantasy story, right, Velma?" Joe said, hoping to get on her side and talk her down. She nodded, but continued staring at her phone. "And in this world, our world, killing or hurting other people is wrong." Velma nodded again, and smack-wiped her face to stop the tears.

Joe looked at her, at the phone, and remembered her panicked tone when she'd dropped it at the panel. It was unhinged, irrational, like when he'd seen her with Xander on Thursday. In that moment, Joe realized two very important things. One: No mother who was so obviously close to her daughter would condone her kidnapping someone, much less inflicting pain or killing. And two: Joe had never actually heard Velma's mother, or even heard Velma speaking to her.

Just as Ron curled his lips to say something dismissive, Joe interrupted. "What happened to your mother?"

Velma looked up, startled. Her eyes slid toward Ron, as if reluctant to speak in front of him. Her eyes came back to focus on Joe and she pursed her lips. She shook her head slightly.

"Did her cycle here end?" Joe asked gently, but he already knew the answer. "When did it happen?"

Velma's eyes brimmed with tears and anger, but this time she didn't smack herself and they didn't leak out. Joe could see a whirlpool of emotions circling in those unfallen tears, and that slow worry rose inside his chest once more.

Velma stood, her eyes fixed on Joe. Out of the corner of his eye, he saw Ron desperately pulling and twisting his left hand to get free, but Joe kept his focus on Velma, hoping she wouldn't notice the movements.

Velma leaned in, her nose almost touching Joe's. Her eyes stared into his, darting back and forth, trying to focus. She was breathing heavily, her warm exhalations moistening the top of his lip. She smelled foul, and Joe wondered when she'd last brushed her teeth or showered. But he refused to look away, trying to convey a sense of compassion that was quickly being overpowered by fear. Finally, she stood and turned, walking into the bathroom with her phone.

"What the fuck are you doing?" Ron hissed.

"Trying to learn her story," Joe snapped back.

"This isn't a God damn comic book where the villain gives a speech about their motivations and then we escape," Ron said. "That's not how the world works. You think you're going to talk your fucking way out of this?"

"Maybe," Joe said, unsure. "I don't think she's evil or she would've blown up everyone in that convention room."

"Jumping Jesus on a pogo stick!" Ron gasped. "You think that thing was going to blow the place up? Like we're dealing with some kind of fucking homegrown terrorist?"

"I don't know!" Joe was losing patience. "But we won't know anything if we don't ask her questions. The more we know, the more power we have."

Ron dropped his head back, muttering to himself. Joe wanted to yell and scream and call him every name in the world. He wanted Velma to hurt Ron, to smack him hard and teach him some humility.

But, no, that wasn't true. Not really. Yes, he wanted Ron to grow up, to see Velma and this situation the way he saw them. And he believed a good hit to the head might be the only thing that could do the trick with Ron. But inside, Joe knew he didn't really want Ron to be seriously injured. Besides, he might need the guy. Like it or not, Joe knew this alliance could be essential if they were going to escape without anyone getting hurt. Joe changed tactics.

"How's that going?" he asked, nodding to Ron's loose arm.

"She died," Velma said from the bathroom doorway. Joe and Ron jumped in surprise, but Velma didn't seem to have heard Joe. "Her cycle didn't end. She didn't pass over." Velma looked at Ron. "That's all made up, isn't it?"

"Well, it's basically Hinduism, but..." his voice trailed off. Velma's shoulders sagged; she looked lost.

"Do you still talk to her?" Joe asked. "I talk to my mom. She died when I was in college."

Velma nodded, then quietly asked, "What was your mother like?"

"She was pretty great." Joe smiled. "She believed in me and in my dreams of being a writer. She liked seeing me enjoying myself at the Expo. She loved coming with my dad and seeing me speak at panels."

"About what?" Velma asked.

"Fan fiction," Joe said.

Ron made a mocking sound and Joe was embarrassed. Ashamed. Part of that came from Ron's response, but part of it was because of what he'd told Velma. It was the standard answer he gave anyone who asked about his mom, but in that moment, it felt hollow.

"I know she tried to be a good mom," Joe said. "I know she meant well."

Silence. Velma sat down on the edge of the bed nearest Joe, forcing Ron to stop pulling at his bonds. Joe knew she was waiting for more.

"She and my dad would come to the panels, and afterward she'd say things like, 'That was a very special day.' And it was, I know. But then she'd add, 'You know, most people don't get moments like this in life.' And I know she was saying it to make me appreciate the moment, but it was like at seventeen I'd reached the height of my success." Joe's mind raced. "It's like when I was in my twenties and I submitted some scripts I'd written to both the Warner Bros. and Walt Disney young screenwriters programs. They were spec scripts for existing shows, and if they liked them you'd go up to LA and get mentored for a couple months and maybe land a writer's assistant job. But when I sent my stuff off she said, 'Well, even if you don't get it, you tried, and that's what matters.' I know she was trying to set my expectations in case I didn't make it, but it was like I'd failed before they'd even gotten the scripts." Joe looked up at Velma and shrugged. "Guess who didn't make it."

"But you work for the Expo," Velma said.

"I work for Superior Staffers," Joe corrected. "They're the company that supplies temp workers and security for the event. I used to volunteer with CBE, and I met the company owners when the Expo hired Superior Staffers for additional help. They liked working with me and offered me a job." And then he admitted the truth. "So, I followed the money."

"Do you regret it?" she asked.

"Sometimes," Joe said. He looked up at her. "How did your mom die?"

"Breast cancer," Velma said. "She never did the boob check you're supposed to do. She..." Velma stopped, started, and stopped again. "She worried about me a lot. I don't have friends. We were friends. She and me. And she would fight for me. Stop the bullies at school. And their parents. And strangers. She loved me."

"She sounds like a force of nature." Joe smiled, eyeing Ron, who was looking up at the ceiling and thankfully keeping his mouth shut.

"I don't think she took care of herself very well." She was quiet for a moment, then went on. "She helped me get a job at the movie theater, and she would leave me messages every morning on my phone so if I got too stressed I could listen to them." Joe nodded, now understanding what Velma was always listening to on the phone. "Moms are good," Velma said confidently. "Your mom was good. She was *trying* to do good."

"She was," Joe agreed.

"Oh, shit..." Ron interrupted. "You're pissed about the Faerie Queen, aren't you?"

Velma stood, turned, and the dark cloud descended on her once more. She bent down, nostrils flaring, and picked up the sword. Joe tensed his muscles, hoping he'd somehow become stronger than before and be able to break his bonds or the chair. He couldn't.

"And that's why you're here," Velma said coldly, holding up the sword. "I need to know why you destroyed my world."

ISSUE #17

"SECRET IDENTITY"

"Beware of Regina Georges bearing gifts..."

—Quote attributed to Frank Svengsouk when asked why he was leaving Marvel at Comic Book Expo #42

"Dexter accidentally killed his parents with the Christmas lights," Velma said accusingly. "Did that happen or not?"

"It did," Ron replied, annoyed by the interrogation but warily watching the sword aimed at his head.

"He went to the orphanage and was haunted by nightmares of their deaths," she said. Ron nodded. "Which we found out in issue twenty-five was the Faerie Queen sending her shadow demons into his dream state."

Ron nodded again; he thought about Sarah's advice to use as few words as possible during a negotiation, and thought it might help in this situation, too.

"She was trying to push Dexter to the left of normal and into the land of the Enduring. It didn't work. It was the headmistress at the orphanage whose abuse eventually pushed him there, but we learned in issue fifty that the headmistress and the Faerie Queen were the same person."

"I'd left the clues there," Ron said.

"I know," she snapped defensively. "She was singing 'The Melody of Marinello' in issue one, like Myranda and Majesty did during The Hunt of the Full Moon—"

"Wait a second," Joe interrupted, and for once, Ron didn't mind him butting into the conversation. It took Velma's focus off him. "I'm sorry. 'Marinello'? Like the beauty schools? That's where you got the name from? The defunct Marinello Schools of Beauty?"

"I will not take criticism from a fucking fanboy who writes fucking fan fiction when he's not working as a fucking rent-a-cop for a fucking comic book convention," Ron fumed.

"STOP IT!" Velma screamed, slamming the sword tip into the floor with a loud metallic *thwang*. But it was the fear and anger in Velma's voice that hit Ron more powerfully than any smack across the face. He glanced at Joe, wondering if the security chief had been right about how dangerous she could be. But as she stomped her feet on the ground and pounded the sword tip up and down, he doubted it.

"I am trying to put everything together in my head, and it's hard, and it's harder when you both keep talking." Velma looked down, mumbling to herself. "The headmistress sang 'The Melody of Marinello,' then Myranda and Majesty did—but it was the Faerie Queen's song. We'd seen her doing it from the start of the series, because it was the song she'd sung to the Faerie Prince when he was a wee child, just before Myranda accidentally killed him—and *that* was why everyone was sure that Myranda couldn't have been the Faerie Queen. It had to be Majesty."

"But it wasn't?" Joe asked.

"It was Dexter's mother!" Velma shouted, clearly distraught. "Dexter loved his parents more than anything, so when he thought he'd killed them he was devastated. But then in issue fifty, he found out it had been a trick: The Faerie Queen had really killed them and wanted Dexter to believe it was he who'd done it. But how could the Faerie Queen have done it if she was also Dexter's mother? That would mean she killed herself. And Dexter's mother was the kindest woman Dexter had ever known. We'd seen that in the 'Mother, May I?' arc in issues thirty to thirty-four, and later when Ariel used the scrying bowl in 'History Repeating' from issues forty-four and forty-five. There's no way it could be her!"

"Okay, yes, Velma, we know it's upsetting," Joe soothed. "But maybe Ron's just..."

"Please be quiet," Ron said calmly. The tone came from his exhaustion, but it instantly garnered both Joe and Velma's attention. A part of Ron realized it had worked because it was so different from his usual screaming or swearing approach. He'd have to remember that for his next meeting with the studio. It might hold more power than he'd initially realized. "Do not act like you have any grasp of what I'm doing in this book."

"So why?" Joe asked, tossing back a sliver of Ron's normal attitude. "Why Dexter's mom?"

"Why did I do it in the story?"

"Why in real life!" Joe snapped. "What happened in Ron Lionel's life that he would paint a perfect mother character, only to have her become the main villain of a hugely popular series?"

Ron sat up slightly and the zip ties cut into his wrists, the muscles in his neck straining to hold up his head in that splayed position. He could feel his cheeks burning as he spat out, "Do not try to do to me what you're..." Ron stopped himself. He didn't want to ruin what Joe was setting up. Just in case.

"Did you make Dexter's mom the Faerie Queen because you're an addict?" Velma asked.

"I'm not an..." Ron almost lost it again. Instead, he took a breath and forced himself to calm down. "I did, I'll admit, go on a bender when I wrote the novel—because *The Enduring* was originally supposed to be a novel." He quickly added, "Writing it high wasn't my fault. I thought I'd bought coke, but the asshole of a dealer I went to gave me crystal instead."

Joe and Velma stared at him. He sighed, exasperated. *Of course they don't know the difference.*

"Cocaine keeps you up and buzzy, but after a while it wears off and you can go to bed."

"Which is why it can become so addictive," Joe said to Velma. *Fucking tight ass.*

"Crystal is much stronger," Ron continued, tossing a look at Joe to shut up. "It suppresses your appetite, can increase your sex drive, and keeps you awake for days. Three hours in, I had my suspicions. At twelve I was certain, and at twenty-four hours—after numerous romances with various adult websites—I was pissed because I wanted to sleep. But I couldn't. And I was writing—like Kerouac and Burroughs and Ginsberg—and that's when I molded *The Enduring.*" He paused, then added, "I haven't done crystal since. That shit will fuck you up for good."

They didn't seem to understand that point. Ron sighed, then went on. "Even when I sobered up, it all felt so exciting. I had tons of other stories to tell after *The Enduring* sold as a book, or a TV show or movie. I knew it."

Ron drooped slightly as memories surfaced. *I never thought it would be the only thing I'd write.* For the first time in a long while, he felt sad. Not frustrated or fearful or angry, like when Sarah had told him about the studio, but really and truly sad.

"I'm still going to get to those stories soon," Ron said suddenly, confidently. "It's just that the movie adaptation is taking so much time.

But I've got this one series—so much bigger than *The Enduring*. That's going to be my legacy project." Ron heard the hollowness in his own voice. He refused to look at Joe.

"You didn't intend to sell *The Enduring* as a comic book?" Velma asked, confused.

Ron looked at her. She was so fixated on *The Enduring* that he couldn't quite wrap his head around it. She knew it was a fantasy, but she took the stories as though they were imparting moral wisdom on society, or stocked with hidden secrets that, if deciphered, could help a person better manage the world.

And that's when it hit him: "Your mother used the books, didn't she? To help you..." Ron searched for the right word. "...navigate things?"

Behind Velma, Joe was nodding. He'd come to the same conclusion.

"I know what karma is in this world." Velma nodded. "When Dexter and Falstaff first met Majesty at the Tavern of Lyre, and we learned that she was the reincarnation of God Karma, Mother explained to me what karma was. She showed me how, when mean kids would do things to me, karma would come to them in this world and mete out justice. And when Whimsy used mirrors on Mount Morenou to teach Dexter to find his inner strength and save his friends, Mother showed me a mirror so I could see my own true self." Velma smiled, looking genuinely pleased. "Yes," she said. "I learned many things from her." She stopped suddenly and pursed her lips. "So why didn't you make it a novel?"

"You don't just write a book and get it published," Ron said. "It doesn't work like that."

"Why not?" she asked.

Ron wanted to scream. And he wanted to leave. And he wanted to smack her on the side of the head as he exited. But he couldn't, so he looked at Joe. "Back me up here, man!"

"Maybe it was fate," Joe said.

"Myranda?" Velma asked. Joe looked confused.

"Myranda is the reincarnation of Lady Fate," Ron sighed. "Actually, she's all three fates from Greek myth rolled into one." Velma stared at him, stunned. "Issue ninety, spoiler alert."

Velma thought about that, turned to Joe, then to Ron, then back to Joe. "What did you mean by it being fate?"

"Comics can reach so many more people than regular novels," Joe offered. "Maybe it was the universe hoping to get *The Enduring*'s message out to more people."

"Jesus, really?" Ron snarled. He immediately regretted it, because now Velma was staring at him, waiting for an explanation. Ron looked at her, wondering how much to say. He decided the truth was his easiest option.

"Look, I don't know about that," he said slowly. "After I came down off the crystal, I got really depressed. And I started to worry that *The Enduring* novel was a waste of time. That it was stupid. But then I heard about a comic book convention back home in Vegas, so I got up the energy, took my manuscript, and went. I figured I could get some editor's opinion and then either listen or not, but it was better than sitting around my apartment watching porn and wondering if I should give up my dreams of being a writer and instead get a job at Target or something."

"You sold it that day?" Velma asked.

"That day," Ron said, wishing—as he had ever since—that he hadn't been so hasty in his decision.

"Without a lawyer to look over the paperwork?" Joe asked skeptically.

"It's how it happened!" Ron said, leaving out the minor detail that he'd snorted his last bump before leaving the house. He'd done it to lift himself out of the dumps and handle the anxiety of showing his manuscript to editors. Even with all the other shit he'd done over the years, he still considered that last bump his greatest creative mistake. It had made him too eager when he'd met the Weeble, who'd read the first five chapters and offered the contract right away. Now he was tied to

Ragnarök Comics in perpetuity; unless, of course, the company was sold.

Ron thought about it all now and chuckled slightly. "Maybe it was fate," he finally said. "Who are we to question the gods?"

"Why Dexter's mother?!" Velma demanded.

"Come on, there must be some reason behind it," Joe suggested. Ron hated the way he looked at him, as if imploring Ron to give up a secret that didn't exist.

"Did you hate your mother?" Velma asked. She turned to Joe. "That's what you're saying, isn't it?"

"Most writers pull from what they know," Joe said. Ron felt his jaw clenching, his teeth grinding. "Their own relationships, experiences, that kind of thing."

"I don't hate my parents!" Ron yelled. "My dad works at a buffet restaurant in the suburbs, and my mom is a blackjack dealer at one of the old downtown hotels because she's too old to work on the Strip anymore. They're good, normal people."

"But...?" Joe asked. Ron wanted to punch him.

"But, what?" Ron snapped. "How could two normal parents raise an asshole like me?" Joe's expression showed that this was exactly what he was thinking. "Dad has these deals that are always going to come through and make him rich, even though they never do. And Mom supports him by working a steady job even though she knows the deals will never come through. And that relationship works for them. They're happy. They love each other. So who am I or you or anyone else to judge?"

Ron paused. Love—he didn't have that, not like his parents did for each other. And they had let him down in the past. Like when *The Enduring* hit its first anniversary and sales were through the roof, so Ron decided to celebrate. He'd booked a reservation at one of the celebrity chef restaurants on the Strip—some bald dude his parents loved to watch on reality TV. But Ron's dad had a meeting for some new business venture they should get into—hot air balloons in Africa that would broadcast wireless service to the tribal people, or some shit like that—and his mom hadn't felt like going with just Ron. She only seemed to be able to make decisions when his dad was around anyway. And so, with no real friends to call, Ron had stayed at his apartment with a pizza and a bottle of red wine, and the reservation had gone to waste.

To be fair, being at home that night had paid off. Cruising online, he'd seen an ad for a small, local convention where fans were hosting an *Enduring* panel...

"No!" Velma yelled, kicking the bed. Ron grew nervous. "It can't be like this! You are Lord Lionel! You are God of this world!"

"Velma, I hear you," Ron said. "I understand where you're coming from, and I truly feel bad about what you've gone through." To Joe, he added, "What you've both been through." *But it doesn't mean I'm going to divulge my entire life story to you two, and it doesn't mean I give a shit about you, either.*

"Why?!" she screamed, picking up the sword. She swung it around the room, narrowly missing Joe and Ron with each swipe. "Why? Why? Why?"

"There is no answer!" Ron finally screamed back. "I'm making this shit up as I go along! I'm maybe six months ahead of the plot." Velma slammed the sword into the side of the bed, the blade cutting into the mattress startlingly close to Ron's leg. Panic flew through him as he rattled out, "I'm sorry, but mom plots make people crazy, they always work, and I needed a boost in sales to keep the buzz going so the studio would keep me involved and not kick me off the project. Fuck, I don't even draw most of the books, I..." He stopped. Velma looked like her world was caving in. Joe's eyes begged him to stop. Instead, Ron feebly added, "I do the thumbnails, but this guy in Venezuela finishes the pages..."

Ron knew he'd made a mistake. Velma was unstable, but he'd never thought she was the kind of violent person that Joe clearly believed they were dealing with. Now, however, Ron wondered if he'd been wrong. Velma's hands shook, and sweat covered her forehead, leaving dark stains on her armpits and underboobs.

"Mother died reading that last chapter," Velma muttered. "She died. It was too much for her to take."

"Velma, it was breast cancer," Joe said with forced calm.

"This got her before that!" Velma said. "I found her when I came home from work. The comic was on her chest. She smelled like poo. She'd pooed herself. She was reading the comic and the story shocked her. Killed her."

Ron's heart raced.

"Velma," Joe said softly, "it may have just been bad timing."

"Dexter's mother," Velma said. Ron felt hot, dizzy, nauseous; he wished someone would shut off the suffocating wall heater. "I took the book from her hands and read it. That was the page she was on when she died." Velma turned to Ron. Nervous sweat soaked the bed under him. "I looked you up. I needed to know why you did this." Velma's eyes darted from Ron to the floor to the ceiling as she recounted her movements. "I took our credit cards and bank cards and flew to Las Vegas to find you, and I met your parents, but they said you had already left for the Expo. And so I came here." Velma stopped, thinking through the details. "But you're saying there's no reason? Mother died for no reason?"

Ron stared at her, not sure what he should say. He shook his head, and felt a slight stinging in his eyes. He was crying.

"Velma, there's something you can do," Joe said, very seriously. She turned toward him. "You can take Ron down. Get revenge for your mother's death."

ISSUE #18

"POWER TRIP"

"What were the Xena and Hercules team-ups, really? I'll tell you: they were just modern retellings of The Shazam!/Isis *hour without the motorhome."*

—Quote attributed to Zack McCullock during the fan fiction panel at Comic Book Expo #32

"What the fuck?" Ron yelled. Joe blocked out the fear he felt in his chest and turned a blind eye to the image of Velma leaving her mother's rotting corpse in a South Carolina living room in July. All that mattered was finding a way out of this situation, and thanks to Ron's revelations, Joe had an idea. He needed to keep Velma's attention on him.

"I doubt you're his only victim," Joe said, trying to sound confident and in control. "I caught him forcing a girl to give him oral sex in public..."

"I didn't force anyone to do anything!"

"...where anyone—even a child—could have seen them."

"She offered to blow me!"

Velma's eyes shifted at odd angles as she tried to understand what Joe was saying.

"I wouldn't be surprised if he didn't plagiarize *The Enduring* story from some poor person who was too weak to fight for themselves. You can picture that, right?"

Velma slowly nodded, and Joe felt a pang of guilt tapping on the side of his heart. He was manipulating her, and that wasn't right, but they were in a very dangerous situation. It was obvious Velma hadn't considered her next steps, like what she would do with the two of them after she'd gotten whatever answers she wanted to hear. If she'd been willing to abandon her dead mother's body to come on this quest, there was no telling what she might do to them without thinking about the consequences.

"Shut up!" Ron yelled. "I created *The Enduring!*"

Just as Velma was about to look back at him, Joe spoke again. "I bet if you came forward and publicly held Ron accountable, you'd find you weren't alone." Ron growled something unintelligible. "Your actions could be the boost others need to find their inner courage and step forward..."

"Give me a FUCKING BREAK!"

"...to find a voice for themselves." Ron rattled the bed with such a vicious, anger-fueled strength that Joe wondered if he could get enough adrenaline pumping to actually break it. He knew Ron was in shape, but assumed it was a "show body" that looked good from working out and a strict diet but couldn't actually do much when pressed into action. Now, as Joe saw a small stream of blood sliding down Ron's loose left wrist where the zip tie had cut into his flesh, Joe realized he may have misjudged him, and hoped that wouldn't mess up his plans.

"What kind of bullshit are you playing at here?" Ron spat across the room.

Joe felt a twinge of panic spark in his heart. Ron was a forceful talker, the kind of person who will either twist your words around to prove he's right or won't let you speak at all during an argument. Both were dangerous in this case. Joe looked at Velma, trying to play it cool.

"Shut him up for a second and let's figure this out," Joe suggested.

"No! No! No!" Ron shouted as Velma dropped the sword and picked up the sock and roll of duct tape from the ground.

"He thinks you're a terrorist!" Ron screamed, and Velma stopped. Almost instantly, that spark inside Joe ignited into full-blown alarm. "He thought you were going to attack everyone in that meeting room earlier today."

"Don't listen to him, Velma," Joe said. He clenched his fists, feeling cold fingertips pressing into his clammy hands.

"How would I attack thousands of people?" Velma asked, confused.

"Hell if I know," Ron said. "Maybe he thought you had a gun or a bomb or something in that bag of yours."

Velma looked wrecked. She faced Joe but couldn't look at him. She began sobbing.

"You made her cry," Ron said accusingly.

"Velma, I..."

Ron interrupted, "You can't trust a guy with no girlfriend who's in a midlife crisis and has failed at achieving any of his dreams. They will say and do evil things because they hate themselves so much. That's a life lesson, Velma. Never forget it."

"I'm not a villain," she whispered. To herself? Him or Ron? Her mother?

Joe's heart hurt. Not for himself, but for Velma. In other circumstances, Ron's words would have stabbed in his chest and left him feeling like a failure for weeks. But in that moment, as Joe looked at the confused girl, he couldn't help but feel for her.

What was it that made her life the way it was? Or Ron's the way his was? Why did some girls get born with the looks, or social graces, or both? How did certain people grow up knowing how to have a voice, to speak up for themselves, and yet others struggled simply to move from shadow to shadow, desperately hoping to avoid any conflicts along the way? Why could some people drink or smoke pot or do drugs and enjoy themselves, while others became alcoholics, drug addicts, or corpses?

Did Velma's parents smoke or drink or have some kind of genetic issue that made her the way she was? Did it matter? Joe knew Pam's parents had messed everything up, at least according to the stories she'd told him. They'd stopped getting along when she was very young but stayed together for her sake—a fact that would slip out in one way or another every time they argued. This eventually led to them "secretly" dating other people (though Pam figured it out) and doggedly chasing their dream jobs. Neither seemed to want full responsibility for Pam, so she learned to take care of herself. Then Pam went off to college and her parents finally divorced and became friends again. It was as though Pam's existence had robbed them of those 18 years. And yet she'd turned out to be one of the strongest, most independent women he'd ever met.

Did Velma's parents do everything by the book and still produce a daughter who just didn't mesh with the rest of the world? Or did Velma's mother love her so much that she'd never learned to live for herself? And where was the father, anyway? Did he know about the mother's death? Was he in contact with Velma, or was she a forgotten part of his past? Was he dead, too?

Was it Lady Fate who let Ron write and sell a hugely successful comic book series when he didn't enjoy comic books, but denied Joe the opportunity to even get his treatments or scripts on the right table? Had Joe done something in a previous life—or even earlier in this one—that made God Karma twist and fold the ways of the world so he would invariably sabotage his own romantic relationships?

Or was it all simpler than that? Was Joe not as talented as Ron, not as loving and open as Robert, not as personable as Xander?

In that moment, with precise clarity, Joe knew there was no answer to any of those questions. Velma's life, Pam's, Ron's, and his—their stories had unfolded the way they had, and no amount of wishing, hoping, or regretting could change that. And the point Pam had been trying to make finally made sense: all we have is now—this lifetime, this moment—and we can't waste it on things we can't control.

Joe's life, his story, was unfolding, right there, in a miserable, dust-filled, smoke-stained hotel room. And not Lady Fate, God Karma, or any other deity or human was going to save them. He had to do it; for himself, for Ron, and hopefully for Velma, too.

"I was scared," Joe said to Velma. "You've been scared before, too, right?" She nodded. "You kidnapped us. That's a really scary thing. And I run security for the Expo, so it's only natural that I would think you may have more dangerous plans."

"I'm not a villain," she repeated.

"I didn't know you," Joe said. "Not like I do now." Then, in all honesty, he added, "I'm sorry. I judged you like those bullies judged you. It wasn't right. I'm sorry."

Velma looked up, a light shining in her eyes. Joe thought he was getting her back ... until she charged at him. For a heartbeat, he froze, seeing Velma's arms coming at him. He closed his eyes, braced himself for the pain he was sure would arrive ... but instead he felt himself enveloped in a bear hug. Velma was strong, her scent sour, and he could barely breathe, but he relaxed, slightly. Then he heard Ron groan in disgust.

Joe's eyes snapped open. Over Velma's shoulder, he locked gazes with Ron, then aimed his eyes at Velma. Ron fell silent, a look of confusion on his face. Joe mouthed the word "Wait!" while trying to convey a larger message in his eyes. He had a plan.

While Joe wasn't sure that Ron understood, he stayed silent for the moment. Joe pulled his head back to let Velma know he was finished with the hug. She didn't get the message.

"Velma, do you have more of that knockout potion you used on us?" he asked.

She pulled back and looked at him, then nodded. "I did get the recipe online. You were right about that." She smiled. "You're very smart."

"Clearly you're the smart one," Joe said. Ron started to gripe again, but when Velma turned to look at him, Joe quickly mouthed, "Shut up!" Ron did, and when Velma looked back, Joe grabbed her focus once more. "You figured out the tunnels, you orchestrated an elaborate kidnapping, and you succeeded. I don't know anyone who could have come up with all this, and I've met a lot of well-educated people at the Expo."

"Mother always said I was smart," she acknowledged. "And she said that someday someone would see that in me. Besides her."

Velma looked at Joe sweetly. Was she crushing on him? Guilt began to wash over him once again, but then stopped. He suddenly felt powerful, and that heat tickled the back of his head and excited his heart. He smiled back, and for an instant, he wondered how far he could take things (not because he was interested in Velma, but because he could). But then the two emotions balanced out and he kept on with his plan.

"Well, I see it," Joe said. "And now, after all that, you've shown me who Ron Lionel really is." Joe stopped himself. He'd suggested too much before, pushed too hard. He needed Velma to make the plan. "So, what's next?" She looked at Joe, not understanding. "You can't keep Ron tied up here forever."

Joe watched as Velma processed the information, her eyes shifting left and right. She opened and closed her hands, then walked in circles.

Ron stared at Joe, glaring so hard it was as if a "What the fuck?" word balloon had appeared over his head. And as Velma turned her back to Joe, he mouthed back, "Relax." Finally, Velma stopped. She had no answer.

"This isn't really about Ron," Joe added smoothly. "There are a lot of people out there at these conventions who think they're losers or rejects because of people like him. When you stand up to someone like Ron, you teach others that they can do it, too."

"I'm not like that," Velma said. "I don't know how to..."

"Be a hero?" Joe asked. "Did Luke know when he joined Obi Wan? Did Elemental before the Earth gave her the powers, or did Dorothy in Oz? Did Dexter when he was first pulled into the land of the Enduring?"

"Jesus Christ!" Ron shouted. "You haven't even read *The Enduring—*"

Velma was instantly upon Ron, shoving the sock into his mouth. She pulled some tape, slapped it on his face, and left the remainder of the roll attached to his cheek. Her eyes grew wide with excitement as she turned back to Joe, and a small part of him felt horrible.

"How do we do it?" she asked eagerly. "How do we expose Lord Lionel and let everyone know who he really is?"

"This is your journey," Joe said. "You figured everything out so far."

Velma thought for a second. "We could broadcast it on the Internet!" she said, then shook her head. "No, he won't admit to anything. Not unless he's scared." She grabbed the sword and swung it at Ron. "Ja'harrah!"

"NO!" Joe yelled. Velma stopped, the sword tip cutting into the wall above Ron's head. She looked back at him, confused. "I mean, yes, that's a good way to get him to talk, but things get faked on the Internet all the time. People need to know this is real."

Velma dropped the sword and thought. Hard. "For a story to go viral you need many, many, many people to share it and talk about it." She looked at Joe, inspired. "An audience! We could take over a big panel in Hall H tomorrow. There will be thousands of people and they'll all be live feeding it on the Internet!"

"Yes!" Joe encouraged. Then he stopped, as if inspired. "Or you could do it tonight..." Velma looked at him, interested. "The masquerade is happening in an hour. In Hall H."

Velma and Joe grinned at one another. This plan could work.

ISSUE #19

"DYNAMIC DUO"

"Truth is in the eye of the beholder..."

—Quote attributed to Marianne Henning when asked why she was leaving DC Comics at Comic Book Expo #42

"Good evening, America. My name is Ron Lionel ... and I've lied to you."

Ron sat on the bed, still in his boxer briefs and still bound to the headboard. Velma had propped up pillows behind his back and head so he could face the laptop.

Ron was not a fan of admitting when he messed up in general, so he really hated being forced to confess sins that he didn't really consider to be sins. But Ron believed that Joe had some kind of plan brewing, and he needed to trust that—even though trusting people was another thing Ron didn't do very well.

"As you know, I lied about being British," he continued. "And, as you also know, I had my artistic reasons for that. But there's more about me and *The Enduring* that you don't know."

Ron paused. How far should he go? He looked over at Joe, who was off camera, still tied to the chair. He glanced up at Velma towering above him, the sword poised to come down on his head if he didn't tell a story that satisfied her. She'd already hit his shins several times with the flat of the blade as a warning against trying anything funny. Joe had talked her out of doing any serious damage, but there were gashes in the wall where she'd slammed the sword tip right next to his face and neck to heighten the threat; she'd actually grazed his skin at one point. Velma was on a new mission, and she'd made it clear that if he didn't tell the truth, as she saw it, he would pay.

Now she tapped the sword tip onto the wall just outside of the camera frame. "Tell them what you had in your pocket."

Ron sighed. "I drink at times and do drugs occasionally," he said. "Cocaine, to be specific. That's it." He knew Velma believed that this made him an "addict." Maybe Joe did, too. Ron didn't care. In fact, he had some thoughts about the subject, and if he was going to be bullied into making this video then he would leave his stamp on it. "This isn't a new phenomenon. From Hemingway to Hunter S. Thompson, writers have had their crutches. In fact, I've met many a comic book professional who has taken a puff of pot here, a snort of something there, popped a pill or ten, and taken a sip of the sauce anywhere they could," he exaggerated.

He didn't actually know many other comics creators, but the ones he had met were good drinkers, and he knew from experience that this was only a step to the left of using an illegal substance now and then. "I don't need booze or coke to write *The Enduring*, just like those others don't need assistance when creating their work. But, really, who doesn't turn to some small joy—like something sweet, or a fast-food snack—to get them through the day?"

"IT'S NOT THE SAME THING!" Velma yelled, and Ron

jumped. He'd been so pleased with his on-camera moment that he'd basically forgotten the larger situation. "Tell them you're sorry!" she yelled. "Tell them!"

Ron looked from Velma to the laptop. With just a tad more sincerity than was necessary, he said, "I'm very sorry if that offends you."

Ron's eyes were drawn to Joe, who was shaking his head in disbelief. Ron knew his apology was tainted, but he couldn't help himself. Why was he being forced into this when he didn't do anything wrong—at least, not deliberately? He'd been himself. He'd always been himself. And thanks to an accident of genetics or bad parenting, he was now being painted as some kind of grand villain.

"Tell them about the art!" she commanded, pounding the sword into the wall. Small specks of drywall sprayed onto Ron's cheek. "And the story."

"I don't draw all of the book," Ron said. Then, off her look, "I don't draw most of it. I tried. I believed I could." Ron paused. He was tired. Drained. "You can't come at a project half-assed. You have to believe in yourself one-hundred percent—especially in anything creative." Ron's frustration bubbled over. "Look, in the Internet age, everyone has an opinion and everyone feels like they have the God-given right to tell you what it is, which means there are a million dicks out there who will tell you that you suck. That's fine. But you can't tell yourself you suck. If you doubt yourself, you've already failed. And I couldn't fail. So when I realized my art wasn't as good as it needed to be to tell the story I wanted to tell, I hired a guy who not only drew the way I believed I could draw, but who could take my illustrations and clean them up. He works using my thumbnail art, under my art direction, he gets paid well, and he doesn't ask for artistic credit, so everyone's happy.

"As for the plot, I know I've ripped into a lot of you fans for questioning my storylines. I've said many times that I know every detail of this saga. But I don't. The truth is that whenever I plot out the story too far ahead, I think it sucks ass. I start to question everything I'm doing, and have done, and..." Ron looked up at the laptop and reminded himself of where he was and what he was doing. He pulled himself together. "Like I said, you can't doubt yourself. The only way I can keep the series going is if I write it just slightly ahead of Dexter in the story. It's the only way to make it work for me. And sometimes that means I make mistakes." Ron paused for a moment. "But that's what fear and doubt does to us, doesn't it? It helps us make mistakes."

Ron and Joe made eye contact for a moment. Then he looked back at the laptop and quietly added, "So the venerable 'Lord Lionel' is human, after all."

"Velma," Joe said, "I think that's all you need."

"That's it?" she asked.

"What else is there?"

Velma thought about it, nodded, then crossed to the laptop and shut off the camera. She checked the playback for a moment, then saved the recording.

"How quickly can you get from here to the convention center?" Joe asked her.

"Ten minutes, depending on the service elevators," Velma said, pacing back and forth. "And homeless people in the tunnels." She stopped. "And any animals that might be living down there."

"What animals?" Joe asked. Ron felt his chest tighten.

"I read online that some activists released animals from SeaWorld years ago and they ended up getting washed into the sewers that are connected to the tunnels," she said as she rumbled over to her Samsonite and popped it open. "But then I read a similar story that activists released some alligators and snakes and duck-billed platypuses and stuff from the San Diego Zoo and *they're* living down there. Which sounds more likely to me because I've reviewed these." Velma withdrew two large map rolls and began unfolding them at Ron's feet.

"I think the zoo may be too far uptown for animals to have gotten into the downtown tunnels," Joe offered. "And is the water deep enough for sea creatures?"

Ron relaxed slightly, but Velma looked up from the papers and said, "I heard noises when I was bringing you guys here. Scraping and growling. Guttural."

A cold, anxious sweat formed all over Ron's body. He didn't necessarily believe that Joe could pull off whatever he was planning. There was just something too ... victimy about the guy.

"Okay," Joe said, clearly ready to drop the topic. "Run through the plan for me."

"The audio-video equipment for the masquerade is at the back of the hall..." she started.

"But...?"

"There's a hookup backstage by the MC podium and the awards statues," she continued. "I sneak backstage through the back loading dock. I then detach the audio-visual hookup from the camera and microphone ports and attach them to my laptop..."

"Like you tried to do at Ron's panel..."

"And press play and show everyone on the broadcast monitors who they've been dealing with." Velma looked so proud of herself. Ron hated her.

"It's not going to work," he said. "They're hosting a show. They're not going to let some random girl start playing with the electronics."

"They won't see me in the chaos," Velma said defiantly. "If I just act like I belong there, like Dexter—"

"Did with Falstaff when they snuck into the tavern! Yes, I know, I wrote the book—literally—and it's just a work of fiction." Ron stopped as he realized Joe was smiling and nodding behind Velma, as if encouraging him to continue. Velma saw Ron's expression and turned just as Joe removed the look from his face.

"He could be right, Velma," Joe said thoughtfully. "I think he's wrong, but he may be right. We should make a contingency plan."

"A distraction!"

"Exactly." Joe nodded. Then, his eyes lit up and he nodded to Ron. "What if he's your distraction?" Velma looked from Joe to Ron, then back to Joe again. "Ron's supposed to be hosting the masquerade, and at this point, there's no way they can hide the fact that he's missing. But if he was discovered backstage, tied up in the trash cart, everyone would rush to him."

"And that's when I'd play the video!" Velma exclaimed, hopping around in excitement.

Ron slowly grew excited, too. He understood now: Velma had made it clear that Joe would not be let go until after the plan was executed, so Joe was trying to get Velma to untie Ron instead. That way, he could overpower her.

"I'll need to knock him out," Velma said, rushing into the bathroom. "I still have a bottle of formula."

Ron's chest tightened nervously. Whatever crap Velma had used before had left him groggy and achy. If she knocked him out now, there was no way he could recover to take her down. Yes, there was a good chance he'd be found and rescued, but at what cost? Would she ever be stopped? And what would happen to Joe?

Ron looked over at him; Joe was puffing out his cheeks and rolling his head around as if his neck was broken. *It's funny*, Ron thought. *When I met this guy, I couldn't give a shit whether he lived or died, and now I'm worried something could happen to him while she's enacting her grand plan at the convention center.*

Velma returned holding a bleach bottle and a dull grey bathroom towel. Joe stopped his cheek/neck thing.

"What the hell? No!" Ron snapped, panic flaring up throughout his entire body. "You drugged me last time."

"Mother's pills were just meant to disorient you," she said, holding up the bottle. "This is what made you stay unconscious until we arrived here."

"Bleach? You used bleach to knock me out?"

"And other things," Velma replied. "Peroxide, hair spray, some essential oils..."

"You'll fry my fucking brain!" Ron noticed Joe puffing his cheeks again.

"You survived before!" she yelled back. "You both did!" She looked at Joe, who immediately stopped the puffing.

"It's like he said, Velma," Joe said, nodding to Ron. "You can't doubt yourself."

As soon as she nodded and looked down to unscrew the top, Joe began his epileptic moves again. Ron finally realized Joe was trying to tell him something: Hold your breath and pretend to pass out.

The liquid glugged onto the towel, filling the room with a harsh chemical cloud. Velma coughed, then propped the lid back on. Joe turned his head away, blinking rapidly as if the fumes were burning his eyes. Ron pulled on his bonds, the fear taking over.

Please, Ron prayed to a God he hadn't spoken to in years, *I know I'm a fuck up. And I know that if I promise to stop being a dick and stop doing coke and all that, I'll just fuck it up. But I do promise to try and be better.* Ron paused. He meant that. *I promise to try and be better.*

Suddenly, Velma had the towel over his mouth and nose.

Ron's timing was off. He'd started taking in a breath, but the chemical fumes invaded too quickly so he stopped. He only had a half a breath in him. His eyes, nose, and mouth immediately burned from the vapors. He shook his head left, then right, struggling to get away from Velma's grip, but she was surprisingly strong. She climbed up and straddled his chest, her weight pushing more air out of his lungs.

Ron felt his ears turning hot, and he could hear the blood pounding in his brain. It reminded him of the first time he'd done poppers, with a couple girls he met at an electronic dance festival a few years back. They'd done some nasty things with Ron that night—touching and sucking and toy playing in ways he'd never imagined a straight guy doing before. The scent-memory of that night and the weight of someone on his chest made Ron horny now, and he relaxed back on the bed. He felt warm, just like on that night, and he calmed down more.

His brain started dancing, flashes of red and yellow light popping in front of his eyelids.

Finally, the weight lifted, and Ron tried to curl up into a fetal position. He couldn't, and he didn't know why. But then his left arm slipped free and he wrapped it around his chest, cupping his hand between his right pec and armpit. He squeezed, enjoying the hug.

"Ron?" someone said. Someone he knew. "Ron?" The voice sounded worried.

"He's fine," someone else said. A woman. The first voice was a man, the second was a woman, and he knew them both.

"RON, WAKE UP!"

Joe.

"What are you doing?" Velma asked.

With a great, gasping inhale, Ron opened his eyes to find Velma leaning over him with a knife aimed at his right wrist. He instinctively grabbed the handle with his right hand and knocked Velma back with his free left arm. She stumbled off the bed and grabbed the rag and sword from the ground. As Velma rose, Ron cut the zip tie around his right wrist.

WHAM! Velma slammed the sword hilt into his head. The pain sent a shock of white light from the front of his brain to the back. She swung the sword up again, but this time Ron crossed his forearms, hitting her wrists and blocking the blow. The reverb knocked the sword from Velma's hand, and the flat of the blade slammed into his shoulder —hard—letting her get the rag over his mouth once more. But this time Ron had inhaled clean air and held it in as he sat up and shoved Velma back. She fell off him, off the bed, and tripped over the open bleach bottle as she fell into the wall heater.

In a flash, the rag caught fire in her hands. Velma screamed and tossed it down onto the carpet, where years of oil and grime picked up the flames. They hit the spilled liquid and a second burst ignited the carpet and nearby faded drapes. The room was instantly engulfed in flames.

Ron scrambled for the knife but couldn't find it, so he grabbed the sword. His arm buckled from the pain in his shoulder and wrist as he shoved the tip between the zip tie and his ankle. Then, with a twist, he severed the bond.

"Ron!" Joe yelled, then coughed, and Ron saw Velma grabbing the laptop and shoving it into her backpack. He jumped off the bed at her, but with surprising strength, she kicked him in the nuts and he crumpled to the ground. "Velma! Stop! You'll kill us!"

Through the pain and smoke, Ron saw her look at Joe with great sadness.

"You tricked me!" A growl rose inside her chest, and Ron knew what was coming next. "TRICKED ME!" Velma lunged for the sword, but Ron shoved her back, slamming her into the wall. He pulled his fist back just as Velma opened the door, slamming the edge into Ron's face. He stumbled back and she ran out, backpack and laptop in hand.

Ron's rage was as hot as the flames crawling up the walls and across the cottage cheese ceiling. Yellow smoke leaked out from behind the wallpaper as it burned and peeled off, down onto the carpet and bed, spreading the flames further. Ron squinted up at the ceiling, but the fire sprinklers sat dormant.

"Ron!" Joe choked out, forcing him to focus once more.

Ron grabbed Joe's chair and dragged it into the hallway. Velma was at the end of the hall, watching him. He could go after her, probably catch her, but his chest was tightening from the smoke and he started coughing. And Joe wouldn't survive if he left him. Ron looked at the zip ties securing Joe to the chair, then raced back into the fiery room. A wall of scorching heat hit his face and Ron worried the stubble on his cheeks would ignite. He grabbed the sword from the ground—the leather hilt already smoking it was so hot—and dove back outside. He shoved the blade down, cutting through one zip tie, then the second, then the two around Joe's ankles.

"Your hand!" Joe said, knocking the sword from Ron's grip. He'd been burning his fingers on the metal.

Ron's knees buckled. The coughing overtook him. He felt Joe shove a shoulder into his armpit, the other on his thigh, and in a second Ron was lifted up into a fireman's carry and doors began whizzing past.

"Fire!" Joe yelled, wheezing, as they raced down the hallway. "Fire! Everyone get out!"

Ron inhaled deeply. His throat was raw. A few doors opened, and dead-eyed residents looked out to see what was happening.

"Put me down," Ron commanded. "I'm fine, put me down!"

Joe slowed, stumbled, and Ron tumbled to the ground. He was sore but relieved, thankful to be out of that room and breathing cleaner air.

He watched as Joe jumped back to his feet and started banging on nearby doors, yelling, "Fire! Everyone run!"

Black smoke crawled along the ceiling and down the hallway toward Ron and Joe. Men and women, some clothed, others barely aware that they were naked, stumbled past them toward the elevators, the same direction Velma had run.

Ron spotted a fire alarm on the wall and pulled it. Two giant fire blisters on his hand burst as the alarm sounded. The emergency sprinklers stayed frozen in place. Ron and Joe looked at one another, a new purpose in mind.

"Get her," they both said, and took off toward the elevators.

ISSUE #20

"INTO THE LABYRINTH"

Get a real feel for America's Finest City amid downtown San Diego's most colorful residents. The San Diego Hotel is:

- **Central:** *Walk to the train station, bus depot, baseball stadium, and convention center!*
- **Historic:** *One of the last 1940s buildings in the city!*
- **Thrifty:** *Near budget-friendly restaurants!*
- **Beautiful:** *Decorated like a delightful New Orleans boudoir!*

Get the best rates in the city for America's Finest Comic Book Expo, or any time of year! Call for reservations!

"She's headed to the basement," Joe shouted above the fire alarm as he watched the numbers descend on the elevator Velma had hopped into moments before. He turned, saw they were on the sixth floor—the top one—and quickly darted into the stairwell. Ron was right on his heels.

"Move, move, move!" Joe yelled as he and Ron shoved their way through the throng of people evacuating the building. The fire alarm echoed through the old cinder block stairwell, which smelled of piss, vomit, and chemically tainted smoke. He took the stairs two at a time, passing drug dealers, users, prostitutes, johns, and pissed-off tourists who'd come to San Diego thinking they'd scored an amazing last-minute hotel deal.

"How do you know she's going there?" Ron shouted.

"Basement has an old theater they turned into a ballroom," Joe shouted back with a cough. His chest ached. "That's where we found the tunnels back in the day."

Sixth floor ... fifth ... fourth ... jumping from stairs to landing, dodging doors as more hotel visitors poured into the stairwell, Joe was vaguely aware of Ron keeping pace, but that didn't matter at the moment. He needed to save Velma before she hurt herself or someone else.

When Velma had screamed at him in the hotel room, he hadn't felt fearful—he'd felt guilty. She'd been ripped open with emotions, moving from confusion to realization to pain then anger and back again. This girl in a woman's body had lost her mother, very likely didn't have a father, and had abandoned everything she knew on a quest for answers —answers that any other sane adult would know she couldn't find. And then, just when there was some hope for her, he had destroyed it.

Joe had done it for a good reason. He knew that. But it didn't make him feel any better. Now he worried something worse might happen to Velma. He needed to make sure it didn't.

"Move!" Ron yelled as they approached a cluster of people at the first-floor door, shoving and panicking as they all tried to exit at once.

Joe grabbed Ron's arm and pulled him back from the crowd. He then lifted his arms and hunched his shoulders up around his neck; Ron mimicked him. They turned, and like two Incredible Hulks they plunged into, through, and then over the dazed and panicked crowd, finally plowing their way to the other side. Once clear, the two men raced down the last flight of steps.

Joe threw open the door to the basement just as the elevator doors closed. He darted into the dimly lit hallway: nothing on the right, but a door was just closing down on the left.

Joe pulled Ron to the wall and they quickly shuffled down the hallway, stumbling over dull pink carpet that was puckered in spots and worn through in others. Faded and chipped lettering for the "Continental Ballroom" hung above the door Velma had disappeared through. Joe motioned for Ron to stay back.

With a quick yank, Joe pulled the ballroom door open and pivoted inside, ready to duck in case Velma was waiting to take a swing at him. The room was dark but empty.

Just as Joe flicked on the old fluorescent lights, a wave of nausea washed over him. Between the original blow to his head, Velma's homemade potions, and the tussle in the hotel room, he wasn't operating in top form. He reached out, grabbing onto Ron, who had entered right behind him, and closed his eyes for a beat.

"You alright?" Ron whispered.

Joe nodded but said nothing. He blinked rapidly and his vision cleared slightly. He hurried to the mirrored wall, pulling Ron along for support. Ron stopped short when he saw his reflection; Joe ignored the soot and bruises on his body and instead studied the glass surface. The room had aged, but it didn't look like there had been any structural changes. He questioned whether he'd actually seen the ballroom door closing or if it was his vision blurring. But if he hadn't hallucinated, and the space was empty, that meant there was still a hidden passage.

That's when Joe spotted Velma's sweaty palm prints slowly disappearing on the cool mirrored surface. He pushed straight on—making sure not to cover up her prints—but nothing happened. Then Joe remembered that it was more of a slide and a push, so he set his hands against the glass and slid to the left. Nothing. Ron started to put his hands out as well, but Joe blocked him.

"Don't touch her prints," he commanded. "Evidence." Ron grumbled but obliged and put his hands above Joe's. Together they pushed and slid the mirror to the right; the panel shifted, scraping open on a gritty metal track. Inside was a dusty metal staircase, and in the faint light, he saw Velma's footprints on the top two steps. He listened, but there was no sound. Joe took two shallow breaths and began creeping down the stairs.

A red bulb still burned at the base of the steps next to an old bomb shelter. Joe squinted, hoping to see movement. Giant metal pipes stuck out from the walls and he felt trapped, with no room to maneuver in case of an attack.

A squeak and violent hiss of steam made Joe stop.

"Fuck! Fuck! Fuck!" Ron yelled as rats scurried over their feet. It took all of Joe's willpower not to scream himself, but having Ron there helped; it gave him something to focus on. He shoved his hand over Ron's mouth and the two waited for the vermin to run away. Joe hoped they would cause Velma to jump and reveal herself as well, but there were no other noises.

Joe and Ron quietly moved down the corridor and away from the bomb shelter's blunt crimson light. The tunnels grew dark again and smelled dank, but the summer sun that blazed down on the asphalt street above all day had made the space disgustingly humid. Sweat quickly covered Joe's face and arms, and he could feel moisture dripping down his back and chest. An eerie lavender light leaked through the purple crystals embedded in the sidewalks above. He could hear cars, horns, and foot traffic above, but even if they yelled, no one would know where they were.

Joe took hold of Ron's arm and continued into the dark. His breathing quickened as it became harder to see. Joe reached out his free hand to feel his way along the wall ... and grabbed a warm, stiff, lifeless hand.

Joe swallowed a series of unintelligible curses and jumped back into Ron, accidentally dragging the dead body from its resting place between two water pipes. The rotten, smelly lump thudded to the ground and Ron let out a choked curse of his own. Joe gasped for air, trying to control his panic, but then saw a shadow moving toward his head. Instinctively, he ducked as something metal crashed into the wall behind him.

Joe let go of Ron, lunged forward, knocked the metal rod from Velma's hand, and grabbed her sweaty body.

"Velma, stop!" he yelled. "It's over!"

"Kill you, you fucking bitch!" Ron screamed as he reached over Joe to punch Velma in the head. Joe threw one arm up to block Ron, confused and disoriented, but he immediately understood what was happening: Ron's goal wasn't to stop Velma; it was to get revenge.

Joe felt a blinding pain and heard the distinctive sound of two skulls connecting. Velma had head-butted him. He fell back, tripping over the decaying corpse and into Ron. He blinked against the pain and flashing lights and reached out to grab hold of something to stop the fall, but there was nothing there. Joe felt blood seeping from his nose. As he crashed to the ground and into Ron's legs, he saw Velma move down the hallway. She grabbed something off the ground that must have been the pipe and ran away.

"Get up!" Ron shouted. "Get her!"

Ron shoved Joe to the side, jumped up, and charged down the stone corridor. Joe struggled to his feet and followed, bumping his bare arms and knuckles against the walls, feeling his skin being cut and scratched along the way. He didn't care. He needed to save Ron—no, *stop* Ron from hurting Velma—and to stop Velma from hurting anyone else.

Haunting slivers of light cut into the tunnels and Joe could make out small details: a rusted metal door that looked like a prop from the Pirates of the Caribbean ride, discarded Styrofoam fast-food containers and aluminum cans from what looked like the 1970s, a sign for another bomb shelter, long-forgotten men's and women's restroom entrances. Ron was only a few steps ahead, and Joe heard splashing water. Two more steps, and it hit his own feet and ankles; the tunnel they'd run into was covered with warm, tepid liquid. Ron stopped, unsure where to go, and Joe caught up.

A metal gate clanged around the corner ahead. They both turned and eased toward the noise. The scent of trash and stagnant dock water greeted them as they came to an old sewage gate. The two men shoved and it banged open, only to be stopped by a giant metal trash dumpster. They pushed some more and squeezed through.

Joe took in the foul, swampy air, happy to be out of the tunnels. He looked around and recognized the convention center's back docks. They were on the far side, in an area that was caged off with chain link to keep homeless people and dumpster divers from sifting through the convention center's waste.

The giant metal doors at the top of a concrete service ramp slammed shut. Ron pushed Joe aside and raced up the ramp. Joe had a bad feeling in his gut, but before he could say anything, Velma jumped out and hit Ron in the back with her metal pipe.

Joe raced toward them as Ron fell onto the concrete with a pained cry. Velma stood above him, ready to strike again.

"Hey!" yelled a security guard who had been patrolling the back of the building. Velma turned and swung, hitting him on the side of the head. The guard collapsed, but in the impact Velma lost the pipe; it clanged down under a dumpster, the noise echoing. She looked back at Joe, then at Ron and the guard. Fear swept over her face and she turned, running into the convention center.

Joe ran over to the fallen men.

"You okay?" he asked. Ron had lifted himself onto his knees. The guard was groggy but nodded. "Can you call for help?" Joe asked him. "That woman kidnapped me and Ron Lionel."

"Who's Ron Lionel?" the guard asked.

"Just call the police!" Ron snapped, grimacing in pain. Joe looked at him. Streaks of blood covered his legs, stomach, and torso from their mad dash through the harsh stone tunnels. His calves and bare feet were dirt-stained, and rings of raw skin wrapped his wrists and ankles. His briefs, still the only garment on his body, were stretched out from the running and fighting. The great Lord Lionel looked pathetic. But he didn't look ready to quit.

Joe reached out to help Ron stand as the guard fumbled for his phone.

"We're here to stop Velma," Joe commanded Ron. "Not kill her."

Ron nodded, but Joe knew it was to placate him. Ron had plans of his own. Killing Velma may be extreme, even for him. But hurting her was not.

ISSUE #21

"UN-MASQUERADE"

Xander Thompson's first entry at America's Finest Comic Book Expo's Masquerade was a musical tribute to Wonder Woman. This was followed the next year by an all-male Jem and the Holograms live performance. From there, the event itself changed, with the contestants' performances being nearly as important as the costumes themselves. While Xander is keeping silent regarding what's in store for this year, we're sure it's going to be a showstopper!

—Excerpt from Xander Thompson's bio in the America's Finest Comic Book Expo souvenir guide

"And now, our final entry for the night: Contestant number forty-two," a familiar voice boomed out over the sound system.

Sarah, Ron thought. *They got motherfucking Sarah to replace me!* He smiled to himself as he and Joe wove their way through the dark, crowded backstage. *She covered for me. Again.*

"I'm supposed to say all this?" Ron heard her ask in disbelief. The audience cheered and laughed. There was an annoyed sigh, then, "He's a living legend at America's Finest Comic Book Expo..."

"You know where the sound system thing is, right?" Ron asked. "You told her where it was."

Joe paused, turning to face him. "I told her where I thought it was, but I don't know where on the stage the MC or awards are located." Ron gave him a look. "Sorry, I couldn't do room inspection while I was tied up!"

Joe took off again and Ron quickly followed, annoyed.

They raced past a legion of Logan's Runners, generations of Justice Leaguers, and a group of naughty-hot girls dressed in colorful Japanese school uniforms from some animated series Ron didn't recognize. Everyone was waiting for this final act, a combination of excitement and dread on their faces. He kept moving.

"...winner of three Most Humorous awards and two Best in Show at the masquerade. And he's been Comic Book Expo's Fan of the Year three years running..."

The sound went out and Joe stopped suddenly, causing Ron to crash into him. They were at the edge of the stage, and Ron could see Sarah looking at the microphone, wondering why it had gone dead. Behind her and slightly off stage stood the Expo president, Sexy Pam, and some redhead he didn't recognize. They all looked worried.

"Xan-der! Xan-der! Xan-der!" chanted the audience. The president walked onto the stage to examine the microphone.

Ron turned to Joe. He was looking across the stage for Velma, in the shadows behind Sarah and the staff. And that's when Ron spotted her —crouched behind them where the backstage sound board was positioned; he and Joe had rushed right past her. As she hooked her laptop to the board, Ron noticed the technician lying on the ground, barely conscious.

A desperate, irrational rage overtook him, and he shoved past Joe. He knew that trying to punch her in the tunnels had been stupid and immature, but he couldn't help himself. And as he dove at Velma now, a part of him thought, *Mistake...* just before his head slammed into a Klingon's chest, knocking the man into his fellow clansmen. They all fell in a painful heap. Ron's outrage pushed down the twinge of stupidity he felt as he rolled himself off the bulky men and women in their leathers and heavy fabrics.

Ron got to his feet as Joe darted past him and between curtained holding areas. When he reached Velma, he pulled her away from the laptop and the sound system snapped back on. Ron followed Joe's path, a sense of relief washing over him. They'd finally stopped her.

Oblivious to the scuffle, Sarah looked at the working microphone, smiled at the president, and said, "Ladies and gentlemen, Xander Thompson and his crew, in a tribute to Elemental!"

"You've ruined everything!" Velma shouted at Joe over the crowd's thunderous applause.

Just then, ten shirtless, muscled men, all wearing spandex pants and boots that matched Elemental's uniform, charged through them toward the stage. Joe twisted in confusion, losing his balance and falling into the curtained wall, while Ron crashed into the table filled with awards. He shoved himself upright, righteous frustration coursing through his veins as he grabbed a statue to hit anyone in his way—and his eyes locked on Velma.

Uncertainty and confusion washed over her face. Ron marched forward. He knew he looked like hell and hoped it would scare her enough to give him an advantage. But he needed a better weapon, something more intimidating than a plastic super hero statue.

And then Ron saw it: a large red fire extinguisher. He offered Velma a vicious grin, threw the award over his shoulder, and pulled the red cylinder off the wall.

"Come on, bitch," he growled. "Just you and me."

She turned and ran, away from the stage and through a door. Ron started to chase after her but stopped when he saw the sign: "Convention Center Catwalk—Authorized Personnel Only." He looked up at the metallic grate that formed a see-through bridge above the stage and out into the convention center.

"Damn!" he muttered. He wasn't scared of heights, but he didn't like them much either. And he'd lost Joe. Ron knew he couldn't wait for him—and this might be the only way to stop the bitch. So he opened the door and carefully walked up the stairs, keeping to the walls in case Velma found something to throw at him.

As he climbed, his arms started throbbing; his traps and lower back ached. It was suddenly tough to breathe. The fire extinguisher was clearly too heavy to continue hauling around—*and it's a stupid weapon, anyway*—so Ron dropped it at the top of the stairs. As the pain lessened, he looked down and found himself three floors above the masquerade stage.

Then he spotted Velma, staring back at him from across the catwalk like a little girl on her first day of school, overwhelmed, lost in a land of strange people, objects, and sounds. In an instant, Ron's need to hurt her evaporated.

"When Mother Earth became too wounded by man's greed to care for Herself, She looked to her greatest creation for help ... WOMANKIND!" The words boomed from the stage below, and more than 5,000 voices rose in unison to join the familiar refrain from the popular TV show.

"Stop running," Ron warned. "Please."

"Why can't you leave me alone?" Velma screeched. She looked to the heavens. "Someone please help me!"

"That's when She found a hero! That's when I became ... Elemental!"

Below, the dancers moved in unison. A flash, and then a bright spotlight introduced Elemental—blinding Ron. He threw a hand down and gripped the catwalk's metal railing.

"Ja'harrah!" Velma yelled, and just as his eyesight began clearing, he saw her charging at him like a tank. He tried stepping to the side but slipped and fell on his ass. Velma ran past, swinging her fist down and punching him in the face—hard—ramming him into the railing.

Ron blinked, trying to see through the flashing lights. In an instant he saw Joe appear on the catwalk, but just as quickly Velma knocked him down before disappearing into the darkness.

Ron's head spun, the softness he'd felt a second before now choked by a snake of hate. He looked down at the dancers and the statuesque woman dressed as Elemental—who may, he now realized, actually be a man. *Is that a remix of the Elemental TV show's opening theme song?* It was like he'd suddenly appeared above a Las Vegas Cirque show. Or a gay rave. All of it pissed him off, and he held onto that anger as he pulled himself to his feet and followed the cow.

He took a few steps, squinting into the shadows, but the only person he saw was Joe, slumped over on one knee, trying to stand up. *Pathetic...*

"Go-go dancers?" Ron yelled at him. "What the fuck is wrong with this convention?!"

He brushed past Joe, pissed—at Velma, at Joe for being unable to stop her, at everything leading up to this point. He couldn't let her escape.

WHAM! Joe tackled him. For a half-second, Ron thought this was some kind of pussy revenge, but then two waves—one fire, the other a stream of icy water—blasted from Elemental's hands. Ron watched as the hot and cold mixture interwove over the heads of anxious attendees and judges, causing everyone to jump from their seats and cheer with excitement. Then a shock wave of steam hit the catwalk where the men had stood seconds before. Joe had saved him.

Ron turned to thank him, then froze. Velma was charging out of the shadows, holding the fire extinguisher above her head like it weighed less than a baby. She swung it down as Joe turned and instinctively raised his arms up to block the blow, but he slipped on the now-slick surface. In an instant, Ron took it all in: Velma missing Joe and slamming the heavy extinguisher into the catwalk's metal supports; Joe's legs slipping out from under him and off the edge, his hands desperately grasping for anything that could stop his motion.

Suddenly, Velma turned and hurled the extinguisher at Ron's head. He managed to duck back just as she slammed it into the opposite railing, but he slipped, landing on all fours.

"No! No! No!" Joe yelled. Ron started to look, but then Velma appeared over him, holding the extinguisher, ready to slam it down. "Velma, no!" Joe screamed.

"Velma, stop!" Ron yelled simultaneously, as she lunged at him. But she wouldn't stop. Ron knew she wouldn't. So he shoved his hands into the metal floor, dropped to his stomach, and pushed himself away.

He slid backward, the metal scratching into his exposed stomach and thighs.

The fire extinguisher hit the catwalk floor with Velma's full weight behind it—and at that precise moment, everything exploded.

The fire extinguisher shot a stream of foam into Velma's face. She stumbled back into the railing, the bar gave way, and she buckled at the waist, reaching out for anything that might save her—but Ron could see that she was alone.

Without further thought, he shoved his right leg into a lunge and leapt over to her in a single bound. He grabbed one arm, then the other, but her sweat-stained limbs slipped through his hands that were grasping, grasping, grasping to stop her fall. Ron dug his fingernails into her fleshy forearms and for a moment her movement faltered. Then it continued on, as if a magic lasso were pulling her away from him.

Help! Ron cried out once more to that God he hadn't spoken to in years. And then...

Joe's arms reached over his and grabbed Velma's right hand and shirt. Somehow he'd pulled himself back up, but Ron couldn't think about that as Velma's body was being pulled down like metal drawn to a magnet. Ron transferred his left hand to her pants pocket, grabbing hold of the fabric, and together they yanked her up enough so that her knees landed on the walkway.

The three held tight to one another, gasping for air.

And with a bang, the support beams and guy-wires on the catwalk broke free, and a portion of the flooring snapped off, tilting the surface downward. The trio scrambled to get their fingers into the metal grate, but it was too late; the entire structure crashed down onto the stage.

Screams battled with crashing metal and blaring music. And then, all was silent.

"What the fuck?!" Sarah screamed over the microphone. "Ron?"

"Joe?!" yelled another woman's voice.

At that exact moment, the hall exploded into applause.

Ron blinked out over the stage lights to see the crowd on its feet, cheering this dynamic ending to the masquerade. Sarah, the Expo president, and the two women with him hurried over.

The Elemental drag queen shrugged to her ten shirtless dancers, stepped in front of the broken catwalk, stretched out her arms, and they all gracefully bowed to the audience as if this ending had been part of the planned performance.

Ron and Joe saw Velma; she was curled into a ball, crying. They looked at one another and shared a nod: job well done.

EPILOGUE #1

"AFTER THE FALL..."

"*Enduring to Live—The Ron Lionel Story,*" Ron announced his proposed book title to the small group of reporters who had been allowed to remain in the masquerade ballroom. He sat next to Sarah in one of the convention center's blue and silver chairs, in the front row, with 4,998 empty seats spread out behind them. He could tell from her sidelong glance that she wasn't a fan of the book title, and that was fine. They could work out those details later. The main thing was that he finally felt safe again. Some fans of *The Enduring* who had competed in the masquerade had even offered him their Falstaff and Myranda cloaks, which now draped over his legs. A hot paramedic bandaged his ribs, while the press clustered in front, recording Ron's every word.

"That's just the working title I came up with while being held captive, you understand. I haven't run it past anyone at my agency. Or the studio," he told the small group. "They have first right of refusal on movie rights."

The convention president, Robert, had tried clearing the area once police and medical personnel had arrived—which was only about three minutes after their "grand entrance"—but Sarah had wanted some reporters to stay behind. She understood the importance of positive press, especially with the current tensions between Ron and the studio, and nothing garners better publicity than a victim overcoming a harrowing experience.

"There are reports that you punched some kids on Saturday. Is that true?" a reporter asked. Ron recognized her as Shannon Spindler, the *Vanity Fair* staffer who had written an exposé on him at the start of his career.

"Shannon! You're looking well," Ron said with a slight grin. Nothing had ever happened between them, but that never stopped Ron from trying, despite the fact that she clearly found him repulsive. Shannon was beautiful.

"We're not prepared to speak about that at the moment," Sarah interjected. "But the timing of that alleged incident coincides with the young woman drugging Ron. We're having blood work done as soon as we get to the hospital tonight."

"I don't remember anything from Friday afternoon until I woke up in the hotel," Ron said, which was basically true.

Ron winced as Hot Paramedic finished taping his ribs. The photographers quickly snapped photos, but this wasn't for show; the pain was definitely real. According to Hot Paramedic, he'd probably broken a couple ribs in the fall. Ron didn't care. A creative rush had filled his veins once he realized this was a story people wanted to hear. He'd felt this way only a couple of times before—first, when he sat down in a drugged haze and wrote the beginnings of *The Enduring* saga, and just this weekend when the Visionary Comics team had invited him to join their ranks. It was excitement. Genuine excitement.

Ron knew it would be a thrilling book, and anyone who was a fan of *The Enduring* would buy it. Hell, anyone who wasn't a fan but had heard about his infamous behavior would undoubtedly pick it up out of curiosity. Horror fans and literary people would both love it because he was a skilled writer. Hell, everyone would read something this fantastic! It would be a bestseller before he even typed his first word!

"Can you tell us about the kidnapping?" a man in the front asked.

"A lot of things went on that..." Ron trailed off as his mind flashed over the past 24 hours. He swallowed, his throat dry. He suddenly felt nervous, like he was in a dream and being compelled to open the door to a room with something potentially dangerous on the other side, but he couldn't stop himself, or speak, or scream, or make any noise in protest. But then Sarah shifted in her seat, very slightly, and he felt himself returning to the ballroom. "I had to step away from what was happening, while it was happening. Mentally. And I'm a writer. So, to do that, I started chronicling the story in my head, figuring out who this poor girl was. Trying to understand her..."

"Why did she do it?" Shannon asked, looking at her notes. "She's not very young..."

"She wasn't well in the head," Ron responded.

"She had to have said something," Shannon continued. "Do you know Velma's last name?"

"What did Velma do to you and Mr. Cotter?" asked another.

"Did you try to sleep with her?" Shannon asked.

"Absolutely not!" Ron snapped.

"You do have a reputation, Mr. Lionel..." she said wryly.

"Okay, guys, I think that's enough." Sarah stood up. "Mr. Lionel's had a rough couple of days, and—"

But now the questions flew like bullets: "How did you and Joe Cotter escape? Did he help you? What's the story with these tunnels? Do you plan on suing the city for not blocking them off? When were you first taken? You came here in your boxers; did she molest you?"

Joe and a wall of five police officers walked up, and the press fell quiet.

"Sorry, everyone, but the police need Ron and me," Joe said. The press tried asking him questions, too, but the officers began escorting people out. "Ms. Cisneros will be setting up a press conference as soon as she's able."

And in less than ten seconds, they were all gone. Hot Paramedic finished packing up the equipment and went to check on the ambulance.

"The police will take our full statements at the hospital," Joe told Ron and Sarah in a hushed voice.

"Thank you," Ron said to Joe, but then stopped. Joe followed his gaze. Two female police officers and two social workers were escorting Velma out. She was in a wheelchair, sitting like a vacant mannequin from a store that had gone out of business 20 years ago. It was sad. As much as Ron hated her, he had to admit that it was sad.

"The laptop is missing," Joe said, and Ron instantly felt his face grow red. Sweat formed on his neck and back, but Joe's voice remained calm. "I have my team working with the police to see if we can find it. It's likely that a volunteer or convention center employee saw a valuable laptop and stole it for the money. They'll probably wipe the drives for resale, but..."

You'll handle it, Ron told himself. *Just like your past mistakes, just like this weekend. You'll handle it. Because you can.*

"Hey, guys, smile!" shouted Xander, who was still dressed like Elemental. As he reached them, he extended his phone out on a telescoping stick, then he and his shirtless dancers jumped into frame behind Ron and Joe. Ron saw the three-second countdown, sucked in his abs—which hurt his ribs, but he persevered—flexed his arms, and looked serious just as the photo snapped. "So happy you guys are safe!"

"Sorry we ruined your performance," Joe said as Pam approached with Robert and a redheaded woman.

"Oh, please!" Xander said with a dismissive wave before furiously tapping away at his phone. "I knew I'd be disqualified for using the fire and ice blasts anyway. I just wanted to end the Expo with a big show-stopping number, and you two helped me do that." He looked up at Joe, his expression somewhat stunned. "I can't believe you, of all people, helped me."

"Not willingly..." Joe said, tossing a look at Pam and Robert.

"You're hotter as a guy," Ron said to Xander. He could tell Sarah was about to scold him, so he added, "What? It's a compliment."

Xander smiled, sent out the photo on social media, kissed Ron on the cheek, snapped another photo as he did it, and took off before Sarah could react. In a fantastic flurry of gauze, satin, and spandex, he and his dancers flew out of the ballroom.

"So, a book, huh?" Joe asked.

Ron looked at him, and the others seemed to vanish. He and Joe weren't friends. In fact, under any other circumstances, they wouldn't even strike up a conversation. But he had misjudged Joe, and he knew that now.

"Gotta work it out somehow," Ron said. Then, with a wink, he added, "I'll make you look good."

"As a fanboy I have to say: That book title is horrible."

Before Ron could snap back at him, Hot Paramedic returned. "We need to get you both to the hospital."

Joe and the others followed, but Ron and Sarah held back.

"You okay?" she asked. "Really?"

Ron watched Joe, surrounded by friends, as they slowly made their way out of the ballroom, laughing at a joke. *About some geeky movie or something, no doubt.* For a second, Ron felt empty.

"Oh, yeah," he said, pushing any sadness aside and grabbing hold of his excitement again. He took Sarah's arm and they followed the others. "I never got to finish telling you about the meeting with Frank and Michele," he whispered. "They're teaming with a bunch of big-name creators to launch a new company, and they want me to be a founder. They're calling it Visionary Comics." Sarah nodded, as if the name sounded good. "They want you and the agency to rep them. Very hush-hush right now, but this could be huge. They also have a young social media guru who's pretty brilliant, and a thought leader who's freaky she's so spot-on with her ideas."

"What the hell does a 'thought leader' do?" Sarah asked. "Besides think, of course."

"No idea, but she was able to read me like you can," he said. "I think this could be huge." Sarah nodded. "And I want the Weeble on board." She looked at him suspiciously. "He's the only guy I know who's actually run a comic book company. And he's learned from his mistakes. We'll need that experience." Sarah raised an eyebrow. "And it may constitute the technical sale of *The Enduring* to another company."

"Which you now have ownership in," Sarah said with a knowing smile. She patted Ron on the hand. "My little boy is learning." Ron laughed. "I love you, kid."

"Me, you too," he said, squeezing her hand.

EPILOGUE #2

"SECOND STAR ON THE RIGHT..."

"I always feel sort of sad when CBE ends," Joe said to Pam. "A sense of melancholy, if you'll excuse the writerly expression."

She smiled, and Joe took in the red, orange, and yellow hues the setting sun cast across her delicate face.

It was Sunday evening. America's Finest Comic Book Expo had officially ended a few hours before, and the last day had been (thankfully) drama free. The two stood at the top of the convention center, where the public wasn't normally allowed. To their left, the stone, steel, and glass structure stretched multiple city blocks toward hotels and high-rise condos. He turned to downtown San Diego stretching out before them. A plane glided over the tops of the buildings, so close you could imagine Batman or Spider-Man grabbing hold with grappling hook or web fluid and soaring in toward the airport below. To the right was the pristine San Diego Harbor, where massive yachts were anchored, armed naval vessels guarded the shores, and the blue-trimmed Coronado Bridge joined two land masses together.

Joe inhaled the crisp salt air and smiled. "Do you smell that?"

"The beautiful ocean breeze," she replied, sighing softly. "It's one of the things that convinced me to move here from Utah."

"I used to notice it all the time before. When the convention center was first built and we moved America's Finest down here, I remember smelling that breeze and thinking it was full of so many... possibilities. Over the years I forgot about it." Joe looked at his arm and saw goose bumps rising under the scratches and scrapes. His wrists were purple and raw, his chest and legs sore and bruised, but otherwise he was completely fine. Louise had called it "a blessing," while Pam thought it was "good luck." Joe wasn't sure what to call it.

Pam noticed his arm, too. She rubbed it and the goose bumps subsided, like she'd massaged them into his spirit.

"It's nice to remember things like that again," he said.

Joe stared out at the city's historic core. It was forever being rebooted—giant, sleek skyscrapers housing high-end restaurants, corporate-owned boutique hotels, and allegedly innovative start-ups consuming the cracked blacktop parking lots that had once served long-forgotten businesses. From where they stood, he could see the charred remains of the San Diego Hotel, burned down in the fire. Two bodies had been found after the blaze was extinguished, both addicts who were either already dead when the fire started, or too messed up to escape. Joe wondered if either of them had loved ones who would care.

What would matter to people was the land, and what could go up in place of the burned-out husk. Joe knew that within two years, a shining structure would stand, most likely a fancy hotel, and the people who stayed there would have no idea what had happened there before.

"I'm sorry," he said. Pam nodded slightly, but said nothing.

A noise below drew their attention: convention center workers were removing the America's Finest Comic Book Expo banners from the cylinders that reached across the front like power conduits. Out in the streets, city workers were already taking down the sponsorship signs from lamp posts. In downtown storefronts and city lots, workers disassembled displays from the various entertainment companies that had been promoting their new shows and movies.

Sadness wrapped around Joe once more.

"Millions of people—living in the city, visiting the city, leaving the city—all with their own stories," he said, almost to himself. "And once again, CBE is gone. As if we'd never been here." He looked at Pam and smiled sheepishly. "At least for another year."

"My college mentor used to say that feeling sad after a big event or trip was okay," Pam said. "The only reason you were sad was because you had a good time." She stopped and laughed slightly. "Not that you had a 'good' time, I suppose..."

"No," Joe agreed, and took her hand in his. "But it was..." He stopped, trying to figure out what his time with Velma and Ron had been about, what it had meant to him. He couldn't. Too much had happened. There had been too many revelations and emotions, and instinctively Joe knew he'd need to write it down to process everything. Only then could he talk about it with Pam, or anyone else for that matter.

"It was good," he concluded. "In some way. For me, I think it was good."

In that moment, he felt a little better. The salty breeze brushed over his face and neck, arms and chest. He inhaled deeply again, and for the first time in a long time, he sensed that there was a future ahead of him.

And in that future, the possibilities were endless.

1

Richard Andreoli is a writer living in Los Angeles. He's written about educational programs at LA County Jail, crafted bitchy dialogue in nighttime soap operas, and launched numerous pop culture websites and online properties. Before all that, he worked for Comic-Con in San Diego, volunteering in their registration, treasury, and events departments, and later producing their monthly member magazine.

In his spare time, he likes to run away with the circus. Learn more at **richardandreoli.com**.

CPSIA information can be obtained
at www.ICGtesting.com
Printed in the USA
LVHW08*2123220818
587766LV00012B/260/P